RECOVERY

*The Lord is known by the judgment
which he executeth: the wicked is
snared in the work of his own hands.
Higgaion. Selah.*

PSALMS 9:16

JOHN BERRYMAN

RECOVERY

FARRAR, STRAUS AND GIROUX

NEW YORK

THIRD PRINTING, 1980

Printed in the United States of America
Published simultaneously in Canada by McGraw-Hill Ryerson Ltd., Toronto
DESIGNED BY HERB JOHNSON

To the Suffering Healers

Oh! I haue suffered
With those that I saw suffer
Miranda, in Shakespeare's
second Redemptive work, I.ii.5

'*My doctrine is not mine*'
John 7[16]

NOTE

*I don't write as a member of the American and
international society, Alcoholics Anonymous
(founded 1935), but as an author merely who has
experienced certain things, witnessed things, heard
things, imagined some. The materials of the book,
however, especially where hallucinatory, are
historical; all facts are real; ladies and gentlemen,
it's true.*

J.B.

John Berryman

BY SAUL BELLOW

He wrote in one of his last letters to me, "Let's join forces, large and small, as in the winter beginning of 1953 in Princeton, with the Bradstreet blazing and Augie fleecing away. We're promising!"

The Bradstreet was indeed blazing then; Augie was not nearly so good. Augie was naïve, undisciplined, unpruned. What John liked was the exuberance of its language and its devotion to the Chicago streets. I had, earlier, published two small and correct books. He did not care for them. In Augie there was a Whitmanesque "coming from under" which he found liberating. I admired the Bradstreet. What he said was true; we joined forces in 1953, and sustained each other.

The Princeton John was tallish, slender, nervous, and gave many signs that he was inhibiting erratic impulses. He wore a blue blazer, a button-down shirt, flannel trousers, cordovan shoes. He spoke in a Princeton mutter, often incomprehensible to me. His longish face with its high color and blue eyes I took to be of Irish origin. I have known blue-eyed poets apparently fresh from heaven who gazed at you like Little Lord Fauntleroy while thinking how you would look in your coffin. John was not one of these blue-eyed serpents. Had you, in a word-association test, said "Devil" to him, he would have answered "John Webster." He thought of nothing wicked. What he mainly thought about was literature. When he saw me coming, he often said, "Ah!" meaning that a literary discussion was about to begin. It might be *The Tempest* that he had on his mind that day, or *Don Quixote;* it might be Graham Greene or John O'Hara; or Goguel on Jesus, or Freud on dreams. There was little personal conversation. We never discussed money, or wives, and we seldom talked politics. Once as we were discussing Rilke I interrupted to ask him whether he had, the other night, somewhere in the Village, pushed a lady down a flight of stairs.

"Whom?"

"Beautiful Catherine, the big girl I introduced you to."

"Did I do that? I wonder why?"

"Because she wouldn't let you into the apartment."

He took a polite interest in this information. He said, "That I was in the City at all is news to me."

We went back to Rilke. There was only one important topic. We had no small-talk.

In Minneapolis one afternoon Ralph Ross and I had to force the window of a house near Seven Corners to find out what had happened to John. No one had seen him in several days. We arrived in Ross's Jaguar, rang the bell, kicked at the door, tried to peer through the panes and then crawled in over a windowsill. We found ourselves standing on a bare gritty floor between steel bookstacks. The green steel shelves from Montgomery Ward's, meant for garages or workshops, for canned peaches in farmers' cellars, were filled with the elegant editions of Nashe and Marlowe and Beaumont and Fletcher which John was forever importing from Blackwell's. These were read, annotated, for John worked hard. We found him in the bedroom. Face down, rigid, he lay diagonally across the double bed. From this position he did not stir. But he spoke distinctly.

"These efforts are wasted. We are unregenerate."

At the University of Minnesota John and I shared an office in a temporary wooden structure to the north of the School of Mines. From the window we saw a gully, a parking lot, and many disheartening cars. Scorched theology books from a fire sale lined one of the walls. These Barths and Brunners looked as if they had gone through hell. We had no particular interest in them but they helped to furnish forth a mental life in the city of Minneapolis. Minneapolis was the home of Honeywell, of heart surgery, of Pillsbury, of the Multi Phasic test, but it was not celebrated as the home of poems and novels. John and I strolled sometimes, about a pond, through a park and then up Lake Street, "where the used cars live!" What on earth were we doing here! An interesting question. We talked about Yeats. The forces were still joined. We wrote things

> Drop here, with honor due, my trunk and brain
> among the passioning of my countrymen
> unable to read, rich, proud of their tags
> and proud of me. Assemble all my bags!
> Bury me in a hole, and give a cheer,
> near Cedar on Lake street, where the used cars live.

He was proud of the living of these cars. That, he said, was "Delicious!" a favorite expression. My offering to him at that time was a story called "Leaving the Yellow House." This, too, he declared delicious, though he found it faulty, inconclusive. (We told each other exactly what we thought.)

Tense, he stood at his desk as I entered the office. He was greatly excited. He said, "Pal, I have written some new verses. They are *delicious!*"

When he broke a leg and Dr Thomes was called in the middle of the night John said, as the splint was being applied, "You must hear this new Dream Song!" He recited it as they carried him to the ambulance.

I would visit John at an institution (not the one in this novel) called, I believe, The Golden Valley. He was not there because he had broken his leg. The setting of The Golden Valley was indeed golden. It was early autumn, and the blond stubble fields shone. John's room was furnished simply. On the floor was the straw *tatami* mat on which he performed his Yoga exercises. At a collapsible bridge table he wrote Dream Songs. He said, "As you can see they keep me in a baby crib. They raise the sides at night to keep me from falling out. It is Humiliating! Listen, pal, I have written something new. It is," he assured me, raising hands that shook, "Absolutely a knockout!"

He put a finger to the bridge of his glasses, for nothing was steady here. Things shook and dropped. Inside and outside they wavered and flew. The straw of Golden Valley swirled on the hills.

John had waited a long time for this poet's happiness. He had suffered agonies of delay. Now came the poems. They were killing him.

> Nitid. They are shooting me full of sings.
> I give no rules. Write as short as you can, in order,
> of what matters.

Inspiration contained a death threat. He would, as he wrote the things he had waited and prayed for, fall apart. Drink was a stabilizer. It somewhat reduced the fatal intensity. Perhaps it replaced the public sanction which poets in the Twin Cities (or in Chicago, in Washington or New York) had to do without. This sanction was not wickedly withheld. It simply did not exist. No one minded if you bred poodles. No one objected if you wrote Dream Songs. Some men of genius were fortunate. They could somehow come to terms with their respective countries. Others had women, the bottle, the hospital. Even in France, far from the Twin Cities, a Verlaine had counted heavily on hospitals and prisons.

John drank, of course, and he took refuge in hospitals, but he also studied and taught. The teaching was important. His lectures were conscientiously, even pedantically prepared. He gave them everything he had. He came in from Golden Valley by cab to address his Humanities class.

He walked up the stone stairs of the University building looking very bad. He wore a huge Western sort of hat. Under the flare of the brim his pale face was long and thin. With tremulous composure, shoulders high, he stalked into the classroom. While the taxi waited, he gave his lecture. His first words were shaky, inaudible, but very soon other instructors had to shut their doors against his penetrating voice. He sweated heavily, his shaky fingers turned the numbered cards of his full and careful lecture outline but he was extremely proud of his dependability and of his power to perform. "Henry" was indeed one of the steadiest men on the block, as faithful to his schedule as Kant, as precise and reliable as a Honeywell product. His talk ended. Then, peanut-faced under the enormous hat and soaked in sweat, he entered the cab and was returned to The Golden Valley, to the *tatami* mat and the bridge table, to the penitential barrenness of the cure. No wonder after these solitary horrors that he was later grateful for group therapy, submitting democratically and eagerly to the criticisms of wacky truckers, graceful under the correction of drinking plumbers and mentally disturbed housewives. In hospitals he found his society. University colleagues were often more philistine, less tolerant of poets than alcoholics or suicidal girls. About *these* passioning countrymen he did not need to be ironical. Here his heart was open.

But everything went into his poems. His poems said everything. He himself said remarkably little. His songs were his love offerings. These offerings were not always accepted. Laid on the altar of, say, an Edmund Wilson, they sometimes were refused. Wilson, greatly respected by John, had written him a harsh letter about his later poems and John was wounded by this the last time I saw him. I read Wilson's letter. John sat at my table, meteor-bearded like John Brown, coughing softly and muttering that he couldn't understand—these were some of his best things. Then he snatched up the copy of *Love & Fame* which he had brought me and struck out certain poems,* scribbling in the margins, "Crap!" "Disgusting!" But of one poem, "Surprise Me," he wrote shakily, "This is certainly one of the truest things I've been gifted with."

I read it again now and see what he meant. I am moved by the life of a man I loved. He prays to be surprised by the "blessing gratuitous" "on some ordinary day." It would have to be an ordinary day, of course, an ordinary American day. The ordinariness of the days was what it was all about.

He had arrived during a sub-zero wave to give a reading in Chicago. High-shouldered in his thin coat and big Homburg, bearded, he coughed up phlegm. He looked decayed. He had been drinking and the reading was a disaster. His Princeton mutter, once an affectation, had become a vice. People strained to hear a word. Except when, following some arbitrary system of dy-

---

* From the second (1972) edition, Berryman deleted six poems.

namics, he shouted loudly, we could hear nothing. We left a disappointed, bewildered, angry audience. Dignified, he entered a waiting car, sat down, and vomited. He passed out in his room at the Quadrangle Club and slept through the faculty party given in his honor. But in the morning he was full of innocent cheer. He was chirping. It had been a great evening. He recalled an immense success. His cab came, we hugged each other, and he was off for the airport under a frozen sun.

He was a full professor now, and a celebrity. *Life* interviewed him. The *Life* photographer took ten thousand shots of him in Dublin. But John's human setting was oddly thin. He had, instead of a society, the ruined drunken poet's God to whom he prayed over his shoulder. Out of affection and goodwill he made gestures of normalcy. He was a husband, a citizen, a father, a householder, he went on the wagon, he fell off, he joined AA. He knocked himself out to be like everybody else—he liked, he loved, he cared, but he was aware that there was something peculiarly comical in all this. And at last it must have seemed that he had used up all his resources. Faith against despair, love versus nihilism had been the themes of his struggles and his poems. What he needed for his art had been supplied by his own person, by his mind, his wit. He drew it out of his vital organs, out of his very skin. At last there was no more. Reinforcements failed to arrive. Forces were not joined. The cycle of resolution, reform and relapse had become a bad joke which could not continue.

Towards the last he wrote

> It seems to be *dark* all the time.
> I have difficulty walking.
> I can remember what to say to my seminar
> but I don't know that I want to.
>
> I said in a Song once: I am unusually tired.
> I repeat that & increase it.
> I'm vomiting.
> I broke down today in the slow movement of K. 365.
>
> I certainly don't think I'll last much longer.

Contents

Higgaion

Every light in the house seemed to be on. At the same time there was a great deal of darkness about—in horizontal bands between bright bands. It puzzled him. He knew he was standing in his entry-hall. Wife facing him, cold eyes, her arm outstretched with a short glass—a little smaller than he liked—in her hand. Two cops to his left. His main Dean and wife off somewhere right, beyond the couch; no doubt others. His baby (qualm sick—he hadn't thought of the baby in six days while they were looking for him as far away as Zurich and Paris) must be asleep upstairs. It must be nine o'clock, it was Sunday night, no doubt about it. The girl had gone. He was looking into his wife's eyes and he was hearing her say: 'This is the last drink you will ever take.' Even as somewhere up in his feathery mind he said 'Screw that,' somewhere he also had an unnerving and apocalyptic feeling that this might be true. Wonder whether to shout with relief or horror. His fingers closed round the glass. Not feeling like making any noises whatever, very tired.

I

FIRST DAY

*Sufficient Vnto the day
is the euil thereof.*
Matthew 6[34]

1

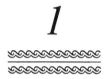

ALAN SEVERANCE, M.D., LITT. D., formerly Professor of Immunology and Molecular Biology, now the University Professor, Pulitzer Prize winner, etc.—twice-invited guest on the Dick Cavett Show (stoned once, and a riot)—found his right arm up under the pillow as usual—not his pillow though, bone-hard—and opened both eyes. He was back in hospital. How he had got there he didn't know. The last thing he remembered was Ruth's hard eyes and the voice of her final declaration. Time shifted. This room was larger, squarer, than last Spring's: he knew the treatment center had been moved from the Main Building, where he had continued in out-patient treatment and AA for the last four was it months, to Ward W, and the number of beds enlarged. The dull cream walls looked newer, the ceiling lower. One wall-length window, or three with the venetian half-closed. Ambiguous in light, 6:45 by his Gruen. His plan of yesterday harked back, and he shuddered. At least he was still alive, safe back in hospital. No gun, anyway. His forehead hurt. Otherwise he didn't feel bad at all. What he felt, as he got his elbow under him and reached for a cigarette, finding one, was determined. This was It. Third time—not lucky, sweat and blood, wasting no minute. His mind was clear as mountain air. Moreover he knew exactly what to *do* this

time: There must have been something wrong with his
First Step. Gus Larson, the savage, had bought it, but he
was wrong. He had taken him in, God knows without
meaning to but 'sincerity' was nothing in this game. Okay.
Start over. It felt he would not be fighting withdrawal this
time, either. He'd find out what the *hell* was wrong and fix
it. Submit was the ticket. He was prepared with all his
power for anything. He finished combing his hair, grinned
his half-ugly/charming ('Mad Charm Severance' his
place-card had read at a party in Cambridge thirty years
ago) stern face at himself with malice, and went out into
the corridor to find the new lounge and coffee. No lights
yet.

A verse from Joel drifted through his mind as he walked
and decided, by glow, the nurses' station was to the left.
'Awake, ye drunkards, and weep . . . for it is cut off from
your mouth.' Even so; 'Sanctify ye and fast.' Light was
pouring from a doorway with a black sign 'SNACK ROOM'
dim on the white wall beside it. A tiny kitchen was all,
with four bodies in it. He went confidently in. Greetings,
smiles all round—a hairy-chested man in a blue striped
wrapper leaning against the freezer-cabinet biting an Eskimo Pie—except from the plump-faced fair girl on the
near side of the little table. She glanced up toward him,
morose, that was all. Chin propped on the heel of her hand,
her lacy fingers. A medium short man, maybe forty, with a
short beard, looked familiar. 'Jasper?' 'Jasper Stone.' Well,
well.

The coffee was as bad as ever, Santa Maria. Discussion
of this fact. Data traded. And where was the lounge? This
was the lounge, frankly: there were three real ones, at the
end of each corridor, but nobody used them. Severance
mentioned nostalgia for the great single central lounge and
fine kitchen next to it in the old Ward D, alas, murmurs of
sympathy with universal (reciprocal) deterioration. He felt
comfortable at once with a wiry perky short Irishman

older than himself seated across from the silent girl. He had been a pro hockey player. Raised eyebrows, an innocent tough look, crinkled. Mild Charley, a goddamn saint (it was to turn out) with an Adam's apple. They swapped yarns, reading the others gently out of the Book of Life, growing excited together. Severance was never much of an athlete, despite the broad-shouldered thin build—too nerved up—but he had won numerals in track and crew, wrestled with seriousness (pinned a 180-pounder in Freshman gym in two minutes, he boasted—at 140 himself), and he had known that year a formidable quarter-miler, classmate named Johnson, nineteen, black as starless country night he came from, two national records already, a streak of light, and softly intelligent. He told Charley the high thing that happened after practice one afternoon when, Severance standing by, some metropolitan reporter asked if he had any formula for the 440, notoriously the worst distance of all. 'Sure,' said Johnson agreeably. 'I run the first 220 as fast as possible to get in front. Then I run the second 220 even faster, to stay out in front.' Everybody laughed— Severance elbowed his coffee over in self-appreciation—even Jeree smiled—but old Charley Boyle looked intensely surprised and gratified too, not just 'dulcedinis almae,' blue eyes sharp among wrinkles. They pointed out to each other the broad relevance of this attack on life's problems but its peculiar application to the present task of Severance, who had been through treatment twice before and ought to be desperate but wasn't, but was. He quoted Lautrec's remark, 'I paint with my penis,' and explained in one fancy sentence (bypassing a Matisse anecdote) who Lautrec was.

Here Severance had a coughing attack. One of these accompanied his first cigarette almost every morning and they recurred with grisly frequence all day and all evening until he dropped his final butt down the toilet, flushed it away, and reeled or crept into bed. They did not for some

reason occur in lecture or seminar, but everywhere else
they convulsed without mercy, horrible to all within hearing. Hundreds had clapped him on the back, men as well
as women had run for water, and to the near-prostration of
the seizures themselves—he often half-expected to *die* at
the third or fourth next hack—was superadded the exasperating need to reassure his stricken company: 'Just cigarettes (hack!)—three packs (hack!) a day for (hack!)
thirty-five years. My internist says I have a (hack hack
hack) chronic mild bronchitis. Die of cancer of the tra-
chea, caught too late to (hack! hack!) operate.' So they'd
all laugh together (hack!). Theatres were worst, sometimes
he gave up and slunk out. Not a problem, really, except
social; and the agony of the throat. He had tried everything, cutting down (many devices), pipes, cigars, even
cold turkey. He had quit once in Rome, for seven hours
after breakfast, during the last two of which his (first) wife
was begging him to take it up again.

Jeree murmured something about Wisconsin. Severance,
a little hard of hearing, bent forward. 'I'm sorry?' 'I was
in treatment before too.' This endeared her to him, the
pretty, sullen smooth-haired young lady with veteran troubles; he felt less isolated, and determined to help her. Feeble
himself, he was a St Bernard or Crusader castle to twenty
other people, hundreds of other people annually. She
couldn't be in his trouble but she didn't look good.

'They drink brandy in Wisconsin,' said hairy George,
roundheaded, goodnatured, early thirties, some sort of
businessman. 'A bartender in that thirsty but fastidious
State once told me they consume more brandy than all the
rest of the States put together. It isn't so. I happened on figures the other day: two and a half million gallons of
brandy. Quite a bit, buddies. But only a quarter of U.S.
brandy sales.'

Severance, though interested to hear this (he bought
facts, like all Americans except Emerson, and found real

ones hard to come by), had decided that he did not like George, all knowing smiles, shallow, glib, too cheerful altogether considering their circumstances, not really passionate about his future sobriety. Severance felt sorry for him. Severance also felt sorry for Jeree, who did not look in any shape to do much for herself, and even for Jasper Stone, the extremely bitter bearded poet, who did not seem to care about anything whatever. Other patients had crowded yawning into the nine-by-eleven cubicle now, and he felt sorry for everybody—except Charley and himself, who meant to do a job on this problem.

So he felt depressed when he learned after breakfast that he had been assigned to Louise's Group. Staring moodily down on a half-empty parking lot, he said to himself: 'I am at the point of death—physical mental spiritual. Highly promising. I have nothing to lose. There exists the lock, my only concern is the key. Is *Louise* likely to help me locate it?' Never watched Louise in Group, a goodlooking pale tall blackhaired girl (thirty-eight?), rather stiff and pleasant, but could she confront? His spirits lifted a little, though, when, looking around the fated room at ten o'clock, he found Julitta down in the corner off right of him—supercilious stare, upswept peroxide, trim ankles, pug nose. She sure could.

When all the chairs were full (nine, eleven, too many, what attention could he hope for in such a large Group? *one* confrontation a fortnight, maybe only one in the whole three weeks, moreover he had been saddened by the lecture, enjoyed it—he admired Father Krueger—but picked up nothing new, after all he'd heard it twice before—if he couldn't depend on lectures, what was there but Group and of course First Step Prep). Louise rose, saying, 'Let's all stand and pray the Serenity Prayer.' They joined moist hands and unisoned: 'God grant me the serenity to accept the things I cannot change' (he relaxed some as he said this—more trust, he needed more trust),

'the courage to change the things I can' (after all, if nothing happened by the weekend he could talk to the Chief
Counsellor about a possible transfer, it had been done),
'and the wisdom to know the difference.' His rich, prac-
tised, lecturer's voice had dominated the chorus, giving
him no pleasure as they sat down, returning each into his
own world.

He found Louise looking at him. 'Alan,' she said quietly
with an appearance of real interest, 'would you like to tell
us something about yourself? I know you were in treatment here last Spring, but that's about all.'

Dr Severance did not find himself as eager to talk as he
had expected. He was pretty sure he was not going to be
confronted—confrontation was unheard of during the
first week, patients being fogged-in for at least that long
(though he did not notice any fog in himself)—but he
felt uneasy. Business had begun. He braced himself and his
eyes sent her eyes eight feet away a rueful message.

'That's right,' he said, 'and before that at Howarden last
Fall. With genuine pain it occurs to me that I am an alcoholic, and it was the opinion of Dr Rome, delivered one
evening last July in Encounter-Group, that I might be un-
treatable. We'll see. I've been an alcoholic, so far as I can
judge, for twenty-three years. I hallucinated one morning
on the way home from an all-night party outside town—
heard voices. No trouble with liquor before that. What
was I—thirty-two. My first adulterous love affair. I'd
been faithful to my wife—despite heavy provocation
which I'll spare you—for five years. My mistress drank
heavily and I drank along with her, and afterward I just
kept on. Not all the time, of course, long periods of social
drinking, in fact once I was sober for four months—and
happy too, so my present wife tells me, I don't remember
anything about it. First wife left me, after eleven years, because she couldn't stand my drinking. Second wife left me,
very shortly indeed, same reason. Married nine years now

to Ruth, she said Treatment or else. Half a dozen hospitals, spent a night in jail, some reporter picked up the news and the most powerful newspaper in that State put it on the front page, just six lines but it was also on radio, and I had to resign—job I hated anyway but never mind that. The usual horror story.' His sense was odd: at once he felt nothing and he was shaken. He heard his voice unconvincingly reeling off the bloody old wives' tale, abrupted it with relief, glancing back at Louise—he had been staring at the empty middle of the floor, not much enjoying the circle of faces felt, not disliking them—let's face it, *bored.*

'Why do you think you're back in treatment?'

He was not keen on this question; but he might as well give her the word. 'One, I'm damned if I know, Louise. Two, I must have conned Gus Larson with my First Step: I don't see how. Gus is fond of glaring at some shivering alcoholic who has just recited his sins, leaning forward with his hands on his thighs and elbows out—a brutal type, coarse with suspicion—and booming at him, "You're a drunken *lying* halfassed bum!" *Or* he leans back, with a tender expression, and says gently: "In my opinion, you're not an alcoholic. I don't know what you're doing here. If I could drink the way you do—or say you do —friend, I *would*." So I don't see how I got away with whatever I got away with. My two treatments—believe it or not—were not exactly rest-cures. The first few days at Howarden—I spent a whole week in Intensive Care, I was in such bad physical shape, before they assigned me to a Unit and began treatment: my first four days and nights—I slept either not at all, or one hour, two hours—so I had twenty hours a day to go over every goddamned evil and awful thing I've done in the last twenty-odd years. The word is "fearless and searching" self-scrutiny, and believe me I held nothing back from myself. Well, that's the Fourth Step; and I haven't suffered greatly from the past since that week. I do still feel very bloody sometimes, but that's simply a menace, there's no use in it, I apply the damned Serenity Prayer to it, no offence, Louise. Then my Fifth Step was one of the most marvellous experiences of my extensive life. I took it with a young priest from New England. It's different at Howarden, I had not only written out the Step but he had studied the account. It was long. Well, we spent the first three hours on my vices and shortcomings, broke for lunch, and then two hours on my up-to-scratch's if any, and I went home and was sober for months until I suddenly got plunged into a brand new, very demanding and inflammatory job of work, finished it (I *thought*) in less than six weeks, at which point I was back up to a quart a day—I drink nothing but bourbon nowadays, only brandy abroad—and half-dead both body and nerves. My wife and our psychiatrist (a joker who knows nothing whatever about alcoholism) pushed me in here.' He stopped, tired, his heart slowed down slowly.

'Well, never mind the rest of it now,' Louise said patiently. 'So you think the trouble was the First Step. We'll go into that again when you've cleared up a little. I expect you are in for surprises. Freddie, what's going on with you at present?'

Severance was prepared for surprises, he considered. He knew something was wrong. He knew everything was wrong. Nevertheless he resented her assurance, and he thought: Not from you, sister. He applied his whole attention to Freddie's problem. Freddie it seemed was better educated (though his education seemed to Severance pathetic enough, as indeed did all modern education, particularly his own) than his hopelessly menial job took any proper account of. He was—afraid, and disappointing his wife —failing to use himself. The rest of the first hour and the whole second hour loitered vaguely by to elicit these meagre data, and even then Severance never discovered

just what the present job was. Still he intervened fre-
quently to offer reassurance, spine-stiffening, advice, for
which the rather timid, long-haired, engaging, hangdog
young man seemed reluctantly grateful. Louise was sharper
with Freddie than he anticipated, but that was not very.
Even Julitta came on only twice, not strong either time.
Sometimes long periods seemed to drag without one word
being spoken by anybody in the entire room. Severance
was not used to this, and it seemed a damned waste of (pre-
cious!) time. In Vin's Group silence had never been pres-
sureless; nobody just sat, for long anyway; either the heat
was on oneself and silence was one defence, or somebody
else was being confronted and one was either suffering
with him—Phyllis, Amos, the high Administration
official—or exasperated with him for either not levelling
or not sticking up for himself. Christ, what hours of minutes charged with fear and hope. Severance recalled with
definite nostalgia the tigerish Keg seething in the wings hot
to support Vin's assault, and crumple delusion.

'A tea party,' he said violently in the Snack Room after the
one-forty-five lecture, to Charley B (Charley R was a car-
roty fag from Houston. Apparently. Severance was not
censorious. Like many or some others, he had endured his
doubts. He heard himself seated in his red leather chair
drunk, desperate, shouting across their livingroom at his
first wife, after seven or eight years of mostly happy marriage and two years of depth-analysis high in a building on
Fifth Avenue in the 80's facing the park, 'I'm a homosexual, damn you. I just don't do anything about it!' and
saw her kind look). 'Louise presides at a tea party. I'll
never get anywhere except on my own. Okay.'
  The sweet hockey pro looked sweetly at him, earnestly
too. 'I hear different, Alan. Take it easy, my boy, as they
say around here. You haven't been in but one day yet. Last

time don't count, you know. Start all over. "Even faster"
but *gently*, son.'

'It's true what you say, pal.' Severance relaxed, dismiss-
ing images of female torsos dismembered and strewn. 'Besides, they've put me in Mini-group, which they didn't do
before and I could never find out heads or tails of about.
Maybe that's something.'

'All roads lead to Rome, as us Romans say.' He patted
Alan's shoulder. 'In the hands of the great God.'

2

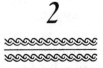

ALL DAY he had been up and down, and up, and down up.
Right now he felt gorgeous; but he wished he could level
off—say on the 'Grehant plateau' of stabilized high alcohol content, not that he wanted a drink. It was odd that in
treatment you never did (exception made for late Sunday
afternoons at Howarden after the adrenalin visits of Ruth
and the baby, and even then only in the first two, as far as
he could remember). He felt good, except for her not coming during the visiting hour just ended, or calling, or even
answering. After waiting until *nine o'clock*, he had called:
busy signal. *Busy* four times. Now she can't be out without
a babysitter there. If the phone was off the hook, she was
refusing even to listen to him. He could kill her. What
conceivable— Could she be unaware that she was menacing his morale at the very outset, when every resource, all
aplomb, might be called on at any second? 'I see a seething
pot.' Renounce. Renounce old Hah, the deity of unbounded time, master of blackouts. Re-enter Christian

time, twenty-four hours, Sufficient unto. The cagey Founders. Dr Bob dry into his casket, half a million prides mourning. Look up his life some time, there must be stuff.

How do you feel, they ask you, until you bite. I feel as follows: Casing the joint. Courbet arrived in Paris, twenty-one, cased the joint. First he decided to ignore and overcome the domestic opposition, which he identified as Delacroix, Ingres, Manet. Then he spat on the Italians, at that point top dog in Paris. He appreciated the Spanish (Velasquez) and the neglected Dutch (van Ostrade, Rembrandt). Not bad. Then he announced his programme, wagging a little beard: 'The only thing to do is to go off like a bomb across all the subdivisions.' Grandiose (a favourite put-down around here)? Not exactly. Painted his first great picture two years later, then vaulted into the Salon—'Self-portrait with the Black Dog.' Loved that dog.

Who did he love? Keen on Charley resolute as himself, a clown like himself. He had been playing the day over, seeking illumination, brooding, and little in it accounted for his strong hope except Charley, hardly older than himself. Middle-aged, physically poor, but strong in brain, indomitable, wipe out the opposition, create as he did in the lab with ballpoint and paper, create sobriety. Almost by himself. Group was a drag.

Now something frightful happened with Dr Severance. He sat erect up on the comfortless hospital chair, nape tingling. He heard himself looking down at the middle of the floor saying 'sober for months' after Howarden, and he shuddered.

It wasn't so.

Not only was it not so but he had been forced to *learn* that it was not so, and now he had 'forgotten' again. He was sincerely lost, relapsed back over ground gained long ago, months ago. He had given the same account of his first slip after Howarden when he came into Northeast in the Spring, and happened to mention it to his wife that evening. 'But Alan,' she said, 'that isn't so, dear. You had your first drink at the New Year's Eve party at the Browns.' 'The hell I did, I don't even remember any party at the Browns.' 'But there was, and you did. Then you had your second drink a week later at the Klosters—when you took it, I went upstairs to the bathroom and cried.' My God, he remembered the Klosters. He could see himself standing in their thronged gameroom with a highball in his hand. Then he had others. So she must be right about the Browns too, and instead of being sober for months and only starting again under work-pressure he had started drinking exactly three weeks after discharge, with no connexion with anything but *whim*, blind will, loss of contact with the First Step. This was not memory-loss, there was some damage of course to his celebrated memory but not much: this was delusion. And now it had taken over, again. One might shroud one's head. Forever. He felt—depressed.

II

THE FIRST STEP (I-IV)

Here are the steps we took, which we suggested
as a program of recovery:
1. We admitted we were powerless over alcohol—
  that our lives had become unmanageable.

ALCOHOLICS ANONYMOUS (1939, 1955)

3

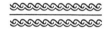

Alan Severance Begins Journal XIX

Shook, but recovering. I feel less defeated than last night. It is true I am nowhere near where I thought I was. Too bad. But at least I know it. Until that date business recurred to me I didn't even know it and didn't have a prayer. In fact it was *good.* The delusion cleared up this time all by itself, without proof-force from outside, and in just a few hours. That is positively hopeful, my friend. However: It was only by deliberately reviewing the empty day that I came on the symptom. I've got to keep in touch with myself, as closely as possible every second. I'm bound to come on more distortion, anywhere. So I've got to keep notes. Disagreeable prospect, when I need all my time for Step One, and besides look at my record of Journal-keeping—are there eighteen volumes so far, kept spasmodically for no reason I could ever make out and never looked back at (as I vaguely at the times intended)? Nevertheless! it's necessary, it's part of treatment, I have nothing to lose but a few minutes a day, the hell with it, let's go. And do read back over, say the weekend. Bet I pick up stuff & poke my head out of.

   Bet, sister. And you know what, Louise, you were right

already. I admit it. So much for the value of *that* judgment of mine. Maybe I'm in fact incapable of undeluded judgment at this time. Ah, unattractive reading. But I've got to know the worst.

Let's just see what this famous but it seems unreliable memory is up to, on a *neutral* subject. Biology 4, thirty-six years ago. Third floor of Fayerweather. Room John Jay sixth, where the empty bottle hurled from the terrace below through his open window met his skull entering the room at midnight from the corridor turning the light on and knocked him out—Crandall found him, four stitches, went wild with rage to the Dean, who investigated. Room impersonal as this one, good for study, wouldn't care for it now, need attractions around not distracting. Okay.

'*Recognition of "Self."* Research in immunology has implications of far more importance than simply the development of new and better vaccines for protection against disease—important as that is. The whole question of how the body recognizes some substances as "self" and others as "not self," which has a vital bearing on the problem of transplanting tissues and organs from one individual to another—'

Lefthand page, two-thirds of the way through the book. I can see it. If five words are wrong, I'll tear the page out & eat it, when I get home, if I get home, if I go home, goddamn Ruth. Not such a neutral subject, though, after all: *my baby!* Both ways. Science, Recovery. The point is to learn to recognize whiskey as *not* my 'self'—alien, in fact, to be rejected by the desire-center in the forebrain. Job no easier than—just the same as—cancer cure. My terrible silence all these years about that. *Cancer is a tissue.* The Serenity Prayer. So far it's been okay. Nobody else has noticed it lying there for all the world to see, just below the surface, if you know it's there and that the tools exist, and are ruthless enough. So far.

Dr Severance's consciousness, during this initial period of his third treatment for chronic alcoholism, was both intermittent and double. Now and then he would catch himself as it were and *come to;* he recognized that, and he attributed his absent-mindedness to his absolute and over-riding (and wise and noble) obsession with the First Step. He ate walked slept (not much) talked listened laughed, he 'admitted,' as usual. But really he was working on the First Step—that is to say, hallucinating. Dr Severance was in withdrawal. In a way he knew this—how could he not know it, with his experience? But when he heard Father Moen on Tuesday say, 'Tolerance to the drug finally becomes so low that a few hours' hard drinking may be fatal,' he did not apply this fact—well-known to him of course—to himself, and it would be the better part of a year before he would stop saying to himself and to others, 'I only drank six days,' substituting instead, 'At the end of the six days I was still alive.'

He seemed to himself acutely aware of everything. True, the lectures were boring—as he put it to Julitta when he happened to sit next to her at one evening lecture, 'I personally *hear things the first time* and I have a memory like a steel trap—except of course for alcoholic distortion and brain damage,' he added hurriedly. But he recog-

nized with intensity that anything (anything else, that is)
might contribute to his recovery: a hint even, overheard,
from another patient or a nurse or an orderly even, and
he went around in perpetual Alert, despite his obsession.
Others might be mentally loafing, not Alan Severance The
Nationally Famous Drinker (*Life* magazine had actually devoted a good deal of space in a long article about him some
years back to his drinking, and among the pictures was a
series of him holding forth to rapt pals in an Irish pub)
About To Become—and remain, remain—Dry As A
Bone.

What did particularly arrest and hold his attention was
Mini-group, which responded three mornings a week for
an hour and a half to the hypnotic voice and diffident
pounding inavoidable insights of Dr Linc Haller. Linc was
as long and bony and slangy, relaxed and even droll, unhurried say, as his great namesake, whom he did not otherwise resemble—imposing a certain jauntiness of style,
from his large round steel-rimmed spectacles to his elegant
dark-brown glossy strap-boots (features, both of them, despised by Severance, but as Marlene Dietrich's Alphabet
said, appointing Ernest Hemingway to 'A is for Arro-
gance,' 'On some people it looks good'). He was unpredictable, Severance decided after the first session. There
was no levelling or confronting. Noone spoke except
whoever Linc was working on, and Severance could not
see the point of having others—eight or nine patients, a
nurse or so—present at all. Session began with a brief explanation, about the tape-recorder 'to be heard only by us
in this room and then erased—Okay?' and Contracts:
'You decide' (he said to Severance across the room, as a
new patient, Linc was very personal, very private and
eye-seeking his communications) 'after a few days of listening, what bothers you most about yourself, what most
completely feels not-okay, and you tell me, and then some-
time we'll work on it together—Okay?'

'All clear,' said Severance. 'Can I propose a Contract now?'

Linc drooped his eyelids a little and did not say anything. Severance was to grow used to this patience, but this first time he felt it, with surprise, as pressure, as criticism even. 'Sure,' said Linc finally and grinned, like a long, lounging, very adult fifty-year-old child of six or seven, younger than Rachel even.

'Well, it's this. I don't seem to be too goddamned happy about my goddamned reputation, "celebrity" it's called. Either I take it too high, which is ridiculous, it amounts to nothing whatever, or I am actually ashamed of it. I even feel it's *right* to feel ashamed of it, since other people a hell of a lot more worthy than I am have no reputation whatever. The same goes for money—I have a great deal at present, and some of my friends don't, and I sweat. But mostly it's "fame." I can't get used to it, and I know there must be something wrong about this, because frankly *it's not my fault*, I didn't ask for it, I have never "operated" for one second in that direction, and in some ways I didn't even expect it, during my lifetime. Also Arita said to me last night, the fat night-nurse, that she was "uncomfortable" with my word "ashamed" and she's a sensible girl, I knew her very well last Spring in treatment. She says, "Learn to live with it." That sounds sensible, but just try it. I arrive in a strange city, even abroad, and there's a reporter and a photographer, God knows how, get used to *that*. On the other hand, there's nothing accidental about it. My gifts are unusual, I take no credit for them, but I ought to be able to take credit for the hardest and most self-sacrificing kind of lifelong work, and certain other qualities too—"daring" is one of my critics' favourite words, and there's something in it, and especially and above all perseverance: when the first volume of my most important work so far appeared, many predicted that I could not continue it and others predicted I could not bring it to a close. I did both—took me thirteen years, drinking like a madman too, some of the time. So why should I skulk around like a sneak-thief or a corporate people-robber who *knows* he is. What about that?' Severance was out of breath with excitement.

'You sound as if you were asking for advice,' Linc said thoughtfully with some irony perhaps. 'I don't give advice, I fulfil Contracts—which may or may not work. You've already had what sounds like good advice from your friend Arita, and it doesn't seem to do you any good. You hurt. Maybe what she meant was, "*Try* to learn to live with your reputation." I am against the idea: *trying*. You either do something or you don't.' (Obscurely, in what perspective he could hardly have described, Severance felt sorry to hear Linc proclaim this. It had an authoritative ring that was both attractive and discouraging.) 'Give it less thought, anyway, and we'll get around to you. There's no hurry of course. If you have a dream, you might let us hear it. Mabel, have you been thinking about your Contract? Are you ready to make one?'

Mabel had not been thinking about her Contract, and he went on to George, a white-faced bald young man sitting flaccidly with his plump bare arms dangling between his knees. He asked questions, switching on the recorder, and George with great reluctance, discounting and apologizing for every admission he made of what was obviously a considerable success in life, responded. At one point Linc broke off to say, 'I'll give the new people some data about the framework within which we operate in TA.' Uncoiling to a great dapper height he crossed the room to the blackboard.

Circling a 'P' with an 'A' under it and a 'C' under that, for the three persons in everybody's personality, Parent, Adult, Child, he said 'Injunctions' for P and wrote the verb 'should' by it, then 'I will' after A, adding 'acts,' and finally 'want' after C. Severance, who had been a rigid Freudian for thirty years, with heavy admixture however from Reich's early work, owing to his seven-year analysis, and immense extension of dream-interpretation owing to a self-analysis several years after that, liked this scheme, at first blush, better than Freud's; the indebtedness was almost complete but not quite: metaphor made a difference, as in Sullivan's explanation of how the universe must be both unbounded and finite. Then Linc went into what he called 'Witch-Messages'—'Don't be,' from the Father, 'Don't be you,' from the Mother. Severance bought this too. Yes indeed. He felt illuminated. Then he heard what interested him even more and would dominate for a long time to come his never-ceasing quotidian explanation to himself of everything that he was doing and everything that happened to him.

The human need for Recognition, Linc said to them: Strokes—the patting and stroking and cuddling of a baby, *without which*—some babies don't live. Clinical data on orphans institutionalized and with fosters. Same situation at the end of life. Man retires at sixty-five and goes to Florida to live it up with leisure, hardearned leisure and shuffleboard—no salary cheques, no praise, no requests, no challenges, no triumphs—all that came to an end with the testimonial dinner (200 plus-strokes, obviating the need for any more ever) and the gold watch—no anxiety even, only no plus-strokes: dead in a year. (One of Severance's older friends, long ago, had made it in six months.) So a lacuna of plus-strokes menaced biology itself. On the other hand, too many plus-strokes menaced sanity (Fame, thought Dr Severance): a swelled head and delusions. Requisite: a minimum. Optimum: a *good many*—because the usual environment was full of minus-strokes—poor pay or unemployment, nagging wife, Sophia Loren abroad somewhere unavailable, the kids' lousy education, banal and useless or destructive work (two friends at General making anti-personnel explosives), no mail, hippies running

riot, you name it. The worst minus-strokes were those you
gave yourself all the time; in the case of the alcoholic, Disgust and Rejection internalized as Shame and Guilt. I
can't win. Everybody hates me, I'm no good, I'll never get
back on the boat, might as well drink myself to death,
poor fellow, never had a chance or if so, blew it, see you
Downstairs, so long everybody, death of the nearest animal, meant no harm, just *worthless*—Okay?

Severance embraced it hook line and sinker.

What was a plus-stroke to one man (a fan letter say) was
a minus-stroke to another (lui-même, mostly). Some
needed *more* plus-strokes than others. He himself was an
Eagle-brand baby—mother couldn't nurse—insatiable
greed for reassurance. He had to *give himself* plus-strokes
when too few came in from outside. And minus-strokes?
Earlier on the way down to breakfast he had waved
a real smile to the nurse's aide on the station, a new
girl, 'Good morning, Miss!' A look of stone, mouth shut.
Well! as he turned down the stairs he swung into play the
oldest scientific award in the country, the stupid Pulitzer, a
Congressional grant with its citation, two honorary degrees, and the 'Severance enclave in Jerusalem' some author there had written to him existed wanting him to come
and talk to them. One minus-stroke (to *him* 56), 87 plus-
strokes; barely even, but he got his appetite back and the
images of slain nurse's aides strewn around receded. As Mr
Frost had admitted to him—slyly, complicity-bit—
across the dinner-table once, after some outrageous de-
mand or other on his secretary's grown children serving
them, 'I require special treatment.' He wasn't that bad, but
it might be coming.

Linc had gone back to his chair and was working with
George.

It gradually became plain that George's father, long
dead now, had not given George the right time; wanted
another athlete, like George's older brother, who also put

down George, who wanted to emulate him but who was
even more streaming with passion to get his father's approval. George no good at football, went out for coaching
though, against all the competition finally in his senior
year (high school) *made* manager, brought the news as a
heave offering to his father and got shot down by a bitter
comparative reference to his brother's All-State history at
left half. Ignominy. Severance burned. At least he hadn't
had that to face, and then the self-put-down. *His* plus-
strokes going for him he was only too familiar with, and in
a way, though he saw that George's problem was phantom, he envied him his humility, little as it was justified.

Linc said, rather offhand but his voice had developed
and increased a certain resonant pressure, Severance could
see that the rest of the group had ceased to exist for
George and in fact George was sitting up straighter, had
uncrossed his ankles, hands in his lap now, 'Would you
like to have a talk with your father?'

'I guess so,' said George doubtfully, "if only it wasn't too
late.'

'Do you have anything you want to say to him?'

'I don't know. Anyway it's impossible. Yes, I would.'

'Okay!' Linc got up and borrowed the nurse's chair to
put in front of George, facing him, empty. He sat back
down. 'Your father is sitting in the chair.' Long silence.
'You can see him.' Silence. 'Can you see him?'

'Yes,' George's voice was far-away, hard to hear. He
was staring at where the head would be.

'What does he look like? Can you describe him?'

'Sure. Just the usual. Like after supper, in the livingroom.'

'What expression has he got?'

'He's smiling at me.'

'What do you say to him?' Silence. 'What do you say to
him?'

' "Hi, Dad." '

'And he says?'

' "Hi, George." '

'And you say?'

' "I miss you a lot, Dad." '

Severance's eyes filled with tears, his breathing was difficult, he could only partly attend as George's father said, "I miss you too," and George said, "I made manager, Dad," and his father said, "I'm proud of you, George," and George said, "I love you, Dad." There was more, but Severance was fighting sobs and didn't hear it, before Linc's voice changed, acquired a snap, 'Now your father's not there any more and you're back here with us.'

George looked at him dazed, his hands braced on his knees relaxed, he leaned back, though not as before.

'Do you remember what just happened?'

'Sure.'

'How do you feel?'

'Wonderful. I feel happy.'

'You know that none of it was real. Your father has been dead for eleven years—okay?'

'Sure.'

'You feel okay about that?'

'Yes.'

'You employ four men, is that right?'

Reluctantly: 'Yes.'

'You're thinking of expanding. Right?'

'Yes.'

'Three other firms like yours have failed while yours has been succeeding. Right?'

'Yes.'

'Did you have any help in your success?'

'Well—'

'Yes or no. Did you have any financial backing or did you do it all yourself? Yes or no. You did it alone?'

With recovered firmness, with actual energy: 'Yes.'

'Climb up on your chair.'

Looking sheepish, but half-grinning, George stood awkwardly up onto his little straight chair and looked down across at Linc.

'Now say, "I did it." '

George hesitated. 'I did it,' he said embarrassed.

'No. Louder.'

'I did it!' He sounded as if he meant it.

'Louder.'

'*I did it!*' He was crowing like a cock, and every nerve in Severance's body was jumping. 'I DID IT. I DID IT.'

Cheers from everybody, general exultation, universal relief and joy. Severance felt triumphant. George climbed down and two or three patients rushed over to embrace him. Out of the tangle presently he sat back down, fists on his knees, bolt upright, eyes flashing.

'How do you feel?'

'*Okay!*'

'It's okay to feel okay, George. Remember that. It's okay to feel okay,' said Linc, turning off the tape-recorder.

5

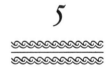

SEVERANCE REMAINED FASCINATED, all through Louise's boring Group and lunch: he wished his problems were as simple. One in fact was the opposite. He had no difficulty indeed in giving himself credit, and over-credit the sky's the limit, for his bloody pathetic achievements such as they were. Still it was marvellous to see a man stop beating up on himself—obeying Witch-Messages—worshipping at the resented shrine of an unjust father. Marvellous! He felt

brought forward, and listened closely to Father Mankey's
one-fifteen lecture, making notes.

> 'aft., 13 Oct   *Guilt*
>   recognition
>   sorrow
>   acknowledgement
>   (restitution)
>   resolve not to repeat the offence
>   *Forgiveness* (based on desire to restore the
>   prior rel'n)
>   David to Shemi, "You shall not die"
>   *insincere* dying instr'n "Oh, yes, and
>   kill Shemi"
>   Reconciliation must be based on sincerity on
>   both sides, *with trust*—maybe impru-
>   dent! *but*—
>   Immense difficulty of the offending person be-
>   coming *convinced* he's forgiven
>   (Peter's betrayal, 3:3 "Feed my sheep")'

Again, not his problem. He had only had one enemy in the
world, so far as he could remember, and he certainly had
been bitter without a ceiling against this man so long as he
suffered under his authority; but after his power over Severance was taken from him by the University President
Severance half-forgot him and was actually sorry when the
man finally had to resign under pressure both from below
and lateral, partly owing to accumulated rage over his
treatment of Severance and similar power-abuses—had
thought of writing him a note, desisted when he could see
no way of avoiding a graceless and cruel note of triumph
he didn't actually feel, though he did feel some vindication
and was happy to see that domain of the University delivered from tyranny. An able scholar too; normal corruption
of office. No, forgiveness was not his sweat, and a lucky

thing; he could see himself, located there, being very very hard. As for guilt, the vast business of that he'd worked through, and survived, at Howarden, in the first four or five days *and* nights after he was transferred from Intensive Care.

He went off, after two hours in his room on Step One, to First Step Prep at four o'clock in high spirits with a sinking heart, determined to Bear All. But when names had been admitted around the circle of eight or ten victims, he found Gus regarding him with unexpected friendliness. 'Alan, it hurts my old heart to see you back' (Gus was twenty years younger than Severance) 'but I'd rather see you back than dead. There's always hope, as the man says. What do you think happened?'

Severance took a deep breath. 'Hell and shit happened, Gus. I went out cocky and never had a prayer. Six or seven slips in the first two months, all faithfully reported —practically every week—to both Dr Rome's Encounter-Group and my AA squad, AND I got hell and hell over again. Never missed a meeting. I figure now the slips not only let me drink but kept me the dead-center attention of both groups. I never enjoyed the drinking, and in fact I didn't even want to drink. It was *whim*-drinking. I remember one noon maybe six days out of hospital—Vin had me still coming to Group—I was walking down Barsnet afterward and I found myself wondering whether I would turn off right towards the University and the bus home or whether I would just continue *right on* to the Circle and up right one block to the main bar I use there, and have a few. *Wondering.* My whole fate depending on pure chance. If that happened now, I would turn straight around and back to the hospital and sign in for more treatment. My God. Well, a few days later, of course, I took a bus to Ashville and had two or three drinks. And so on. Then after two months of this, I put my foot down. I decided I would rather die than walk in on Wednesday

night and look at Dr Rome and confess another slip. No
No, not for Baby. So I went two months, and that in-
cluded a trip to Mexico far from easy. I sweated in the
plane—my wife and daughter were in seats together behind me—and I sweated in the airports, especially San
Antonio, and I sweated the week in Mexico City. It was
no Programme whatever, it was pure pride and rage that
kept me sober. Then I went on a trip East—trips are
hard on me—and drank six days; shacked up in the end
with an Arab girl here in town, totally out of touch and
entirely out of my mind; formed a perfectly satisfactory
suicide plan for yesterday morning as soon as the gun-
stores opened, for no reason at all changed my mind, had
the girl drive me home and here I am. It must have been
the First Step, though God knows you seemed satisfied
yourself, and brother, I'm at it.'

'Well,' Gus said amiably, 'there's no hurry about the
First Step. But why do you think this time will be any different from your previous treatments?'

'I had a heavy diminution the other morning of: self-
pity, rage, resentments—a load so great I've spent two
well-known volumes on it. I *don't* depend on AA, I went
every week and drank almost every week for those first
two months. A new view and practice of Steps One and
Three. I pray a good deal.'

'What are you going to *do* when you want that drink?
—just pray?' and Mike—his old friend Mike from last
Spring sitting in, formidably dry: 'How about the gradual
building up over *months?* How do you plan to fill all that
time?' Other questions, too, and he answered them but he
sounded uneasy and he felt even more uneasy than he
sounded, and he was amazed when, after the meeting broke
up at quarter past five, Gus took him aside in the corridor
and actually said, 'I'm counting on you to help me some,
Alan? Do you think you can?'

'Christ, Gus,' Severance was overwhelmed, 'I would not like anything better in the world, if I thought I could.'

'We're all sick in our degrees around here,' Gus said warmly, 'but we can help each other even where we're blind ourselves. You're a nice guy, Alan. I'm counting on you, then.'

Severance was too choked-up to speak. He went to his room and sat unnerved till the gong went for dinner. 'How's it going?' Charley asked, looking up as they clattered downstairs together. 'Terrific,' said Severance. 'I'm not so keen on myself but Gus thinks I may be able to help him with the others.'

*   *   *

Though not exactly a street-angel-house-devil like his grandfather (according to his grandmother, who hated men), Severance was a man of intermittent and irreconcilable virtue. One of his heroes was some priest once read about, who 'treated everyone with the utmost kindness: if he favoured anyone it was the most unfortunate, and especially those who rebelled.' Severance liked that, it was just how he treated his students, and its coincidence with how he thought he *ought* to treat his students—and not only his students but his colleagues' students, for Dr Severance was much applied to, his office was a sort of problem-clinic on Tuesday afternoons from three to four-thirty or six— gave him deep satisfaction: there was one corner where he was okay. He gave himself credit, vigorously. His wife he did not see in either of these positions—though he recognized daily and with bitter remorse her misfortune in having married *him* and he sympathized (secretly) with her rare up-on-her-hind-legs revolts against his tyranny. He was very much afraid of her and he gave her a hard time. She often complained that any damned student, especially

if female, had his automatic undivided attention sooner
than she did, that he was a louse, that he did not care anything about her. None of this was true, he considered. He
thought about her night and day, for instance her problems
and inadequacy as a teacher (for she had finally finished her
training and was teaching the 6th grade in a suburban
school, her first job ever). It was true he felt some contempt (carefully concealed, and he was ashamed of it) for
her cowardice in not standing up to her students, of whom
she was mortally afraid, every third morning at breakfast
she was half-in-shock at the prospect of facing them again.
On the other hand, how could he expect her to cope with
aimless brutes? One of her boys, a bright little fellow
named Drake, had broken a little girl's arm in class one
day; another had hoisted an atlas heavy as a boulder and
slammed it down on the cranium of the little girl sitting in
front of him, he might have given her concussion; the
Generation Gap was real, Severance's blood boiled, he was
fertile with devices against these monsters, only he de-
plored her helplessness, doubted if she had any vocation.
He looked at her with rage, seated on the edge of his hospital bed that evening, and said, 'Where the hell were you?
I called four times.'

'Did you? I'm sorry, Alan. I was so exhausted from the
six days' strain I just went to bed right after dinner, even
before Rachel did, taking the phone off the hook so I
wouldn't be wakened by one of your damned fans ringing
up from distant States in the middle of the night.'

'That's not my fault, for Christ's sake—'

'Well, you complain, but in my opinion you get a
charge out of it. I don't.'

'Didn't you know I'd want to see you and Rachel?'

'Frankly, no. You were so weird that night, I didn't
know whether you'd *ever* want to see me again, and—
even more frankly—vice versa. I'm grateful for your
coming home at last, but I was half out of my mind. And

I'm not going to reproach you about that girl but that wasn't an entirely agreeable experience either.'

'I know, Ruth. I was insane. She took care of me.'

'I bet. Actually though, I was sorry for her later. It probably wasn't her fault and it can't have been pleasant for her having *you* agree with me—finally—that she really had to leave. If I knew how to reach her, I would have called to say I understood and didn't blame her. Do you happen to know how?'

'No,' he lied, 'it's all very vague to me. She's somewhere in Ashville Heights, all I remember. Never mind. How is Rachel?'

'Well, I didn't tell her you'd called from the airport, she thought you were still in the East. She's sorry you're back in hospital. Alan, she knows far more than you think, and hurts more.'

'It kills me. I know. I've remembered things. At Howarden, when I was working on the Fourth Step, I said to myself: At least my drinking hasn't done the baby any harm, she's too young. But last Spring, here, I woke up. I remembered two little things. When she said to you once, "Daddy dinks too much," and you told her, "You mustn't say that, Rachel," and you and I laughed. Ha ha. Then when she said to you, "Daddy never plays with me," and she cried, my God when I heard that I thought I would die.'

'All past, Alan,' she said looking at his bowed skull kindly. 'You've been very good with her all summer. Much much better. Do you want to go down and see her.'

'Better not. I feel torn to pieces. They've had me going like a maniac all day. Listen, will you bring my old First Step over tomorrow, it's in the pile on top of Webster up in the Study.'

'Yes. It does seem to be the First Step, doesn't it?'

'What were the goddamned cops doing there, anyway? And Oliver, for God's sake.'

'All that was pure coincidence. I hadn't asked any of them. Oliver had alerted the campus police and two just stopped by to see if I could give them any pointers. We didn't know *where* you were, except something you said to Floyd over there one night drinking and something you said to Amy. They'd only been there five minutes. Wilbur and Rose had come to hold my hand. Nothing was *planned*.'

'Well, I nearly went crazy. My own house!'

'It's our house.'

'Okay!'

They patched up a hostile reconciliation. At least she hadn't been planting authorities on him and he had been forgiven (maybe) the six days berserk and the Arab girl and you name it. Wince for the baby. He lit a cigarette, blanketed his feelings, and went to work. Rapidly he listed his qualities—his equipment, after all:

> 'arrogant
> sensitive & madly nervous (except
>   performances etc)
> hard-working
> authoritative but *suum cuique*
> witty
> loyal
> kind: cruel as Pharaoh
> indifferent, bored; procrastinating
> devout; & "national"
> ambitious
> guilt-ridden
> obstinate
> an attentive listener; impatient
> "daring," "courageous," "dangerous"
> blunt
> *"original"*

> learned
> resourceful
> power of *connexion* (the point, for my type
>   of mind)
> despairing, afraid of suicide
> *tired*'

Not so bad after all. Better than he expected. Promising.

*   *   *

It was eleven at night in the Snack Room and Severance and Jasper Stone were seated at the little table walking stiff-legged around each other. Jeree sat with them, looking inert. A shitass orderly lounged against the freezer. Severance could tell you something about *him*.

'I don't think much of your *Nation* stuff,' the poet said airily, 'when I see one. I admit your Courbet a while ago was amusing but your attempt to supply the jerk with a spiritual life was pathetic.'

Severance, pleased but stung: 'So you're an expert on Courbet, are you?'

'Are you?'

'No,' he admitted. 'But isn't it *likely* I know more about him than you do? You haven't seen Boudaille's book.'

'Isn't it a fact that he never painted a religious subject in his greedy life?'

'Depends, Stone. I read a valley-scene in Des Moines as a spiritual allegory. Road rounding the foot of a bluff, tiny figure on it, heavy rockmass overhead threatening but not falling, menace but no sweat, weird bright light around the bend right, out of his sight, he doesn't know he'll make it but he's willing to try and in fact he'll make it. Like you and me maybe, me this time.'

'Never been in Des Moines. Had an insolent review there once. How do you come to be writing about art anyway?'

'They'd been looking for a man for years, they said, and wrote to me out of the blue, just on the chance, after some remark I threw off on a talk-show.'

'Quite the Universal Man, aren't you?' Jasper Stone was sneering, not slightly. 'Alberti and Pico della Mirandola bit. Leonardo bit. How does it feel to be omnicompetent, Doctor?'

'Screw you too,' Severance smiled at the poet. 'I know practically *nothing*, my boy. Take Hebrew. Never minded my Jewish friends knowing Hebrew but when Edmund Wilson took it up—after Russian—at fifty-odd, I thought God damn it. Visiting job at Indiana eighteen years ago, nothing to do but drink, made friends with the Hebrew instructor (an interesting guy, Hamburg Arabic scholar, greatest expert living on the date of the Alhambra, asked to lecture on it at Madrid and Cambridge England, when Israel got independence thought it his duty to go there and work as an architect—he was trained at that too—for ten years, built houses exactly ten years, quit and brought his mother to the U.S. and began teaching elementary Hebrew at Indiana)—okay, I sat in. Only two students, one couldn't learn the alphabet and dropped it the first week, the other was a dope who had to take it for Divinity School; and me. I did six lessons each assignment, *Ivreet Chayah*. But Peretz's responsibility was to the dope, not me, so he had him recite the whole hour, and I gave up. No staying power, Stone. Same with Classical Chinese. I ordered a new Introduction from Oxford and sailed into a passage by Meng-Tzu. What a textbook. No translation, only linguistic notes and a glossary in the back. It was when I learnt that in order to look up a character you had to know the *order* in which its strokes were made, I tell you my mind reeled. Not like an English professor one of my students once told me about: decided to learn Mandarin: walled off part of his livingroom, laid in books and a toilet, left an opening for his wife to pass food in, and *set*

to. Seven weeks later, walked out saying, "I know
Chinese." '

'Your name is against you,' the poet said thoughtfully.
Severance stared at him. 'What?'

'Your name, old boy. We might render it as "The Har-
monious Inter-breaker." Not so good. Epithet hangs not
with noun. Plink.'

Severance did not follow, but he heard satire and being
as sensitive as the next man about his name (he didn't like it
much himself, but he had made it a going concern and
moreover children, who never got it right though, liked it)
he thrilled resentment. 'Explain,' he said coldly.

' "Alan" is *harmony*, right? Celtic, I believe. Your last
name is wide open. Tearer-apart of people, disrupter.'

Stung, the scientist ran through a dozen counterstrokes.
He felt an absolute horror for those sinners. 'Sowers-of-
Discord' Dante had a circle for, deep deep down. He often
thought of a monster named Rainey—couldn't recall her
first name—who had gained the confidence of a simple
young housewife in uptown New York and persuaded her
to arrange the husband's murder for his insurance. They
put it up to a cabdriver, to crush him against an El pillar
on his evening walk with the dog, but the cabbie lost his
nerve, and testified against them after a second cabbie was
less—say, scrupulous? He shuddered. Nothing like that,
at least, on his awful conscience. One thing he was—
His mind stopped. Eve's husband had finally left her for
one of their friends, and worse still, Harvey just last year
had walked out on Bea and shacked up with a twenty-
year-old psychiatric patient of his. Long afterward, it's
true, and Eve had had at least one other lover since, to his
knowledge—but even if neither husband had suspected
(*one did, though*—'Bea, there just can't be any more of
this,' when she got home once again at 4 a.m.) what responsibility could he escape for these ghastly breakups? He wondered if he was sweating.

He was. Jasper was offering a paper napkin across the table. 'You look ill. Get the nurse?' Even Jeree had an expression, wide light eyes.

*   *   *

Northeast Hospital's first Repeater's Group slunk together at the appointed hour—*la Roche de dix heures* overhanging Courbet's village, by which the peasants told time, the existential hour in Ward W when one's fate hung in a balance until noon or even on past noon, the bastards. Severance looked round the room at the other old lags. Jeree lifted him a glance half-recognition. The others were strangers, except, to his mingled sense of challenge support fight, Keg G——, the Knife, most fearsome of confronters, who had been with Vin in the Spring as counsellor-trainee. On the whole, Severance was glad to see him; an ally against himself. Bony, with bright eyes, a sharp intellectual teutonic look, a high narrow forehead under brush-hair, a new goatee. It was hard to imagine Keg drinking—it was hard to imagine most of them drinking (Jeree? grandmotherly-groomed Letty?)—though he had only been out of treatment a few months when he came back for training. Thirty years old maybe, Severance's height (five-ten), leashed. The Counsellor was apparently named Harley, new from Renton or somewhere but a legend. It was not hard to imagine Harley drinking, and word was he had been jailed 256 times, not to speak of hospitals from Nevada to Kentucky, lost wives, near-deaths. Droopy-eyed, hardbitten, long-chinned, with a loose slouch and nervous fingers; ageless; you'll get away with nothing, I've been there before you. After the Serenity Prayer, and everybody had said his name around in turn, he began casually.

'It's been decided on high,' he said slowly, looking slowly from one tense face to another, 'that you Repeaters need special treatment. I'm a Repeater myself, been in treatment five times in three States, so maybe we can work something out. But this is your Group. Keg and I are just here to help out. And Group is not just here in this room two hours a day five days a week. Don't you believe it. Or you'll believe till Easter. Treatment goes on every minute you're awake. Only you won't believe till Easter. Every one of you is on trial: if you don't show definite progress by the end of three weeks, you're out. You can go some-where else, if they'll take you, or you can drink, just as you like. You've all got to seek each other out and level with each other and take the risk of confronting each other, namely give each other hell. It's your only chance to get well. Well, we don't say "well": well*er*. Now the first thing is that nothing said in this room goes outside. Noth-ing. Got that? Nothing. And the other thing is that we're not going to do any treatment today.' Severance seethed amazement and chagrin: why the hell *not?* 'Keg will take over from here.'

Keg rose and stood with his back to the blackboard. He looked bitter. 'You've got to have some disciplines. The other patients may not need them—in my opinion they do—but certainly you do. I want everybody to think and write out whatever things he thinks he or she ought to do every day. Don't take on too much, but take on any-thing you think is necessary to create a chance for your so-briety. Tomorrow I'll tally the results. That's all for now, people. Get to work on your Programmes.'

The patients seemed, some uneasy, more stunned, by the rapidity and unexpectedness of this development—or lack of development, as Severance put it angrily to Mary-Jane in the corridor, 'What do *you* think about it?'

'I suppose they know what they're doing,' she said look-ing up at him in a reserved, friendly way. She did not seem at all sure of herself, and he felt a moment's pity for this low-voiced ruin of a young gentlewoman, haggard and el-egant even in old jeans, a shapeless sweater over thin shoulders. Thirty-two, say? surely she had been beautiful and recently, with her highpiled rich brown hair wispy over a pale creased forehead and large concerned brown eyes. 'It's a cinch we're no judge of anything, or I know I'm not.'

'It's a goddamn waste of Group-time,' he said savagely. 'And it's so unlike Keg. I don't know anything about this Harley but I was in Vin's Group with Keg last Spring, He's not about to let anybody off any hook. Why this vacation? I'm very busy myself.'

She smiled. 'Don't be, Alan. Easy does it, if anything. When did you come back in?'

'Sunday night. How about you?'

'This is my second week. End of it.'

'How does it seem to be going?'

'I didn't get anywhere for ten days.' She paused and then went on reluctantly, 'But I made a breakthrough last Friday.' She sounded dubious.

Severance heard reality, though, and spurted excitement. 'Marvellous. What happened, if you want to tell me? Come on in my room five minutes if you're free. We've got the whole damn morning.'

She sat gently on the side of his unmade bed, crossing her narrow jeans and locking one meagre ankle behind the other. Her cheeks were hollow, less pale than her brow. She looked very calm. He tapped her out a cigarette and lighted it.

'I was having a war with Julitta. I hated her guts. I wasn't thinking of leaving, but really I felt awful, pure bitter. Then a friend I made at Howarden last year came to see me and gave me the word: Julitta was trying to help me. My God, that was hard to accept. But somehow she seemed all different the next day—Friday—or I just was seeing her with different eyes; and we made friends, and I broke down, and that was it. I've felt changed since. I have a long long way to go, new friend, but I've got some hope. I *love* Julitta.'

'Well, Christ, I can't imagine loving Julitta, but I see what you mean. The same thing happened to me with Vin, or even more so. I *admired* him all right—he's spectacular, blazing with invention and knowledge of life, wonderfully creative and quick—but I thought he was arrogant and cruel and I wasn't at all clear that he was *sincere*. I'd watched him and Keg brutalize first a poor woman and then two men, one a high Administration official whom Vin made Indian-wrestle with a pathetic young schoolteacher, a guy named Jim who hated the Administration from the word go, and of course crumpled the official, twice. It was ghastly. I couldn't understand it. Then, in the most dramatic way possible, the exact opposite happened —to me. I was in a crisis—not psychological—it was exterofective (forgive my jargon)—*real life* I mean, not Group-stuff; and *Vin* came to my rescue, my worst enemy. At first I couldn't believe it, and when I finally had to, I burst into tears and cried like a baby for two hours. I'll tell you the whole story some time. Anyway—'

'Why don't you tell me now?' Mary-Jane said. 'I'm interested. You don't look as if you would cry very easily.'

'Well, I do and I don't.' He looked at her doubtfully through his bifocals. He was moved by her interest, though long and sufficiently used to people's being interested in him, but he wasn't sure he could make himself clear. He found he wanted to. After all, they had both been through Howarden and not made it, and they had both had breakthroughs, only his hadn't stuck, would hers? He felt close to her. 'All right, but I'll have to abbreviate it. Besides there were things I didn't find out until later. The situation was this: I was giving an odd course over in the Arts College and I had permission from my psychiatrist to taxi across town, give my afternoon lecture, and come back. Two hours, that's all. I've done the same thing from two other hospitals. Well, the first thing Vin did in Group that morning—second Tuesday in treatment it was—was turn to me and say, "I've just talked to Dr Gullixson on the phone and he's withdrawn his consent to your pass." I was horrified. I am not sure I have ever been so shocked in my life. I said, "You and he have no authority over me, I'll just call a cab and go." Then the heat began. "You're shaking like a leaf." I said, "I don't shake when I lecture" (and on the whole that's true). "You can't walk." "I can walk well enough. There's an elevator." "We're afraid you may have a convulsion." "A convulsion," I said grimly, "That's science-fiction, I've never had a convulsion in my life." (Ha ha, I had my first seizure a week later, alone in the lounge at midnight, and might have died if people hadn't been in the kitchen ten feet away from my chair behind the wall. In the third week of withdrawal, mind you. Another one and Dr Rome telling me I'd have had it.) Well, then the whole Group was at me for an hour and three-quarters while I tried to make up my mind what to do. The special trouble was that my students were in crisis themselves, the nation-wide wave of strikes had just hit the University, of my seventy-five kids only one-third had shown up the preceding Thursday and my assistant was lost, he didn't know what to tell them, I had to hear them and tell them myself, the President is a very capable guy but he was handling this particular business all wrong, in fact he was *not* handling it, he had just put students and staff alike on their "consciences," what a way to run a vast institution. Well, I couldn't get anybody to see that. They said, "What if you were flat on your back with cancer, what about your duty then?" I said, "Friends, I'm not." The Chief Counsellor, sitting in, after some speech of mine about my duty to the kids, said, "I read: grandiosity and false pride." Later he described me as a blind man who has hold of an elephant by the tail and gives a description of it; I looked at him bitterly and said, "You're witty." "Judgmental as ever," he smiled at me. I can't describe that

phantastic time, Mary-Jane. It's like a girdle on the old
Times building in New York telling the crowd some night
"JESUS RETURNS 10:37 EDT SPEAKS ONLY ARAMAIC CHICAGO
SCHOLAR SOUGHT." It was the most intense two hours
maybe I ever put in. At one point the schoolteacher said to
me, "Here we are, all trying to help you, and you just sit
there." I can see the face of the empty son-of-a-bitch. "I'm
busy," I said. During the first five minutes I had appealed
to the official, as a responsible outside authority, indirectly
in fact over me, and even he had said I ought not to go.
Santa Maria. It seemed years. At last, about a quarter to
twelve, I gave up. I turned to Vin and said, "All right, I
submit to your judgment. I won't go." ' He drew a deep
breath and looked at the woman, whom he hadn't seen for
some time.

'Why?' she said earnestly, leaning even further forward.

'God knows. It wasn't them. Maybe I just got worn out
with the dreadful back-and-forth passage between. I must
—I mustn't. Anyway, then I was *really* in despair. The
goddamn class met at one-fifteen, it wasn't even clear that
I could get my secretary on the phone in time, much less
the Director, and besides what could they do? *I sweated.*
Meanwhile the tone of the Group had metamorphosed in
one second. They were all consolation, advice, sympathy,
even praise. I couldn't understand it and did not give two
ounces of gerbil-dung. I simply did not know what to do,
in my opinion nothing *could* be done. In response to some
suggestion from Billie Rome, I said angrily, "We don't
even have a Department of Religion, there's no Divinity
School as they have at Harvard and Chicago, there's nobody to replace me." You see the lecture was on the
Fourth Gospel, I give a weird course over there sometimes,
outside my own College. Somebody suddenly said, "Vin's
trained in divinity!" and there was Vin looking hot-faced
at me saying, "I'll give your lecture for you." I felt

stunned. I said, "You're not serious." "Oh yes I am," he
said. I still couldn't believe him—*him*. I had hit him very
hard two times that morning. "You're not kidding me?" I
said, having a sense of about to fall off my chair or just fly
out the window backward. "No, no, I'll do it—if necessary, I'll teach it in Greek!" I saw he meant it, Mary-Jane,
God Almighty. I said, "I could kiss you!" He said—he's
a maniac—"Well, do," and so help me I leaned across
Keg (who, it vaguely and irritably even in that moment
came to me, was *laughing*) and Vin and I embraced and
kissed cheeks. "Well!" I said sobbing, "Come down to my
room, I'll go over my notes with you, it won't take two
minutes, they're full and my texts are marked." Everything
was confused, but I heard somebody say as we all stood up,
"He really *cares* about his students," and I thought as if far
away, "Damn you so you doubted it." I thought Keg was
going to crush my knuckles during the Lord's Prayer and
somebody told me later there wasn't a dry eye in the room
and I briefed Vin, who said he was "scared to death" (*Vin*
scared). I said, "Some of my kids are marvellous, you'll be
completely at ease with them," and described several in the
front seats, with their names, and off he went, in plenty of
time, and I went and sat in the Lounge and wept and
wept. Everybody was at lunch, but Keg came from somewhere and knelt down by my chair and gripped my knee.
"You were so cruel to Phyllis and Amos," I got out between sobs, "I don't understand." "We're hard on delusion." For the first time I saw what treatment was about.'
    The man and woman sat in silence in the dishevelled
room.
    'It's an amazing story, Alan,' she said softly. 'I have a
feeling you didn't finish it.'
    'Oh no. I hadn't even reached the point. That afternoon
as I thought over what had happened I saw that a direct
intervention had taken place and I recovered one particu-

lar sense of God's being I lost as a child. My father shot himself when I was twelve. I didn't blame God for that, I just lost all personal sense of Him. No doubt about the Creator and Maintainer, and later it became quite clear to me that He made Himself available to certain men and women in terms of inspiration—artists, scientists, statesmen, the saints of course, anybody in fact—gave them special power or insight or endurance—I'd felt it myself: some of my best work I can't claim any credit for, it flowed out all by itself, or in fact by His moving. But I couldn't see Him interested in the individual life in the ordinary way. Now I did. Vin was his angel if you like—emissary, agent—I've never had any trouble with angels. Or what they call "miracles" either. I became a different man.'

After a little, 'How,' she asked, 'did you come to get in trouble again?'

'Well, the First Step,' he said but he felt a strange uncertainty as he heard himself say it.

'I don't see any connexion,' Mary-Jane said. 'But never mind,' and she came up off the edge of the bed and embraced him tenderly.

'That was the *Second* Step. "Came to believe that a Power greater than ourselves could restore us to sanity." '

'Sanity?' he was resentful, 'who was insane? I could have talked to my students and given the lecture easily, I've done it fifty times in worse shape.'

'But you had a convulsion a few days later?'

'Completely abnormal, one chance in ten thousand.'

'And you think you should have risked your life for your students? Alan, you're a sweet guy but you are still *lost*.' She kissed his cheek. 'We're not supposed to Give Advice in this game, but I'll tell you the score. Maybe, anyway. Your trouble is the Third Step.'

Extract from Dr Severance's Journal

Incredible. Changes everything. I couldn't understand why
she hadn't told me before. 'I didn't know whether you
were going to leave me. Or me you.' Ugh. But it's marvellous. In May, eh? Name up to me again. David or Rachel.
Rebecca n.g. Consider.

Funny I can't remember the interview with Dr Rome
Tuesday. See him, hear only his word 'numb' at some
point and, 'You'll be like this for some time.' That's what
he thinks.

God's doing.

Group all on Les's leaving. Him: 'disappointed' and 'no
progress after six weeks.' Poor show, poor guy. Problems:
1) business, 2) family, 3) sobriety, 4) self-misinterpretation.
I wish I had more hope for him.

Will power is nothing. Morals is nothing. Lord, this is
illness.

6

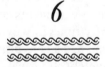

SEVERANCE HOPED everyone else was as well prepared as he
was. He looked around the room eagerly. Maybe they
could pop through this in fifteen minutes at the outside—
it wasn't likely that anybody else would have a list of disciplines as long as his, after all—and get down to busi-

ness at last. He burned to level and confront, be confronted, learn, suffer, and break through.

Keg at the blackboard held a piece of chalk in the air and said, 'We'll go around the room. What have you decided you have to do to get better, Wilbur?'

Wilbur looked up surprised at the tall rather grim figure standing almost over him, hesitated until the atmosphere was tense with exasperation, began to say something, began again, and Keg wrote.

Severance picked up something about his fellows as the master-list of disciplines lengthened down the board and started a second column and started the third column. Both in Wilbur's long, defensive face and whited eyes under the bald dome, and in the hunched-over elbows-on-knees defeated ingrown posture, he read: Self-pity. He was pleased to hear anticipated, confirmed, some of his own disciplines, though not many. Mary-Jane was extremely definite: (1) Accepting Ward responsibilities (Severance uncomfortably could see her sitting on his unmade bed yesterday—in fact he hadn't made it today either), (2) After the day's page in the 24-Hour Book, read 20–30 pages in the Big Book, (3) Seek people, (4) JUST FOR TODAY (she told Grant to put it in caps, and he grinned) I will have a Programme. Severance was impressed, against his will; his opinion of his own great list weakened. Only Jeree was diffident and vague. 'Try to think good about people,' she said, and, 'not to eat too much at meals or between meals.' Several patients laughed at the second, Severance among them, for Jeree was hardly over-weight, but he was touched, even in some way humbled by her first proposal. So this mild creature had been sitting across from him in the Snack Room bristling with criticism. Of him? He was suddenly aware of a great distance between himself and her, of her independent existence, with problems he didn't know of and making efforts he ought to make himself, for she could

hardly be as censorious as he was, and yet there was nothing of the sort on his list. Nothing like Letty's either: 'Tell
myself three times a day I am not a bitch, though I know I
am.'

Severance's list, when Keg got to him, was grandiose
and tyrannical. Four hours' reading a day, thirteen physical exercises every morning (seven isometric, four barbell,
hopping, running in place), and so on. Eleven in all (and he
had omitted many more). He was rather proud of it, to tell
the truth, though he tried not to feel pride in anything. It
covered everything. A man would have to be Jack London
to drink with disciplines like that!

'I don't suppose, Alan, you expect everybody to keep up
with all these?' said Keg sweetly, as he turned back from
the board finally. 'God no, it's just for myself,' Severance
said with some insincerity, since that had been exactly
what he did expect. He didn't want to *lead* anything at all
but he had his duty to the Group as well as to his recovery.

Keg wound up at last with Marge, who snapped out her
ideas as if she hated him and everybody. Then he stood
back and considered the columns. So did they all.

'Let's get rid,' he said suddenly, 'of everything we can.
St Francis and Napoleon put together couldn't run such a
Programme, or he'd go bats on the third day trying to. You
are suffering alcoholics. Some of you are still in deep withdrawal, without even knowing it. None of you has been
dry a month. All of you are hospital patients in treatment
for at least the second time. Almost the only thing I do *not*
see on the board is, "TAKE IT EASY." In fact the whole pre-
posterous accumulation *attacks* that primary law by
merely filling the wall the way it does. I'll begin with
"thinking good about people." Do it if you can, Jeree—I
personally can't—it may get you to Heaven; but in my
worthless opinion it will not help keep you sober. Well,
help maybe. But what happens? Say you succeed even,

then somebody slobbers on you or wipes you out—as does occur in this world—you're back to booze. We've got to lower our sights, all of you, except Mary-Jane. Alan, you are the most deluded person in this room. Eleven disciplines, eh? Some with many parts each. Perhaps you think you are pitching for the Nobel Prize? You are only trying to create a minimal possibility, my friend, that you won't be drunk ten days after you leave hospital this time. You were drinking by the end of the first week, last Spring, weren't you. Can't you see that you'd simply fail at all this noble crap, grow discouraged with yourself, despair of the Programme, and—guess what.'

Severance, who had aged somewhat during this speech, stared at his terrible demands flashing and rocking on the board. He wished he was elsewhere, and did not hear anything for a while. Then he took in that Keg had prefaced Mary-Jane's 'JUST FOR TODAY' to groupings from other patients' items and was calling for comment. He heard intermittently, 'I will do at least two things I don't want to do —just for exercise,' and, 'I will do somebody a good turn and not get found out; if anybody learns, it will not count,' and, 'I will have a quiet half hour all by myself, and relax,' and 'ask for help,' and 'trust my impulses,' and 'not tackle my whole life problem at once,' and, 'self-forgetfulness.' The more he heard, the more uncomfortable he felt; at one moment he wondered dazedly whether he had somehow wandered into the wrong room. He seemed to have nothing in common with these sensible and aspiring people. Then Letty, the wide-eyed Jewish young-looking grandmother on his left, leaned over and patted his knee, murmuring, 'Never mind, dear.' His pained eyes met Mary-Jane's quiet eyes and she winked. By twelve-ten when they rose to say the Lord's Prayer, he was able to seize Letty's hand with a feeling that the unusual comfortless morning had not after all been wasted. There was plenty of time after all. Glad it wasn't worse.

7

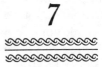

Extract from Dr Severance's Journal

Thurs. Interested, happy.
    1st Step: Gus and Mike alike: *Humility*
        Must be: I am at the end of *my* resources:
           Help me.
        R with all my mail—Pride! letter from V, R.
        Cantor's letter, Heisen's.
    My job is somehow to conquer my Pride. I have
    been *getting away with murder* all my life—
    not only *allowed* to but vehemently *encouraged*
    to. (making up for my lost childhood?? irre-
    sponsible, counting on *over*love??) Only here's
    a subject, liquor, where I can't.

*　　*　　*

Friday afternoon found him writing laboriously. '*Comment:* If this statement has literary merit, that I think is not a con, only the product of the fact that a lifelong effort to put things shortly and forcibly is unbreakable, and harmless, except insofar as it may persuade others to share the patient's delusion and so support his illness (any writer's, or even scientist's permanent message perhaps is really just this: *come and share my delusion*, and we will be happy or miserable *together*) THIS ATTEMPT *is right here. Otherwise* I have made no conscious effort to impress you, only to

tell you how I see myself with the First Step *at this moment.* I am certain to improve that relation as every morning I include it with the 5 to 30 min. I spend (with whatever courage and every trace of humility I can summon)
on the 24-Hour Book. *That,* at any rate, does lie within
the power of my eroded but surviving will: I am almost
bound to skip some mornings at first, but I hope to notice
it and gradually make the habit instinctive—wake up,
out of bed, *book & 1st Step*—I've done it four mornings
anyway, deluded as I am. Every now and then, lately, a
few scales seem to fall from my eyes. Maybe, with your
help and God's, I will some time see something as it is,
then something else, and finally enough to keep me sober.'
He stopped there, too tired to select any more from the
wealth of observations and conclusions that were roaring in
his mind, and it was twenty-four hours before, looking at
it again with a view to going on, he was horrified to find
that it was *crap*—mere evasion—delusion, in short,
pretending to recognize itself but actually having its feet
planted firmly in mid-air, as one of the counsellors had
once said about somebody. Atrociously written too, and
that mattered.

'This is my last chance,' he said grimly to Ruth that Saturday evening. 'If I don't make it this time, I'll just relax
and drink myself to death. There's no better treatment
available, I couldn't be in better condition. That would be
it.' Fanatical determination.

'I don't agree.' She looked solidly at him. 'There's hope
until you're dead.' And he didn't buy that either, but it
made him feel better, and after she left, when the gong
went for visitors out, he slaved on.

At half past ten he jotted down, 'I seem to be moving
with the speed of light but I also seem to be standing
stockstill,' and went off to the Snack Room for coffee.
Eddie was jittering by the freezer, Jeree looked softly up,
Jasper and Mike were arguing. Eddie had come in about

four o'clock, in frightful shape, and driven everybody
crazy by trying to hold conversations when he could
hardly stand up or jabber intelligibly. His white face was
spectral and lopsided, thin lips working, shoulders shaking
in a torn light blue dressing-gown, hands twitching, knees
tottering. He was not in DT's but otherwise he reminded
Severance of a cadaverous lawyer he had seen on the
locked ward at Werewolf Hills, jiggling back and forth
along an imaginary tenfoot runway gibbering to his imaginary wife. Asking the orderly about him, with dismay, he
was told carelessly, 'Oh he comes in two or three times a
year like this. In three days he'll be back in his office giving orders.' It was hard to see Eddie back anywhere in
three days. Somebody had gathered, and reported at dinner, that Eddie had drunk most of a case of Scotch since
Tuesday. Charley Boyle, in whose room he had been put,
came in now and persuaded him back. Everybody sighed.

'Still, it doesn't seem to be the *amount* you drink,' said
Mike. 'A woman in my Group was minimizing as usual,
yesterday, and Sandy couldn't get through to her. She
thought: no bottle-a-day, no Skid Row: no alcoholic, she.
It's pathetic. But what *is* the story?'

'Intake has nothing to do with it,' Severance declared
out of his lore acquired from a hundred and twenty lectures at Howarden and Northeast, and much dogged reading, 'so far as they can tell. It seems to be Loss of Control.
That's the only pinpoint difference between your heavy
social drinker, as I thought I was until a year ago, and the
alcoholic, like me and I suppose all of you. There's a marvellous Churchill story to this effect.' He was happy not to
be slogging away at the goddamned First Step. Truth in
wit. 'The great man was introduced to a big audience over
here, after the War, as a great brandy-man. "Yes," the jerk
concluded, indicating with his arm a point halfway up the
sidewall of the auditorium, "it is estimated that if all the
brandy bottles Sir Winston has emptied were collected in

this hall, they would fill it halfway full!" Churchill rolled to the lectern—his son's biography says he had a natural sailor's gait that made him look intoxicated, along with his slur—anyway, he studied the audience, then shifted his gaze to the indicated point on the wall, studied it, lifted his eyes slowly to the juncture of the wall and the ceiling, and rumbled into the mike: "So much to do. So little time left to do it in." '

But in the midst of their laughter—even Jeree smiled —a strange thought came to him. Or did it? What was it? He steadied and looked. It was *lack of control. That* characterized the alcoholic. As an alcoholic he had no control over the First Step. He had been wasting his time, without ever even *reaching* the Step itself. Put-ons, nailed by himself a day or so afterward. Three of them, with all his (deluded) strength. Clearly this matter was beyond him at this time. The thing to do was *admit* it. He felt lurched by his guardian angel into business. With his head on fire he said goodnight abruptly, patting Jeree's shoulder, and went out down the corridor.

'I doubt' (he wrote hurriedly) 'if this will be an acceptable First Step; and I don't care. I doubt if any man can exactly "take" the 1st Step; maybe some can, but I know I tried hard and failed. Last Spring I wrote one which Gus Larson—a severe judge—recently called one of the best he had ever seen (it was a comprehensive account of twenty-three years of alcoholic chaos, lost wives, public disgrace, a night in jail and a lost job, injuries and hospitalizations, a blacked-out call to a girl student threatening to kill her, involuntary defecation in a public building, DT's once, convulsion once, etc., and it was completely sincere); and a month later I had a slip, four or five more over two months, two months' sobriety, six days drinking, and here I am again—in spite of dead seriousness, never missing either an AA meeting or Dr Rome's Encounter-Group, always confessing all, and every sort of other help, including daily prayer and the 24-Hour Book.' He struck out the last phrase, as being not quite true. So screw *that* First Step.

'This is only a short true account of my *present* thinking on the subject.

'It seems that the memory of experience will not keep me sober; and determination will not; and reliance on God, and all the other helps available will not. But what else is there? So my case seems hopeless. But I refuse to submit to the view that it *is*, because I do not wish to die insane and in fact I even desire the remainder of my life to be very different from the last twenty years.

'On Riverside'

But somehow there he lost heart and broke off, took a new sheet and scribbled at the bottom: 'As you comb your hair in the morning, say to the mirror, "Severance, you are going to have to make out today, as usual, with one arm. You are lucky to have it. God is interested in you, and conscious of your struggle and your services. Good luck." '

His elation had faded, and he couldn't understand it, because he seemed to have reached terra firma at last. Hardly happy ground, admittedly, but real. His week of failures hadn't been wasted after all. He was making progress. Mike had said to him last night, 'You're too ambitious, Doctor. I figure if you pick up just one thing a day, really get it, say you're in treatment the average four to five weeks, that's thirty-odd things: you're in business.' He expected to shock Gus etc. but he was doing his duty. Okay. Free now to concentrate, amid the gruelling ward routine, on his Contract with Linc—nothing had happened there —and on the new (old) problem increasingly worrying him and threatening his treatment.

Going down at midnight for an Eskimo Pie, only that pig Herb had cleaned them out, he learned that Eddie had had a seizure. 'In and out of bed ten times he was,' Charley grumped amiably, 'staggering over to the window, as if there was anything to see. Get him back down in, up again. Arita looked in presently with the news that he had had another seizure and been taken across to Intensive Care, 'God bless the sinner.'

Severance slept like the dead for a change and only Buck and Delores were still eating when he drifted down for breakfast—ad lib on Sunday, eight to ten. 'Do I look as if I self-destructed at 3:18 a.m.?' he asked them gloomily. 'Eddie died,' said Buck, 'about then.'

'So he made it,' said Severance.

'God damn it,' angrily, 'I said the nurse said he *didn't* make it.'

'Exactly. What we're all up to, aren't we? Suicide.'

Then the softboiled eggs were cold and hard. He made it, all right.

III

CONTRACT ONE

Change your life.

8

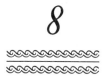

W<small>HEN</small> <small>AMONG</small> nine or ten other patients Severance pushed through the heavy doors into a bright cold afternoon, he felt excited, relieved. Deep breath, cigarette hack. So the world still existed! Both Wednesday night and last night the lectures had been across in the main hospital building, but the dark short mob-scurry gave no sense of freedom, only two minutes' realization of the universal oppressive ward-fug, absorption in all the facetings of treatment, para-military constriction hardly less than Howarden. Out! The sun was by no means burning down and the grass was greying but the air was rich with leaf-smoke in this rundown neighbourhood. Fall was his season, had always been. So you still wish to get famouser, one of the eleven or how many Franckens of Antwerp, every one of them a noted painter enough in his age, mostly now inextricable? Delores' long legs were pretty ahead, smoothly. The other women were slacksed except the nurse. Towers above the trees across the river reminded him he was University Professor Severance not the craven drunk Alan S who had been told by an orderly that his room smelled like a farmyard ('you, you . . . you, you utter/You wait!') He fell in step with Mike M, hunching a little—outer coat next time—against ruffles of wind. Mike was a

heavy-set black-haired attractive man of thirty-four or
-five, with his head lowered. Mike had problems: whether
his stunning new wife would leave him like the first and go
back to airline hostessing (eight months later, to everyone's
dismay, she certainly would), whether to kick his business
partner out on his ear after six years of tyrannical but
faithful service, whether his AA group, called the Whitney
Chapter (who ever heard of such a thing?), would take him
back.

'Why not, for God's sake?'

They were far ahead of the others lounging along. A
hippie napped under an overpass, or maybe stoned. He was
glad not to be stoned, as he had been at this hour and
every hour last Sunday (indecent?!), with immediate Monday morning suicide in mind moreover.

'They're a peculiar outfit. Nobody has slips. They own
a fine club building out on Whitney and when you're
elected—you have to be elected, you can't just join, and
believe me they look you over for weeks beforehand and
you have to have two sponsors—they give you a key
and say, "If you ever feel like having a drink, put the key
in the mail." '

'Well, there are groups all over town. So what? AA isn't
supposed to be selective: the desire to quit drinking, that's
all, isn't it?'

'Not with them. And I admit they have a very bad
haughty reputation with other groups around the city. But
partly it's envy, Alan. Many of them not only have a great
deal of money they're very generous with, but have been
dry twenty thirty thirty-five years. It was the second
group established here. You don't get that kind of security
in most groups. Christ, guys turn up stoned, actually for
meeting. A friend of mine who'd been through Hollins
told me about a counsellor of his who once drank steadily
for seven years, never missed a meeting. He'd stash a pint
in his glove-compartment, drive to meeting, sweat it out,

and when he got back in the car, open up and bottoms up. Arrive home bombed. His wife used to say to him, "What is this AA?" Funny—but what support would you get from a group like that?'

'I see that. Also the authority. Frankly I hate authority including what I have to exercise, but unfortunately I respond to it. It wasn't AA kept me dry two months this summer, it was fear of Dr Rome. Christ, I could have gone on reporting slips to my AA till Armageddon, some of the men even defended me when Ted and Mike Lewes gave me hell.'

'That's another thing—the wives. Wives *come to meetings*. They don't speak to the Chapter—it's big, by the way, maybe 150, and *twice* a week, not once, and everyone comes unless travelling—well, the wives sit around the wall and talk to each other. Nobody gets away with anything at Whitney. I don't mean *drinking*, of course, but the hang-ups that lead to it. Watch out for the root.'

Severance stepped over, hating the word 'hang-ups' and 'up-tight' and 'get the garbage out': 'I buy that too. My whole idea is not to be able to get away with anything whatever. Not that I can imagine concealing a slip. Oddly enough, I never did that, though of course I used to lie like the next jerk before I went into treatment. It's slips I'm afraid of, not serious drinking. That's out.'

'How do you know?'

'Well, I *don't* know. Just trumpeting, as usual,' said Severance lightly, though he hadn't been wholly pleased by Mike's friendly but realistic and stopping question. He was willing to laugh at himself, slightly; God help anyone else who did. 'I wonder if they'd take me.'

'Two of the men come to see me, I could tell them you're interested, they could look you up. Only remember, they've been dry since the Flood, they'll be suspicious.'

Severance did not like the idea of being suspected, or in fact looked over. With *his* determination? Still, he was impressed almost out of his mind with records of decades of sobriety. Anything that would improve his chances. Ruth might like it too, give her confidence. She was familiar with his polar positions: rebellion, awe. Both seemed built in, he was ready to defend both to the death. You had to have both. He saw damned little of either in most other Americans at the moment: just cop-out or sheephood, no independence *or* emulation. Hyperdemocracy, the sovereignty of the unqualified individual, added into a mass. He did sympathize with the young militants, enough to have addressed six thousand of them on Moratorium morning, but he saw them as *incompetent*, a threat to their own causes in abler hands: deluded by Thoreau's hostility to the lessons of history, unable to *use* tradition modified. Even their bloody bombs were so inefficient that they went off too early and killed people. What he approved, what inspired him even, was their hopefulness, which he did not share, and their hatred of technology, which he did.

Turned back now toward the hospital, he and Mike waited for the rest to straggle up. My word, Hasty's was just two blocks north of here, the slowest liquor store in the city, 'two quarts of Jack Daniel's green, please—Dr Severance,' Ruth once reckoned he spent over a thousand dollars a year there alone—well, he could afford it, except physically mentally morally and spiritually. 'How are you, sexpot?' He patted Delores' sloping shoulder. 'Stroll languorous enough for you? I like to *walk*.'

'EXTENDED CARE' came into view, so labelled in stone over the big glass doors. Everybody slowed down, if that was possible, except Severance keen to get back to work.

'When I first arrived in London,' he said to her and Mike, 'the sign "FAMILY BUTCHER" over shops alarmed me. That portico ought to read: "RECOVERING ALCOHOLICS"

SLAUGHTER-HOUSE" and under it "DEFENCES PENETRATED, DELUSIONS VAPORIZED." ' He did not feel witty.

*   *   *

Sunday was Dull Day for most of the forty-one patients on Ward W of Northeast Hospital, C——, Ohio, founded two years before, the first alcoholic rehabilitation center in the United States, or anywhere, with an out-patient family programme (estimated average degree of in-patient recovery: fifteen percent, the rest to be dealt with over two years of weekly Encounter-Group therapy). Dr Marc Rome's latest guess was that half the graduates would make it—that is, never drink again; half the remainder would drink off and on, and the final quarter would die. Severance was suspicious of these figures, being hypnotized of course like everybody else in the country since General Washington by statistics, but capable of moments of lucidity and resistance. Some in-State patients had visitors, in their rooms or out in the crabgrass hospital grounds, boasting of their progress, pleading, joking, begging forgiveness, manipulating, rejecting, threatening to take off. At four-thirty Mary-Jane was reading Chapter V of the Big Book for the seventeenth time (she kept track, having gone back to pills after eighteen months clean and dry), bald Wilbur now sixty-three who had lived with his parents hating them since his first wife left him was arguing with his intoxicated father on the only ward telephone, Jeree was sitting on her bed screwing up her courage to go down to the Snack Room and get coffee, Letty was resenting her daughter's not having called and her husband's having called, Severance was writing obsessedly in his Journal.

'*St Paul's.*

'Fear. Weak, it never occurred to me to go out for football. Fatal "sissy." Bullied by Bone II and Frischer. First eve-

ning Assembly, name called: rose against the wall, expect-
ing congratulations on my job (swept hall in New
Building)—called down for dustpile put there unjustly
after I'd finished. Have I ever recovered? Love (fear) of
Fr Kemmis—long English walks—Mrs Dulon's teas.
Awe of the Old Man. Cameron mocking my "de prus en
prus" and throwing erasers; rumor he fathered Effie's
baby—her husband's first day in Latin III, "My name is
Robert Denzil Hagster-Collins and I am here to teach
Latin"—we roared—day we locked him in the classroom closet where we had a gramophone playing. Joe
Laker the paddling Prefect. Mr Woodward's story about
Bill the S.A. savage and the poison berries—unknown
death—later used, cooked, as therapeutic—man's giant
step; "sun-worshipping," crawling on bloody knees with
books open down the board-walk, across flagstones,
around flagpole, and back. Finishing black coffee (sweet)
after the masters left the lounge after lunch. Butts in ice-
house. Reading after lights-out in slanted eaves-closet and
under covers with flashlight. (Reading *what?*) Erection
over Cornelia the matron in Latin II, suddenly called on,
had to stand in aisle half-crouched. My jokes in the infir-
mary *I* didn't understand (Boom-Du Rail-on, Boom-But
Rail-er). Respect for John Ward. Wittenberg a friend?
"Assume the attitude," Moose-jaw used to say when we
lined up in his room for paddling after lights-out. Sneakin
Jesus the mathematics master coming up the stairs in the
dark. Bobo (Effie's Bobo—we held each other by the
legs one afternoon out the windows in the dorm to look
into their bathroom upside down) waving his arms gently
to get us down from the window-seats—"Don't take off,
Bobo"—flit idea. Sucked off Dopey Compson in the
tool-shed one winter afternoon, he made me do it, largest
pecker in school, once he had an erection in the showers
and we came from everywhere to wonder. Suicide-attempt
lay down across the rails, train coming, hauled off.

'Scarcely anything else.

'I do not remember *one book* read in those *four years* except that Latin grammar, though hundreds up till then (14) and most of all the many thousands since (not all). A fraction of zeal in physics.

'Weird. Look into it into it, intuit into it, weird.

*   *   *

'Ruth last night: "Your model was your *very* powerful mother . . . you have many feminine qualities (as I have masculine qualities—my father was my model)—I love them in you." 1000 quarrels with Mother; utter admiration—my first literary subject, after the ASPCA gold-medal essay, my first prize eh? Or was it the state-wide spelling award? *Second* prize. The taller dark girl made "syzygy." '

9

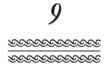

'WELL, STACK,' Harley began Group on Monday morning, 'what happened this time? I've known you how many years is it, but you better fill the others in a little. You've been in treatment how many times?'

'Eight times, Harley! Eight times!' His heavy voice managed to be at once explosive and sad. Severance was shocked by that record and moved by the powerful ruinous sight of him: a large fierce face, furrowed and bald above slit eyes with great hollows under them, large working hands clenched on his thighs, elbows out. 'I don't know, I just don't know. Thirty-five years with the company and they fired me the day I was discharged from Howarden this time. I guess I just started drinking! The wife was on my side but I just couldn't stop!'

'Wait a minute,' said Keg. 'Why did they fire you?'

'I can't understand it! Every week Eric sent in a report on my progress. It came as a blow, Harley!'

'How many weeks were you there?'

'Seven. They just kept me on and on. I guess the company couldn't understand why I didn't get out in three, like always.'

'What's that? How many times have you been at Howarden, Stack?'

'Four times, Harley.'

'And you still expected to be discharged in *three weeks?* How many patients are discharged after three weeks?'

'Nobody!' Stack sounded angry.

'How about you, the previous times?'

'Well, four months was the longest. They gave me a kitchen job but I went on going to lectures and all, they didn't think it was a good idea for me to leave.'

'And your boss put up with that, he took you back?'

'Sure. We was good friends.'

'But after all that history, you still expected to get out in three weeks?'

'I just don't understand it.' Stack shook his big head.

'Neither do I,' said Harley. 'But why did they let you go then this time, after sticking by you for so long?'

'I'll tell you, Harley: it's a mystery. The wife and me couldn't understand it!'

'How did you feel about it?'

'Oh, I may have been a little resentful at first. But right away—'

'For Christ's sake,' Keg broke in. 'A *little* resentful! After thirty-five years they suddenly let you go—what reason did they give?'

'No reason, Keg. They just said fired.'

'And you took that? Did you go see him and ask why?'

'No, I didn't.'

'Why not?'

'Well, I just—I don't know why not! Stop picking on me!'

'I never heard such crap,' Keg said with disgust. 'You're unbelievable. First you expect to get out in three weeks when *nobody ever has*, then your company fires you on the *day* seven weeks later when you actually do get out, and you're "a little resentful." Right this minute you're boiling with rage.'

'No I'm not, Keg,' Stack said in a strange, even sweet voice, glaring murder. 'It was only because I couldn't understand it, that's all. It was a big disappointment to me and the wife, so I started drinking.' His body was trembling with anger.

'Well, God knows we sympathize with you, Stack,' said Harley gently, 'only there is not one single part of your story that makes any sense whatever. How do you feel about coming back into treatment for the eighth time?'

'I'm going to try hard, Harley!' shouted Stack. 'I'm going to make it this time. I gotta! The wife is with me!'

'You've got to get in touch with your feelings. If you *knew* how resentful you are, maybe you wouldn't drink. You've got to learn to level with your feelings—get them out in the open. Do you see yourself as an angry man, Stack?'

'Me? No, Harley. I am the quietest man there is, even drinking. Ask anybody.'

'I seem to remember you drove to Illinois with a gun after your first wife left you. Is that true?'

'It was only because of my daughter. I just couldn't stand to have her taken away like that, with that other man.'

'You didn't plan to shoot your wife?'

'Oh no, Harley. I put the gun in the glove-compartment and I never took it out, the whole time I was in Illinois.'

'Did you see your wife?'

'I couldn't find her.'

'What if you had found her?'

'Well, I would have talked to her a little, just reasoned a little, about her taking my daughter like that, without saying anything.'

'Then what was the gun for?'

'I'm not sure I did have a gun, Harley. It might have been . . .' His voice trailed off lost.

'You're still fogged-in, Stack. But think it over, about the feelings. You've got a lot of work to do.'

'I know it, Harley! The wife is with me all the way!'

Severance's Journal

To become a Jew—the wonder of my life—it's *possible!* Rabbi Mandel is coming at 2:30.

My uneasiness w. Xtianity came to a head in Mass w George this morning—but where? how? *want company* (Geo.—Mike praying in his room *with his wife*)

Passion over Rose's Frank saying to her *at last* (Linc was him) 'I love you'—L: 'You never could say it to her before, could you?'—I thought of David's *wanting* perhaps to say it to *me,* but held off by disappointment with me (rage, eh?)—baffled, hurt—how will he take my letter?!?

Left and came to my room and incredibly thought of *becoming a Jew.* Always held it impossible because of inadequate concept of God—OK since Vin's rescue—but hostile to Trinity—dubious of X, hostile to BVM—anti-Pope, deep sympathy with Church but *not for me* alone w God, yet *not* alone, one of many worshippers, *like* them exc in blood (who cares?)

Somebody in Snack Room even said to me recently, 'You ought to become a Jew'!!? (Irish and Jewish wives—my *son*, etc) perh nexus just now

I feel apprehensive—joy but—can I? Will He receive me? I know I must prepare, be ready for all.

The cantor's letter of admiration helped me, unknowing by me.

And: Jews *don't drink!*

S! D! (even the Mexican Jew in the Greek islands etc etc)

All has pointed HERE.

In my old story, *a confrontation as Jew* is resisted, fought, failed—at last given in to, symbolically. I

So the 'desire' (was it?) is at least 25 years old.

After that, the work on the Nazi doctors—abandoned —obsessed—perh now take it up again? *my position certain.*

Unique horror of anti-Semitism.

Closeness to Ed C, Erich, many, Riegels, Blooms, the Steins.

Excitement over Isaak Babel! Buber! the Hasidim! Bloch's music! Pascal's Hebraism in 'conversion'! WCW's Jewish blood!

How did I come to buy (found it lately in the attic) a very expensive leather-bound 4-vol *Josephus?!*

For years contributed to, eagerly read monthly cover to cover half-unintelligible, *Commentary?*

Love for Shafarman, first therapist I ever felt *anything* for. *flourishing* of Freud & Einstein!—'die unverlierbaren Freunde' *special* interest in Isaiah Berlin, Meyer Shapiro, Hannah, Mlle Weil etc Jewish girls—Sylvia B, Pearl K, Marilyn L, Judith R, Harriet R + my Hebrew effort—studies with Peretz Bargebuhr (write—still

alive?) regular O.T. stint daily, at last, this year (till
lately) unique devotion to *Job*—text, Stevenson's
Schweik lectures, translation fooled with for sixteen years
    People often think I *look* Jewish—resentment, liking

10

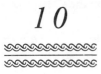

NELA, THE HEAD NURSE, was firmly constructed, a fresh-
faced intolerant woman of forty with grieving eyes whose
husband had wrecked a sky-rocket academic career with
drinking and drugs and died of them. Severance took a
dim view of head nurses and the prospect of her lecture on
ward-discipline, which he had twitched through twice, did
not turn him on; but he was in a do-or-die frame of mind
this morning, alert to the possibilities of help lurking in the
very motes eccentric in the sunbeam bright on Jeree's
hair-bun slumped in front of him, as he readied his ballpoint and pad.

'You all know who I am,' Nela said calmly, smoothing
her uniform. 'My subject in this part of the treatment-pro-
gramme is Responsibility. You are all suffering from the
lack of self-confidence which is common to this illness;
from feelings of inferiority ("someone else," you think,
"could do it better"—whatever it may be); from self-
consciousness (this is *paralyzing* in some of you); from fear
of rejection—often so powerful that it leads to consideration of suicide, a plan which if adopted will leave you
really invulnerable, quite safe at last. Your confidence in
yourself has got to be restored, little by little. We can help
you, but we cannot be responsible for you. The first per-

son we must be responsible to is *ourselves.*' Severance, who
had been rejecting every item as he wrote it down, sat
mentally up to the note of an old accusation. He had heard
this before, when he could not get out of it.

From Vin. The whole elaborate situation flooded back.
A young writer had telephoned from a distant State one
Sunday morning and kept him on the phone for half an
hour with an insufferable amalgam of hero-worship and
megalomania—Severance had been patient, and patient,
and tried to get him off the line, and tried, finally said,
'No, I'm afraid I'm going to hang up now, goodbye,' and
did so, and thought no more of the matter (but somebody
had told him later that he had seen him looking like a
thundercloud, so abstracted that Severance did not recognize him or speak) until that evening when suddenly for no
reason he burst into flame against that young man, he tore
his wife to pieces during her visit, sat cursing through some
female ex-drunk's AA talk ('I fell down the stairs and hit
my head on a marble table-top, I took the First Step')—
screw all these humorless bastards sitting around congrat-
ulating themselves on being sober, what's so wonderful
about being sober? Great Christ, most of the world is
sober, and look at it! He was still raging when after a
sleepless night he took up the matter in Group next day.
Vin accused him of 'insincerity.' Severance was baffled
and furious: 'I did not say a damned *word* to him that was
insincere.' 'You should have told him where you stood, and
hung up.' 'Well, I had to spare his feelings, for God's sake,
you don't know what young writers are like.' 'What do
his feelings matter?' said Vin. 'It was your feelings that
should have mattered to you. You were irresponsible.' 'Irresponsible?' cried Severance. 'Yes. To yourself. You did
not accept responsibility for yourself.' After infinite nego-
tiation and resistance he finally saw this, and it so changed
his behaviour that when, after he got out of treatment, the
same damned young man—and other readers—rang

up from California and then Massachusetts, he cut him off
short. Now as he sat half-listening to Nela ('When we are
tired or hungry, we do irresponsible things') he made the
connexion with his submission over leaving the ward to go
give his lecture on the Fourth Gospel. His responsibility
was not to his students but to himself. Well, well. At last.
By God's grace he had done the right thing without even
knowing why. There was hope for everybody. He said a silent prayer for all the patients including himself. Teach me
to give in.

'. . . Then: the other people in this treatment center;
then *everyone in Extended Care*—our elderly people,
upstairs—and in the whole hospital. Only *then* our beloved ones outside, and those suffering everywhere—for
your beloved ones are suffering with you—in the war in
Vietnam, in Biafra all this time, everyone everywhere.

'Now for your particular ward-responsibilities . . .' My
job! he thought with a qualm. In ten whole days I haven't
done a damned thing about it. I don't even know exactly
what it is or how to go about it. I'm listed as 'supplies for
the Snack Room.' Where are they anyway? Things seem
to be getting along all right without me. But he determined to get hold of Rose right after lunch and *find out*.

                    *   *   *

'Well, Alan,' Dr Gus Riemer was asking buoyantly, 'what
do you think made *you* take your first drink after your
second tour of treatment?' Dr Riemer, replacing Gus One
in charge of the new-formed Repeaters' First Step Prep,
with Julitta sitting stiffly in, was a big radiant young Ne-
gro-surgeon in white buckskin shoes. After booming out
with satisfaction and joy his own fearful history ('Oh, after
a few months I thought I'd just have a little *wine* with dinner, nothing wrong with that—maybe pop some pills
before an operation—quite okay—and pretty soon I

was back on the hard stuff and brainsick with amphet-
amines and lying my rich ass off not only to Rhoda and
my trusting colleagues but myself. Oh, I "could handle it"
all right!') he had been going round the Group with this $64
question, friendly to Jeree ('I see you're still in hopeless
withdrawal, dear'—news to Severance) and Mary-Jane,
formidable to Wilbur and Letty and Stack. Severance had
overlapped him in the Spring and admired him all Summer
in Dr Rome's Encounter-Group, where he dubbed him
Augustus the Chemical Adventurer, but he experienced
now a thrill of anxiety. Still, he was ready for him.

'I've given it a bundle of thought. I told Louise last week
I didn't know, and that was honest, but now I've cleared
up some and I see it was obsession with a woman. I half
fell in love with her in treatment last Spring—it was
terrible—I felt ghastly about it—we only embraced
and touched each other, and kissed once in the corridor
late one night—but I didn't know what was going to
happen when we got out of hospital. I did *not* call her up
but I sweated. I felt unspeakably guilty too, toward Ruth.
Finally about two-thirty one afternoon I had to get out of
the house to think about her, *really think* about her, and
try to decide what to do, maybe write her a letter. I'm a
good letter-writer, I often find out what I think *during* the
letter. Anyway, for some reason I waited until Ruth had
gone out, perhaps at three?—why I waited I don't
know, I could have gone out for a walk any time, but I
did, then I took a bus to Elmwood just to think, and that
was it. What permitted it, so far as I can see, was *omnipo-
tence*, the feeling that I could get away with it, besides I
didn't plan to *do* anything—and self-pity, because I had
been so damned righteous about my really almost unbear-
able desire, plus guilt about the desire itself.'

He stopped, satisfied. He had levelled with them, by
God. But Gus was shaking his head at him, saying softly,
'Deluded,' and Julitta was beginning something off to his

right. He turned toward her, hurt. Her voice was high and controlled.

'The only word I can find in my vocabulary, which is pathetic compared with yours, word adequate to this marvellous and airy intellectual construction, is: HORSESHIT!' Severance almost reeled back in his chair. 'We're not here to discuss your sex life or your psychologizing, but your *drinking*.'

Then Gus was asking, 'What about *feelings?*' and uttering, 'You're computerized,' and, 'Why do you drink?' and Severance was speechless and finally the focus shifted to Hutch, his old friend from Vin's Group who had come back into treatment, to Severance's amazement ('I started drinking the day after I got out'), just the night before.

Severance's Journal

Humbled (I hope) and *shook*.

This morning I felt fine, *confronted* Les with his, 'If there's anything left over from here, it'll be taken care of in my Friday Encounter-Group,' said to me on the way over to lecture Sunday night—he denied it, Harley and Keg at him arguing, defending (major threat to sobriety: quarrels with wife)—I joined in too much, too confidently, and shouted as usual (Mary-Jane vs me, dyad after lunch about it and my flirting joke rejected by her last night at Dr Rome's lecture). Now I see—*correctly*—myself as a patient again, ill, deluded, and whether I've made any progress at all I *don't know*.

Why *do* I drink:

         Defiance (= Fuck you. *I* can handle it.
         Grandiosity (Insecure)
         Self-destructive   = I am just as great, *bec.*
         Delusion: 'I need it'   as desperate, as (etc)

+ Calm down excitement (after lecture,
lab, good news)
Dulling pain (loneliness, self-pity, bad
news)
To animate boredom—but is this really
so?? Screw this usual idea, in my case
(I feel as if scales were falling from my eyes. Surely
this can't *all* be wrong?)
Hysterical laughter at dinner, after Gus and Julitta.
A *defence* (Arita said just now at midnight) against fear of
what Gus read: but not only better than rage and defiance
(which Ruth said she would absolutely at all points pre-
viously have from me expected) but *okay*
= harmless to myself and others
—even useful, as amusing (without laughing we
wd all go mad on this ward, no wonder I
am so goddamn popular, the W Clown # 1)
New idea abt 1st Step. I think: we are in no condition
to make a serious step now: just give *a* version of *present*
view: then two others: 1) after 1 month
2) after 3 months

From Severance's Journal

2nd Mon., 8 a.m.
Have I been wrong all these years and it was *not* Daddy's death that blocked my development for so long?
Could this have been mere separation from Mother?? (cf.
my agony those Fall weeks at school in Chickasha—
and the unbelievably mawkish and cozy tone of my letters to her even as long afterward as Edinburgh. Perh. of
even the emptiness of my Canadian sep. fr. her.)
Because
(I forget the Missouri visit, the trip north
from Florida—exc. seeing him on the street

in Wash., summer in Gloucester and 89 Bedford—typing lessons)

the following year, in Hyde Park, was *the* happiest and
most active of my life up to that time!!? Close friend (*first,*
after Billy Ross and Richard Dutcher): Archie Lamont.
Valerie Paquit. William and Eleanor Garden. Pet of Mrs
Danahey (Engl), Miss Steele (math), even liked Shop
(made footstool for Uncle Jack—damn bad job too). Did
the hydrogen job on my own, the seventh way. Wrote the
Venus 'novel.' Prizes, the bit.

What happened the summer then? Move to East Egg?
Teddy Armstrong was *after* the 2nd Form wasn't she? Yes,
bec. I had a list of bks to read (obviously fr St Paul's)—
which I took out of the library and Bill read.

DID I IN FACT TAKE HIS DEATH IN STRIDE (it all bulges
that way) and succumb over a year later to something
else? or is *so* delayed a reaction possible. Bet it is.

(Check! Dr G: It's rare but I've
seen cases, two longer still)

So maybe my long self-pity has been based on an *error,*
and there has been no (hero-)villain ruling my life, but
ONLY an unspeakably powerful possessive adoring
MOTHER, whose life at 75 is still centered wholly on *me.*
And my ('omnipotent') feeling that I can *get away with
anything*—e.g., slips!—has been based on the knowledge that she will *always* forgive me, always come to the
rescue (Fall '53). And my vanity based on *her* uncritical
passionate admiration (letter ten days ago on my lectures
twenty years ago!)—rendering me invulnerable ('indif-
ferent'—a *fact,* too) to all criticism, and impatient
with anything short of total prostration before the products of my genius (though: much reality too, as my
ironic view of the hyperbole slithering around in recent
years, *Time,* Yale, London, Madrid, wherever).

My debts to her immeasurable: ambition, stamina, re-
sourcefulness, taste (in a small Missouri town, Faulkner's

first novels, how in God's name did she get them, Stein-
beck's), faith (not so clear that), originality, her sacrifices
for my schooling and 1938–9, blind confidence in me.

But she helped destroy my father and R; affairs w JA, JL,
G—others? (>my promiscuity?); horribly weakened my
brother; would never, and *still* hasn't let go of me in *any*
degree—e.g., *in*terminable letters, clips, incessant batter-
ing harangue.
SEDUCTIVE—'beautiful,' forcible but v. feminine (S's
amazement), vanity (yet), self-pity (+ great courage, indomitable), frustrated despite her immense successes.
  Good Lord I can't make head or tail of anything theres
the bell

*   *   *

If life on the ward became *really* existential only from ten
to noon five days a week, and in Mini-group three days,
still high moments were possible during Eye-stare and even
animal/vegetable/mineral on Saturday morning, while
flamboyance featured the Reverend Hill Manson every
Thursday evening and the chilling intellectual height of
the week was Dr Marc Rome's Wednesday evening performance, or *demonstration* rather. Severance had heard
many famous lecturers, knew himself not in the category,
but neither Harold Nicolson in England nor Reinhold
Niebuhr in this country seemed to him Rome's peer, the
first deficient in sheer pressure and Dr Niebuhr unstable in
his exordia, striding about flapping his arms and gibbering
until he steadied, whereas Dr Rome began high with re-
lentless control which he then, and menacingly, though
with what Severance had to admit was actual charm, even
increased until the subject was *wiped out*. He was flawless,
non-rhetorical, only the terrible facts spoke. This week it
was the Digestive Tract—the ulceration and/or hemor-

rhage of the mucus membrane lining it from the mouth to the rectum.

Dr Rome was a little under average height, dark-blond hair immaculate, faultless grooming altogether, though often a sweater under his tweed jacket, nothing medical about him, large gentle eyes, a no-nonsense nose and chin, manner very very calm as he drew fearful diagrams on the blackboard and supplied them with horrifying statistics. His bulky attractive wife, dry three years, was in the row ahead of Severance's, to his right.

'. . . heavy vomiting of blood in an hour or so: acute hemorrhagic alcoholic gastritis. Forty to fifty percent die, of shock. Ulcers, same mortality rate, depending on age, length of condition, etc. . . . The alcoholic reacts to stress very badly, besides *having* more stress. . . . Cirrhosis of the liver accounts for one-seventh of all deaths from all causes in the United States. In San Francisco, for some reason, it is highest of all.' Severance knew he had no significant liver damage. Amazing. It was nearly all functional —Ruth often had to tie his shoe-laces before she rushed him off to lecture, wondering whether he would be able to negotiate the two flights of stairs—except the brain damage. He couldn't *feel* that himself—some cloudiness maybe—but Dr Rome's even more spectacular lecture on the CNS (next week) left no room for speculation. 'It has seven hundred known functions, mostly vital, including detoxification: the liver is the body's *only* way of getting rid of alcohol. Under damage to it tolerance decreases. One drink will have the effect of ten formerly. . . . eighty-five to ninety percent of all you patients have fatty infibulation of the liver—a rare but bona fide cause of death.' Preliminary to the scarred-down, small, hard liver of the sinister slides in one morning lecture. Severance shuddered. Then Dr Rome went into pancreatitis.

*   *   *

He had cut his toenails that morning after showering (softened the things, a little). This always made him feel old—made of horn—'cut'? hacked at, rather, slabs off. The right big toe was worse than the left big toe. He mentioned these facts of life to the poet as they sat morose in the Snack Room later that evening. 'Your time will come, Bucko.'

'They say we have weak wills. Do you know about the two drunks who went to the film of *The Lost Weekend*. Came staggering out. "My God I'll never take another drink," said the first. "My God I'll never go to another movie." How's that for commitment? one-track all-powerful, same energy do the *Critique of Practical Reason*. Protecting his habit. Plink.'

'What do you do for a living, Jasper?'

The poet considered, smiling in his beard. Attractive son-of-a-bitch. Doesn't look his forty-is-it. Very bad reputation, women, so Ruth had said. 'Well, I sell, you know. My books sell. Christ, my last royalty cheque from New York was nearly eight thousand. I nearly fainted. Also I give readings. Teach around the place.'

'What place?'

'U.S. How do you make out? I expect you're fat.'

'I support a good many people,' Severance said awkwardly, very nervous about being, indeed, 'fat.' Sounded awful. Was awful. 'Good many books in print still but only the Harvey sold really well, and my last book.'

What was he doing in a literary conversation. Give it ten minutes.

'I bought it one time,' Jasper confided, 'secondhand paperback. Hope you're not miffed. Haven't read it yet. I stock-in biographies for my old age. Some title: *The Secret'st Man of Blood*, eh? Scientist deep in medieval Scots gore worked up for James First. What turned you on to the guy?'

'Not the circulation-of-the-blood business, though I *was*

angry about a great man almost utterly neglected. I got interested in his later work, on generation. Related to my own work then, now, all the time, on cancer-growth. Besides, there hadn't been a biography for fifty years. Flood now, since mine. France mostly, California, Germany.'

'You opened the field. I do too. Make things possible for other people. Screw my own stuff.'

Severance was moved. It was how he felt too, but he never thought of artists that way. He looked at the poet with brandnew almost loving eyes, very touched. 'My wife used to read me some of *The Screams* when it came out. She keeps up. Three four years ago?'

'Six. Plink. Turn you on? Or off?'

'Frankly—'

'*Don't* tell me anything frankly, you lab-hound.' The poet was grinning however. 'Just report gently your wonder consternation rapture grief exaltation and crucifixion.'

Severance really laughed. He did not mind being had by a pro. 'How about the Harrowing and the Resurrection?'

'Settle for those. Tell me, were you interested, at all, in that very weird stuff?' He looked as if he cared.

'Yes. Not as much as Ruth, but I read some myself afterward. You sound better aloud. Good deal of authentic mania there, black and blue wit, pain—the fellow going on to fresh defeats, flappable, flappable. Surviving however. I bought a lot of the little I could understand. Do you write when you're drunk?'

'Not necessarily. You know, I prefer your capsule to most of my American reviews of that book. Not all, but you *heard* my little man. I'm touched, Alan.'

'Well,' Severance swallowed, 'you touched me just now.' He felt as if they were suddenly locked in a death-grip of amity. Neither man was smiling. 'The going-on bit. Groundwork. Hacking entry-points to the sensitivity Group.'

'Quite so. It's real. Plink. On the other hand, I am a raging egoist. Tell you a story about Bertrand Russell. Back home in his castle or whatever, year or so before the end, some strangers were shown in when he was looking at an article about him in some shitass American newspaper. "You will simply have to *wait*," Bertie said to them. "I am *reading about myself.*" Marvellous. That's me, pal.'

The scientist was overwhelmed with admiration and envy. 'I really wish and wish and wish and wish and wish I could make it. I'm probably even vainer than you are, but I'm *impeded.*' He had never confessed this before. 'My *vision* jumps when I find myself reading a complimentary sentence. I can go back, I can read doggedly through. Then memory takes over: five minutes later I've forgotten who wrote the article, I can't even remember, except vaguely, whether it was favourable or not. A phrase may stick; that's all. Same for speeches. I *don't hear* remarks as soon as I smell genuine praise underweigh. My ears skip. Not that I wouldn't *love* to hear: I just don't. And go back and ask? say "Would you mind repeating that extravagance, so that I may not only savour it to the full and recall it forever but repeat it to my wife the next time she shoots me to pieces or treats me like somebody met at the corner of 4th and Broad?" Not bloody likely.'

They were laughing together and the spell was broken. But Severance felt that he had made a deep ally in a most unexpected quarter and it was with sorrow as well as pleasure that he reflected Jasper was taking his Fifth tomorrow and would probably go home by the weekend, wherever home might be for that bird of passage. He pressed the younger man's shoulder hard, warm, as he left to get back to it.

*   *   *

Severance sat in his grey Japanese kimono with his knees wide and his big scratchpad on his left thigh and his cigarette burning in his left hand and wrote: 'Tu. nt.

'First Step (5th version?)

'I see absolutely no hope unless I can learn to accept the First Step (and then keep in daily contact, both meditative and behavioural, with it and Steps 2 and 3, and 12). But with my infinite self-cons and mental distortions, many recognized in the last ten days but how many recognized and *going strong?* how can I know whether I do or not? All I can say is that I finally *seem* to believe as *solid facts* that I am *powerless* over alcohol and that my life is *unmanageable*, out of all control, insane, has been for many years. For Christ's sake tell me whether this belief of mine is real, and whether I can depend on at least *it*. I *am* a dependent man, I need something besides God.'

Here he broke off and leaned back. Suddenly he hacked. He read it over. No Style: good. Still, it didn't sound too good, exactly. But it was only a beginning. Deciding that he wasn't up to the thing itself tonight, he left the rest of the page blank, turned up the next, wrote '3' up in the corner (hoping that would do—it meant to keep this last one short, so that nothing could go wrong) and then:

'Now, *I* am satisfied with what I have said. Where *you* are not, shoot me to pieces. I am deluded. It is not wrong to be deluded. What is tragic (*and unnecessary*, given divine and human help) is to be a drinking alcoholic. Wherever, in whatever points you can discover, my delusions *right now* may lead me back to drinking, I desire to be rid of them. If my many character defects can also be crippled, good; but that seems to me to be secondary.'

He read the two sheets over, and over again, very slowly, and then very slowly detached them and ripped them across and across and dropped them in the wastebasket beside his right arm.

From Severance's Journal

Levelling is so hard because it opens you to confrontation: it gives your address and telephone number.

Maybe if you report puzzlement *when* confronted, and you reply 'sincerely' and are shot down, *without feeling anger:* you're levelling! You're open! *You* don't know (yet) where you stand—perhaps you are outside the window hanging on by your toenails facing toward Jerusalem; but at least *somebody* does, in fact *they* do, and can tell you, *reaching* you, and you can then (POSSIBLY) accept it, and you're in business—advancing, recovering—one delusion *dead* (although, I note depressed, it may always regroup and take over, as last week—just trap again and again), pray, hope.

** ** **

This damned Inventory is valuable though. I find I'm not doing (acting) as well as I *thought* (an instruction in Humility—that thing so uncomfortably far beyond me) but *better* than I feared (encouragement).

Ζεηό δα ηος Κριστος.

With Potts and his tape-recorder I was far more open —about my drinking and my ambition—than I've ever been before in public. I call that a gain. I wonder if it is. Did I avoid pomposity? I hope I can *see* it if it's in the transcript he promised before he sends the interview abroad. Nice boy. A bad moment: though so concentrated on his sometimes rough questions and the mike, I noticed Ruth come in at one point, waved hello, and when I finally said, 'That's enough for today,' I looked and she wasn't there—went off angry, he said, at the 'two male egos ignoring' her. Professional business, curse her. I might as well have been in a television studio.

11

'DON'T READ IT,' Linc said, 'just tell it.'

Severance saw his point but was not having any. 'I think I'll read it,' he said calmly, 'if you don't mind.'

'Go ahead.' Linc was sprawled out, with, as usual, another pair of fancy high shoes on. Perhaps he had ten? Keg and one nurse were sitting in.

Severance unrolled the sheets in his right hand, leaned forward, and read in his clear, powerful voice, keeping the volume down but not neglecting the drama of his spectacular dream, which enshrined, in his opinion (he had deliberately not tried to analyze any of it), at least three concerns—his First Step secret, his fear of Dr Rome, and his ungovernable sexuality—even if it didn't bear, obviously anyway, on his Contract.

' "I was out on a pass—at one point I went back and a man was signing in, I saw his name but forget it (W——?) and realized I could think of no excuse to get out again at 10 p.m. Throughout the very long dream it was just past 10 p.m.

' "Dream begins: *I cannot accept the 1st half of Step I.* (*Fact*, just realized, with shock and horror, this evening) —went to talk to Mary-Jane, others with her, drunkalogues, left to return later. Out on pass I tell Ruth (after perhaps telling others in the same building—she is not as dismayed as I am, doesn't say come home, 'go tell Dr Rome's Encounter-Group'—I say give me some money, I've only pennies (but in fact I had maybe 50¢, enough for bus home but not for drinks at the Masters—she gives me a one and a five?)—walking toward *corner* building on campus where Group is meeting up on 3rd? floor—walk in, very *few* there, all men—I go into room behind—forget

'"Then I am walking campusward *again* past a very large building not right—find corner building—have to go to my office, 3rd floor, to get my *2nd* half of 1st Step to show Dr Rome and ask them for help (which I don't expect to get—will go to Masters and drink—hours till closing)—stop at door of banked theatre down left inside building upstairs (where I am *supposed* to be, to find empty but people are there, even at that time of night and on campus a film is to be shown—ask some girl on left what—girl coming up aisle says German film—now I have SEEN this girl before, know her well—middle height, straight hair, pretty—we talk, she stands against doorway, people passing—I am excited, I stand close to her, find her excited—we half embrace, her one eye is blind—she says excitedly, 'Do you recognize me? Do I exist?' We go hurriedly down dark corridor, turn right, then into my office, she is on bed—I say, 'But you *knew me too*—we *must* have met—I meet so damned many people.' To my amazement, in the *other* bed in my office a TINY boy is awake, in middle of counterpane, *under* it, just showing through hole, I say, 'little boy, it's time for you to go home' (I'm mad to be alone with her)—he says, 'No,' and I realize that his father, a colleague of mine possibly, has *told* him to spend the night here—so no sex, reluctantly resigned to this, but she's under counterpane and says, 'Come under'—I do, she has stripped, she feels for me, I worry about my clothes, begin to touch her breast

Wake up."'

Severance looked up flushed and expectant, rolled the sheets, sat back in his chair. His cards were on the table, whatever they were. He felt ready for the Antarctic.

'A nice dream,' the analyst said lazily. 'Lots of emotion. Do you remember anything more about the theatre?'

'Surprisingly large. Sort of amphitheatre. Not many people in it. A few onstage, but not getting ready for anything. Maybe twenty scattered through the front rows, with nothing to look at.'

Linc thought for a while. 'Do you think you could *be* the amphitheatre?' he asked suddenly.

Severance, not a man easily taken aback, was taken aback. 'What?'

Linc did not say anything.

'*Be* the amphitheatre,' Severance said baffled. 'I don't know.'

'Would you like to try?' Linc's voice was not casual at all. It had assumed the tone of intimate command Severance was very familiar with, used to others. He felt pressure.

'All right,' he said doubtfully.

'Go ahead.'

He closed his eyes, and in five or six seconds, to his speechless surprise and unsurprise, he felt exactly like an amphitheatre. To show the group just where he stood, he raised his arms to shoulder level, stretching them out ahead of him, wrists and hands curved inward, and became immobile.

He heard Linc's voice say, 'Are you the amphitheatre?'

'Yes,' he said with decision.

'How do you feel, Amphitheatre?'

He reflected. 'Fine!'

'Good. Can you see Alan?'

He looked, without opening his eyes (he really had no eyes, though he could see all right). 'Sure.'

'Where is Alan?'

'Right here.' He jerked his head an inch to the right and moved his right thumb. 'Just behind my shoulder.'

'Can you see him clearly?'

'Yes.'

'How does he look?'

'Not so good.' Severance considered. 'He's tall, very thin. He's badly dressed, I can't see why he came. Inappropriate. He looks like hell.'

'How does that make you feel, Amphitheatre?'

'I don't give a *damn* about it,' he exploded.

Other questions, many questions, followed, and he responded without hesitation, clearly and fully, but afterward he could never say what any of them had been. His concentration was complete but his consciousness was double, he both was and was not in the Mini-group room, aware and not aware of the people seated around it. Linc himself was only a voice. He explained his position on the topics proposed to him. He felt quite happy—remote, austere, interested but uncommitted, semi-circular, almost empty, expectationless, patient. He felt that he was being understood, at last.

But at last the discomfort of his extended arms mounted toward actual pain. 'I've got to put my arms down,' he said irritably.

'Okay! You're back in the room now, you're Alan Severance, and you remember everything that has happened.'

He opened his eyes and saw Linc, dropped his arms in his lap, and sighed. 'The next time you have me be something, I hope it doesn't involve *that* muscle-strain.'

'*I* didn't ask you to raise your arms,' Linc smiled at him, and the group roared with laughter.

Severance grinned sheepishly. My god, the witch-doctor.

'How do you feel now? Do you feel okay?'

'Yes. Yes, I do.'

'Our desire here is to find out whether you are an okay

person or not an okay person. As for what *kind* of okay person, that doesn't matter—okay sad, okay mad, okay vain, anything is okay so long as you're comfortable with it. All clear?'

'Maybe,' said Severance. 'I'll think about it.'

'Don't think about it. Does anybody else want to say anything?'

Keg put a question: 'Why do you suppose one-eyed women are seeking their identity from you?'

'Faintest idea,' Severance said shortly. 'Never knew one.'

Apparently the young man didn't know a castration symbol on sight. Not my job to pass that back here.

Nobody else spoke.

'I do want to extend our Contract, though.' Linc was looking sharp at him. 'Over the weekend, will you make up your mind about two things. One, why you were surprised at your *comfort* in being an amphitheatre. Two: supposing you had entire control over it to re-invent it, is there anything about the dream that you would like to *change?* Okay?'

'—'

While Linc swivelled toward Rhea and her doomed competition with her Mother-of-the-Year mother, Severance adjusted his thoughts. Compare my surprise, even incredulity *still*, about the *Irish Times* people waiting for me on the tender at Cobh: I have *not* come to easy terms with my fame etc—I am *not* an okay person. For no reason, this notion, with which he had begun the Contract, struck him with fresh and depressing force. He laid it aside to consider the second part. I feel that I *ought* to make the theatre feel guilty about neglecting poor Alan; but in fact I *won't*: screw him. *I give shows*, all day and even late in the evening (no?), *of all kinds*. Let him solve his own problems—I'll schedule him if I'm free. I'm sometimes free, he only has to ask the authorities that govern me—

but I won't *feel sorry* for him. I am a busy amphitheatre, glad to be one, useful to many.

Then he put the matter out of his head, attended to the confrontations of Hutch (very depressed: 'I'm afraid— after four weeks it will be just the same thing over again.' Severance, who happened to know that he had started driving immediately: 'You'll be a *different* Hutch— otherwise, no hope') and Letty, wide-eyed innocent grandmotherly minimizing, bolted lunch, let the lecture flow unregarded around him, and was so busy with the First Step that he just said, 'No thanks today,' when some-body looked in for the walk at four o'clock. 'I present this' (he had begun, for the nth time) 'without much confi-dence, but also with great confidence, as merely the pres-ent stage of my feelings on the subject after nearly two weeks of my third treatment period in one year. Obviously my other two 1st Steps were worthless, though "sincere" enough to deceive a good judge at Howarden and Gus One here. I think I now know why. If this is an improvement on them—you will judge, and help me where deluded —it is because I have decided or learned to stick here to bone-sure emotional *facts*; so I may not get far but (I *think*) I can hardly go wrong.'

Feeling that he had not made any mistakes yet, he began a new paragraph. 'I take the second half first; I used to think this the harder half, but have changed my mind. The unmanageability ought to *prove* the powerlessness; but it is horribly possible to "admit" the first without *accepting* the second, and in fact that was my situation until night before last, though I only realized it that afternoon.'

He had a good deal more to say before he really got going, but he felt unaccountably tired and went down the hall for coffee. Hotcha in the Snack Room half an hour, joking with Gene S, the new beanpole of Ward W. A minute after he'd returned to his room, Harry knocked and came in for a dyad. Severance was touched by such consideration from a man about to be discharged, but during the desultory talk—Harry was a tall lean heavy-lidded man more thoughtful than articulate—he experienced some twinges of worry about Harry's unruffledness, facing The Outside so (attractive but) menacing to most patients including Severance. Harry seemed not to have a care in the world. Severance thought of confronting him, but decided: If their judgment is he's ready, what's mine worth. He left, and the weary scientist took up his pad to read over what he had written before PUSHING ON.

With sick dismay he saw that he had n o t   s a i d *anything*. He slashed a savage diagonal with his ballpoint down through his laborious and deluded paragraphs. He was sweating lightly. He looked at nothing, like a wall, without interest.

After the evening lecture, he had recovered sufficiently to start exploring his feelings again, to see if he had any, and he found himself writing something very different. 'It is true that I am only an amphitheatre,' he began. 'But I have a certain power of criticism over the shows that are put on in me. I don't allow shows that are merely entertaining; in fact I insist on shows that are so interesting or difficult that they are put on again and again. Only certain spectators are willing to come so often, but that is quite all right; I am a very ambitious and demanding but not a *greedy* amphitheatre. How about the seats? Not too comfortable, lest somebody drowse. Adjustable? Yes, decidedly; so long as' Here he broke off bored.

The following afternoon, Saturday, hard on a dramatic evening and a harrowing morning, he scratched quickly, 'Yest'y, *fine* as amphitheatre. Today, not so good—in fact, unhappy, since Casey's wife saw the amph. as just a *container* for (my) "tumultuous" emotions. Now I'm struck by: Amphitheatre *never sleeps*. An amph., it's true, doesn't *need* sleep, but I am *not* an amphitheatre

'*I am a human being*—Alan, in rags, "thin, woebe-

gone"—arriving where he was *"supposed"* to be—Alas!
(self-pity)

> 'This dream was supposed to be a picture of my
> true life; but all it is is *a picture of my illness*
> and delusions (grandeur etc).'

As on wore the long day, dreary, and a pitiless dinner,
and a three-drunkalogue 'lecture,' the worse he felt.
Shortly after ten he took the pad on his thigh and set
briskly down:

> *'Revision of Dream*
'Practically everything in the dream is wrong.
> 1) I would put together the borrowing of money
>   to go drink, and the *not* telling Dr Rome's group
>   (which I minimize and bypass); interpret them
>   with Gene's idea that my "honest" last-minute
>   doubts about the first part of Step One was a de-
>   fence to get out of treatment.
> 2) I would wipe out all the sex stuff as a pathetic
>   attempt to prove to Julitta that my sex life *is so*
>   relevant here. (It's not.)
> 3) I would refuse to be the amphitheatre; or, if I
>   agreed to try, I would fail. Alan looks like hell,
>   with his mysterious mission (*"supposed* to be") and
>   then his con-man outfit (vest and all); but as a mat-
>   ter of fact, *I* am *him*. We need an entirely new
>   dream. I leave that up to my mangled (by me) but
>   surviving and adorable "child."

'I was *surprised* Friday by my *surprise* at being so comfortable as an amphitheatre; since "that is what I am."'

'Yesterday and today, I *am still* surprised, but for a very
different reason: didn't the deluded son-of-a-bitch *recognize* his delusion?!'

He relaxed in his chair with a sense of angry out-of-the-
woods triumph but also with disappointment at the level of

grief. Just one failure more! Many months would pass, not until one rainy morning nearly ten months later would he be able to write, with sudden realization: 'Yes. Contract One *was* indispensable. So long as I considered my self as merely the medium of (arena for) my powers, sobriety was out of the question: no care for self ("You were not responsible for *yourself*," as Vin said).

'The even deeper delusion that my science and art *depended* on my drinking, or at least *were* connected with it, could not be attacked directly. Too far down. The cover had to be exploded off, then the under-madness simply withered away, for lack of sustenance and protection.

'No effect, maybe, on the *apparent* difficulty, the stated Contract. So what? Who ever *died* of mismanagement of his fame or lack of peace with it or my impediments to its shameless enjoyment? It's only Whiskey kills.'

Severance was a conscientious man. He had really thought, off and on for twenty years, that it was his duty to drink, namely, to sacrifice himself. He saw the products as worth it. Maybe they were—if there had been any connexion.

An electrical storm, trivial compared to Long Island's but a very decent try on its own (B−), imposed the survival of the outside world briefly on Ward W and Severance was interested in the duologue that ushered Harry out into it— Old Harry, he thought of him as, though it was to turn out much later that Harry was several years younger than Middle-aged (Old he thought of himself as, but Younger) Alan.

Harley began Group on Thursday with, 'Harry. You took your Fifth Step yesterday.'

'That's right.' Harry looked like a benign lizard, long, half-drowsy, low-keyed, Permian.

'How was it?'

'Seemed to go all right. He gave me some advice. Not bad at all.'

'We're discharging you today. You'll check in with Ray right now—you know where his office is? and then the Cashier over in Main and you're off. How do you feel about going home.'

'Be nice, I guess. Never liked the food here.'

'What are your plans?'

'No great plans. Work a little maybe. Keep out of trouble.' He grinned.

It seemed to Alan Severance a *hell* of a Programme but he had to admit Harry was utterly relaxed. He wished he was. After all, he took it in as if afresh, *tension* was required to make a recovering alcoholic drink. How could tension be avoided—his life was built on it.

'No problems, eh?' But Harley was smiling too.

'Oh, I'm very worried, but I don't let it worry me none.' He winked at Mary-Jane, actually winked. And that was it.

Long afterward, when he had grown to feel the power of Harry's long, distinguished silences, this little scene recurred to Severance's mind one afternoon and without knowing why, he applied to it the remark of some great conductor, that he would require a far larger orchestra than had ever yet been assembled, in order to produce real silence.

IV

THE LAST TWO
FIRST STEPS

The eternal gates terrific porter lifted the northern bar.
Thel enter'd in & saw the secrets of the land unknown.

12

IRREGULAR PROGRESS but, undoubtedly, some. Too many plus-strokes pistoning in from qualified sources for entire doubt. Of course the big tests had not come yet, and his private struggles with the ack-ack First Step were, so far, private—he reported faithfully, without any attempt at fullness, to Ruth every evening or so, but she did not take in at all what he was talking about in that stratosphere. Otherwise they were getting on brilliantly. Cozy over the on-coming Him or Her. Only one blow-up: the interviews. In Group, the red heart after all, it was impossible to avoid the conclusion that he was going like a house afire, confronting and levelling, helping everybody reachable. No doubt he was talking too much, as ever, but not only had nobody said so but Keg had actually complimented him while leaving one twelve-fifteen, though he couldn't recall what on. Ten o'clock was almost a pleasure. His Jewish studies were fascinating Severance, his disciplines were rigorous, his room was shipshape, his talks three mornings a week with Dr Gullixson were banquets of approval, only (really) his scrotum was bothering him to any serious degree. It was so sensitive he could hardly walk. He widened his thighs and went slow. Why hadn't he complained to anybody, he wondered. After all he was in a hospital. Severance was aware that he stood pain remarkably well, considering the delicacy of his nervous organization, short of course of the crushing of his greater occipital nerve (in a muscle spasm apparently) that had put him in hospital for two months the year before, out a few weeks in daily massage-and-heat and then when they began traction, back in hospital on Demerol; he gave himself no credit for this; he considered his stoicism (various people had used the word off and on for years) idiotic; he knew he was a fool for not seeking help. Why suffer? But he did. He had not examined it, even in the shower either yesterday or the day before or today. He had not, certainly, examined it. No indeed. The less he heard thought saw imagined and above all *felt* about it, the better. It would probably *not kill* him. In fact he expected it to go away, any minute, and felt hurt, or outraged rather, as it mysteriously and worseningly didn't.

He sat with spread legs in Group while Wilbur tried to explain to Harley and Keg, especially Keg, why he called his even more elderly parents two or three (or four and five—the number magnified with the pressure on him) times every single day. The telephone was a topic on Ward W. There was only one, and its use was discouraged. Severance had tried to get the Group to agree to just one call a day, limited to five minutes, for the Repeaters that is, and had had some support but not enough; Harley had asked him, with a twisted happy smile, if he was applying for a job as Counsellor. The point was: *associations outside*—there should not *be* any. Everybody, or all who spoke (Jeree and Mary-Jane, at their opposite ends of the well-ing spectrum, were silent), agreed; except Wilbur. After he had finally been harried and battered into the admission that he spent *a good part of every day* on the phone to his goddamned parents (Wilbur was sixty-odd, and, believe Severance, it was hard to imagine that he had ever been married, though two wives had left him), the question could be taken up of Why. 'They need me,' he said many times. His father, drunk from morning to night, was urging him to come home, and Wilbur was anxious to go—although they fought like madmen right through every call and it was perfectly clear to everybody but Wilbur that he got a *bang* out of holding his own against his frightful Dad from a safe telephone distance (Father's ax, kept in the kitchen where *he* drank: 'I'll chop you, Wilbur, late one night, I'll chop you.'), revelling too in the fact that he himself was not only sober at the moment but being *treated* for the disease that was killing them both. 'They need me,' he said stubbornly. 'They need you sober,' Keg threw him. 'Next time you drink you're fired for the last time, right? How the hell at this point in the U.S. economy, with your record, do you expect—do you *ever* expect, Wilbur—to get another job. You'll all three starve.' 'Dad has his pension.' 'You can live on it.' 'No. No, he won't give me a cent.' 'So *you'll* starve.' 'They need me!' 'You need yourself, you fucking deluded bastard. You'll be drinking within twenty-four hours, and we won't take you back. That's a promise. You've got to get your mind off your parents and work on a Programme that will give you, after five treatments isn't it, here and in Illinois and Minnesota, a ghost of a Chinese prayer of a chance to stay dry long enough to be of some real *help* to your miserable parents.' It was never possible to be certain whether Keg was really angry or was making with it to bring the patient out, but Severance saw him here as exasperated, at a loss. He glanced at Harley. The senior Counsellor was staring at Wilbur with what the scientist realized, with a start, was something like hopeless love. He had never seen anything quite like it. He saw that Harley the Hound, Author of Drouth in this part of the death-prone addicted country, saw himself, saw Harley of old a hundred and a hundred times, where Wilbur was—and hurt. The guy had a heart of gold, for God's sake, he was

full of *grief* for Wilbur. So was Severance, he had to confess, but not in that degree. His not-responsible heart was
comparatively a stone, he just felt *sorry* for Wilbur.
There was pain all around the room.

But everybody was his own hot topic too, and you
could almost see pain—recede. They sat there. Nobody
said anything. Gradually everybody forgot about Wilbur,
including Wilbur. A long time passed. Nobody was looking at anybody. A sense began and grew in Severance of
Trouble on both sides of him and across and around and
up and down and outside and *inside* and Harley said pleas-
antly, 'It's nice to know that all of you are cured. Why
don't you all go home?'

Stung under the general lash of this, Severance let go.
'I've been *fed up* for five minutes. We're all cowards. We
might as well be in the Lesser Antilles, slopping rum.' To
his surprise, nobody hit him. But nobody else spoke, either.
Mary-Jane was slumped over, grim, depressed. 'Tout le
monde, ou du moins bien du monde allait dans ce salon,
et il n'avait rien de banal' (not exactly!); 'on y respirait, en
entrant' (and *staying*), 'un air de discrétions et de mystère.'
Sainte-Beuve on Mme Récamier's. That was the trouble,
nobody dared *in*discretion. 'What's with you, Letty?' Harley finally asked tiredly. It was the worst session they had
had, and noone looked at anyone after they joined hands for
the Serenity Prayer ('the courage to change the things I
can') and went slouching out.

At lunch, which reminded him of the two most unpopu-
lar dishes at his preparatory school (fisheyes-in-glue and
Purple Passion), he listened with relief, for the fourth time,
to old Alice's frenzied, gleeful recitation of how she had
once done Hildegarde's hair when the singer was in
Akron, 'and she was just like you and me—so *sweet*.'
Severance and several of his cronies could not understand
how Alice had become an *alcoholic*, a concentrated resolute person after all, with a certain malign dignity, whereas

Alice scattered in all directions like her own white wisps and flagrant streamers, but like everybody else he was fond of her and hoped to God she would make it, if they ever let her out. (They did, a week later, and she wandered in, the following afternoon, blind-drunk, 'just to make a phone-call,' she said, as they locked her in her not yet occupied room, safe with anti-convulsant and sedative, before transferring her to Seven—psychiatric.) Poor old Alice, probably a better human being than he was, and in fact he knew it.

Brooding on a passage in one of his Jewish books ('Even selfishness, the most dangerous of human traits, has its proper place. A modicum of it is a *sine qua non*. "If I am not for myself, who will be for me?" asked Hillel, going on, however, to add, "If I am for myself alone, what do I amount to?" ') he underscored 'for myself alone' and was late as usual to lecture, had to sit in the back, heard only random words, not enough to discover what the subject was—no doubt he had heard it before, though he couldn't remember the lecturer, an intense young-middle-aged woman with a long nose and a forefinger—and was thoroughly bored. Impediments!

He spent an hour in his room with the Big Book, Chapter V. Meat all over. If only he had had his brain with him at Howarden. Easing his awful crotch—not the crotch precisely, somewhere southwest on the scrotum, an acre of the scrotum—he read slowly. 'We were now at Step Three. Many of us said to our Maker, *as we understood Him* (no trouble there, thank God himself, Father Boniface, and Vin): "God, I offer myself to Thee—to build with me and to do with me as Thou wilt. Relieve me of the bondage of self, that I may better do Thy will. [Double margin-marks.] Take away my difficulties, that victory over them may bear witness to those I would help of Thy Power, Thy Love, and Thy Way of life." ' (*Thy* Way of *my* life. A heavy saying, as Origen described, 'Many are

called, but few are chosen.') ' "May I do Thy Will Always!" We thought well before taking this step making
sure we were ready; that we could at last abandon ourselves
[double underscoring] to Him.' The opening words of the
Step drifted into Severance's open mind, and he realized
—with a physical start—that he had never actually
'*Made a decision* to turn our will and our lives over to the
care of.' He had tried to *do* it, all right, off and on, off and
on, but the *decision?* He *stood up*, feeling quite unlike himself, and went and opened the door and hurried down the
corridor to the nurses' station and right and crossed in
front of the elevators to the chapel door and opened it and
entered and without genuflecting knelt down in the first
pew on the right and without even crossing himself leant
his elbows on the rail and clasped his hands very tightly
and bowed his head and took the Third Step. Christ. Afterward he probably prayed for a long time, who knows,
feeling easy and light and amazed at not having ever done
this before and, 'just the *decision*—now it's up to Him
too—I can't do it all—He *knows* that, for Christ's
sake, He made me up, He knows what's possible to me and
what's just *not* (at this point) possible—God and I are a
majority, as somebody said,' and when he finally stood up
in the dusky empty chapel he felt as if a weighty knapsack
had been hoisted off from between his shoulders, he felt
possible. 'Hurrah,' he said in a low voice to the light on the
altar as he genuflected and turned back out.

   Bravo you tardy bastard, he bade a happy farewell to
himself, wondering if maybe one-sixteenth of it would
stick. Submission, eh? Not so clear sailing for *pricks* cursed
with intransigence and power like Baby, but anyway he
was on record, and he didn't plan to forget it. Returning
to his neat room for one minute, he wrote the Third Step
below the First Step inside the front cover of his 24-Hour
Book, where he had already put the names of the thirty-
odd people most prominent in his treatment. Slogans were

jabbed in there too, and 'Amends' notes, and he read it all carefully every morning before he read the three texts for the day. Then he trotted gaily down to the Snack Room and told Jeree, Mike M, George, and Delores stories.

Severance was, though he had never developed a special system of breathing-just-*before*-concluding (like his old friend Jean Stafford) to keep from losing the floor, an able storyteller. He said that most of the time Ward W reminded him of the legend carved on W. C. Fields's gravestone—'I'D RATHER BE HERE THAN PHILADELPHIA' —though on the other hand he also felt about it what that elegant veteran Maurice Chevalier replied to a reporter: 'Old age is not so bad, when you consider the alternative.' Nobody knew the pineapple-juice story. 'Fields not only had a refrigerator-bar built into his limousine, to ingratiate himself into his role—that is, himself—on the way to the set, but he drank steadily on the set: martinis. A pitcher of them. He did not however call them martinis. He called them pineapple juice. One day some wag, while Fields was on-camera, emptied the pitcher and filled it with pineapple juice. When next he went to his throne to refresh himself, he sputtered, gagged, and—having, like most great comedians, no more sense of humour than a flatworm—exploded. "Who's been putting pineapple juice in my pineapple juice?" ' This pleased one and all, so he went on to mention a personal experience of the sincere delusions of quite ordinary bar-drinkers, most of them probably not even alcoholics. He had done some devoted drinking in West Side bars around 23rd Street after his first wife left him, and was fascinated in some can by the column of graffiti about a certain 'Mary Jane.' (He winced at the incongruity of name but it was out, and true, and no matter.) Outstanding and epiphenomenal sexual qualifications, tastes, and achievements were attributed to her, beginning about seven feet high on the wall and descending, in many calligraphies, to below one's knee—where some

realist had knelt down to record at the bottom his opinion.
' "I don't believe," he wrote soberly, "Mary Jane exists." '
Non-alcoholic stories were at a premium on the ward, so
this too made a hit, and Severance went away recharged to
further his newest campaign against the First Step, glad
that he had refrained from boasting about his Third Step
insight—where in his chair at the end of half an hour's
work he looked up suddenly from his note-making with
incredulity: all his labours had been wasted or nullified.

He realized at last where he stood, and it was in the
worst place a patient could be.

He did not speak during dinner except, twice, to a scary
scrawny frozen-faced woman named Luriel who had come
down the day before from Seven looking so wretchedly
that Severance had sort of taken her on, at meals. She
hadn't answered him yet but he kept at it.

                              *   *   *

It would be hard to say why Severance took Gene into his
confidence about a matter so capital, when Mike M or
Charley or Mary-Jane would have been natural. So much
happened by accident on the Ward, who ran into who
where when in what stage of progress, regression, torpor,
despair, or mania. Even the deliberate seeking-people
which was mandatory for the Repeaters' Group turned
largely on whim, in these early days, before their Programmes (some of their Programmes) had hardened and
before they (some of them) finally grew back lax. Severance later read miracles here and there in this matter. The
immensely tall lazy intelligent young man, maybe twenty
years his junior, who had just come into treatment, was relating from his great height, in the Snack Room, his first
confrontation. 'They're just trying to make me mad,' he
concluded.

'Did they?' Severance asked.

'Certainly not. What do I care?'

'You didn't feel angry?'

'Of course not. It's just a game.'

'It's not a game, Gene, and they weren't just trying to make you mad. They meant it. That's exactly what Daisy said to me in Group her first morning last Spring, when I called her a lousy superior bitch and asked her what there was so superior about her. Vin had been playing psychodrama and she said, "You're all freaks." Everybody was furious. I hit her and she looked at me across the Group and said, "You're just trying to make me mad." It was ten days before she caught on.'

'Caught on to what?' Gene asked with interest.

'Caught on that I wasn't kidding. Found out *she* was a freak.'

'I don't understand. You mean I should have pretended to be angry?'

'No. You should have been angry.'

'What about? I'm very easy-going.'

'The hell you are. What do you drink for?'

'That's a question,' Gene said seriously. 'That's a real question. I haven't the faintest idea.'

'Do you get mad at work?'

'Sure. But I don't do anything about it.'

'Why not?'

'Why bother?'

Severance, peering into the thickets of the newcomer's delusion, saw he might be of some real help. 'Come down to my room and chat a little, want to?'

They took their coffees down the corridor. Severance sat, Gene stood at the end of the bed.

'Listen,' said Severance. 'You're nowhere.'

'I know that. God almighty, my dear new friend, I know that. Something is going on that I cannot get a clue to. I feel as if I were in fairyland. What in the name of Christ is the *point* of all this business? What does it have to do with *drinking?* I'm here for *drinking*, not because I happen to be a tranquil type, with everything under control.'

'Everything under control!' Though he knew it was foolish, Severance felt his heat rising. 'Hospitals, accidents, blackouts, your wife's left you twice, you tried suicide at least once that you told me—' He drove down the list.

Gene was standing white-faced, holding the bedrail.

'God,' he said hoarsely.

'It's true, it's true, isn't it? Your life is a nightmare. You are an *alcoholic*, pal. You are almost as sick as I am, maybe more so. You are *insane*, and you tell me everything's under control.'

'I tried one other time too ' Gene put his left hand to his face. His left lid was jumping. 'I know I'm mad. I see it must be. Can you help me, Alan?' He was pleading. 'Can you give me just one point of connexion. I'm absolutely lost. I don't know what's happening. What *ought* to *happen?*'

Severance felt terrible himself. What could he do? 'I can't really help you yet, Gene, God knows I would. You're going to have to get in touch with yourself. It takes time. It takes miracles: two or three or four *miracles.*'

'I don't understand—"get in touch with myself." I *am* in touch with myself. That's the trouble. I see the whole story and I wish I were dead.'

'You do not see the whole story. You do not see any part of the story. You are deluded. Look, two minutes ago you said you were absolutely lost, now you say you see the whole story. *Put* the two things together, will you?' He waited. 'But you *can't.* They don't *go* together. They come out of different worlds.'

The temperature in the room was 112 degrees. Total darkness at the end of the bed.

'Listen. Even in my condition, I could take any one of your statements and tell you the entire score in about five minutes. But you would not understand, much less, accept, *one word* of it.' He tried to think. He thought. It was possible. 'I might just be able to give you an opening. Listen closely. If you can see where you are, or rather are not, on just one point, it might help a lot—if you could hang onto it.'

'That's what I've got to have. Just one point.'

'Okay. Here it is. What do you do at five o'clock?'

'I get stoned.'

'I knew it. *Why* do you get stoned?'

'God knows.'

'No doubt. He knows everything. But the point is that *you* know too.'

'I do not know. I swear to you.'

'I know that. But you also do know. Look here, do you remember that you said to me a minute ago, when I asked you why you did not *do* anything about your rage at your bosses, "Why bother?" Do you remember that?'

'Yes, I do.'

'Okay. *Crap.*' Severance's voice was as hard as he could make it, which was not as hard as either titanium or zirconium but hard.

Gene flushed. 'What do you mean?'

'I mean that you are *lying* when you say you do not do anything about your anger. You get bombed. It is called medicating the feelings, pal. Every inappropriate drinker in the United States does it, and in France, Chile and Norway. Cause and effect. Visible to a child. Not visible to you. Don't you see how weird, how *unacceptable*, your little put-off, "Why bother," is, in the light of the fact of your daily self-destruction and progressive ruin?'

'I don't see the connexion. I admitted they made me mad.'

Severance gave up. 'I know. It was just a try, Gene.'

They looked at each other, Gene entirely reconstituted —regrouped, the term was—intellectually puzzled, disappointed, skeptical, condescending, quite okay now. Severance felt something like despair, though he knew that in a few weeks this would (probably) all be mere history. Anyway, he had tried. Having been there so often and so long himself, he felt very close to Gene—though very distant too, undeluded in that particular corner—and he was inspired to put his own insoluble sweat before the younger man. Besides. Help was about as plausible here as a Biafra airlift from General Foods, or rather from Appalachia— edibles from the starving to the even more starving— but you never knew.

'You don't even know you're in trouble. I know I'm in trouble, and it's worse than yours. When I admit it they're going to throw me out of hospital. I don't buy the first half of the First Step. I just realized this afternoon. I've had it.'

'How do you mean? You don't accept it?' Gene did not sound greatly concerned.

'How can I? It's not a fact. "Powerless over alcohol" —horseshit. I drank and drank and drank and drank and drank, and stopped and stopped and stopped and stopped and stopped. Six or seven slips in two months. Dry two whole months after that. What the hell.'

'But here you are.'

'Pure accident. I'll tell you what happened. It will be nice not to be confronted about it, for a change.' He actually did smile, with bitterness. 'I started drinking on the plane to Buffalo to give a lecture, first part of week before last. I forget why, God damn it. Trips are hell on me; I got through ten days in Mexico without anything, but I had my family with me and even so I sweated in airports; if I ever get through a trip alone, that will be the day—I may have to give up travelling, though I have a bloody tour agreed on, damn it, this December. Anyway, I slipped off and on in Buffalo and some other city upstate New York, got through a TV interview etc., tapered off and arrived very much in order back here, something past ten o'clock

Thursday night. Called Ruth from the airport not to meet me, she was just going to bed in any case. Well, suppose she'd met me, that would have been the end of it, no? back on the programme. Okay. I got a taxi. The taxi happened to take the long way, around through Bristol Square—*happened*, mind you—and by pure chance I happened to look up—I was hunched down in the back brooding without pleasure on my imminent confession—*happened* to see across the Square, we were stopped at a red light, my favourite bar. *Bad luck.* I was willing to *postpone* a bit the unwelcome announcement of my new slip—first in two months—maybe she'd go to sleep and it could wait till morning—so I said, "Drop me over at The Masters." I admit that, then, from that point on, I was doomed. I blacked out around midnight and woke up next day in the bed of an Arabic poetess, sent her out for a bottle, and was holed up blind until Sunday afternoon when I formed a detailed suicide-plan for Monday morning when shops opened, we went downtown and drank in a bar until suddenly for no reason whatever I abandoned my plan and told her to drive me home. Chain of accidents, Gene. Suppose Ruth had collected me, *or* the flaming cab had gone the usual route, Lake Circle, *or* I hadn't glanced out and seen *the one* of only two bars in the city that menaces me, nothing—*nothing*—would have happened. I would have been safe!' His tone was triumphant. Q.E.D. Irrefutable.

'Until next time.'

This small phrase, pronounced sternly by his deluded new friend, produced a cataclysm in Severance. He felt his brain might burst out of its cradle. He felt: *It's true.* His very heavy momentum either reversed itself in a split-second or came to a dead stop and then tore off in the opposite direction. All doubts departed. He could stay in treatment without a qualm. This sense of irresistible conviction, as real as an abscessed tooth, was not new to Severance. He had experienced it in science, in life, and in literature.

But it was very very rare in his long history. Only two instances flashed as he stared at his instructor. After an awful night-flight from London with his first wife (layover five hours for repairs in the makeshift airport at Reykjavik, Deirdre just out of hospital with a slipped disk trying to rest on the narrow red imitation-leather hard bench-cushions), she had turned to him in their hotel room as the bellboy closed the door and said, 'You know I'm going to leave you.' These were the worst words ever spoken to him, and although the idea was in fact absolutely new he felt no doubt whatever from the instant he heard it, it even seemed to him that she was as usual right and he *had* known it, forever, or at least during the second half of their marriage, the six years of his uncontrollable drinking. Horror and assent. No protest, no attempt. Just so, at the climax of one of Cervantes' most convulsive tales, he saw again 'Rindióse Camilla, Camilla se rindió.' It was intolerable and unavoidable, the product of the siege to her laid by her husband's best friend:—Camilla gave in; she gave in. Severance succumbed to this truth in the same way, with agonized satisfaction. He could never, comfortably, never comfortably, drink again. 'It must be by his death,' Brutus' *First* words, after the long wait and underground wondering where *he* stands on the tyrant (his best friend, maybe his father, governor of his will). No half-measures: Rejection. Christ's horrible gesture against the damned on the end-wall of the Sistine Chapel.

'Ye-e-es,' he said very slowly. 'I see that. I am obliged to you, for pointing out to me that the earth is not flat. If I live twenty years, as I may do now, I will never be able to render you thanks.'

'Maybe you were just trying to get yourself off the hook,' Gene suggested.

They talked on, like thieves making common cause against their own (stolen) property—raids planning—

and certain things were not quite the same for Severance after this particular dyad.

When Gene took himself off, Alan opened his journal and closed it again, too tired to write. He lay down and passed into a weary but not unhappy half-hallucinatory state. His body flat out, his scrotal state neither contunding nor quite still, he wandered through old adventures. He was in mid-town Manhattan one evening twenty years ago, unusually drunk, convinced that he was an FBI man with Communist agents after him. He fell into a taxi and told the driver to take him to the Bronx 'by the most indirect route.' As they zigged and zagged north he kept a terrified watch out the rear window. Finally the driver stopped at a light and asked for the street address. 'Never mind,' said Alan urgently, 'Take me to Greenwich Village. Bedford Street. Hurry.' The fare was formidable and luckily he had it. He gave the driver an extra five 'for saving my life.' He saw a marquee and went in and upstairs and along a corridor until he heard gaiety behind a door, held his finger on the bell. Two men opened it. 'I'm an FBI man and the Communists are after me. Can I come in and hide?' The man on the right gave him a grin. Severance loved him. 'Well, I don't believe you're an FBI agent, but come in and join the party.' He did, and had a ball. Then he was lunging through the hot streets of Calcutta in the middle of the monsoon night, unable to remember his address and dying of thirst. Embassy party, maybe; got separated. Hours passed, nowhere to sit down. Dawn was already full on when a pimp picked him up and wafted him to a brothel. The madam brought Danish beer and two girls, one short and fat, one thin. He liked the iced dark beer better than the Hindus and liked the thin girl better than the fat girl. He *drank*. The madam brought him a pack of Craven A he must have demanded. The girls took off their saris and knickers, lay down on the carpet, watching him, and handled each other. Presently the fat one got from somewhere a long dildo, attached it to her brush, and inserted it with great lunges of her great tail in the almost hairless cunt of the delicate slim girl. She fucked her. The girl underneath waved her arms and legs. Alan, who had always felt rather turned on by phantasies of lesbians, was not much interested by this *fucking*, but despite his exhaustion and his skipping vision he grew excited by the thin girl. He would have liked to be on her himself. She simulated orgasm, grimacing, heaving. The madam came back and it was clear that he could have one of the girls. Unfortunately he was unable to speak—not much Hindi he had anyway, and no Bengali—and somehow he found himself alone with the dildo-wielder, screwing her. This sobered him so quickly that he remembered his address (Harrington Mansions, just off Theatre Road, third floor). Getting there, he slept until just barely time to leave for his 5 p.m. lecture at the Royal Asiatic Society.

He came off his bed in Ward W sweating. It was eleven-ten.

There was a gang in the Snack Room. Luriel was leaning into the refrigerator, her narrow back active. Jeree had gone to bed, Edith was gossiping with George and a new man, slight build, slack-faced, in a dressing-gown. Charley and Bill S were arguing across the table. Alan drew coffee and stood behind Charley, leaving the third chair for Luriel, who brought salami cheese mayonnaise butter bread to the table, paying no attention to anyone. Edith laughed her suburb terrace laugh. 'Getting ready for a greedy night?'

Luriel dropped her empty hands, looked at Edith, lowered her head, and rushed out.

Now Severance could not bear Edith, a pretty, dark-haired, offhand housewife who had been more or less confided to his protection—'Show her the ropes, she's resistant and scared'—by a mutual friend who had just left the Ward. She seemed to him neither scared nor resistant; just not here at all. Most patients were for their first week or ten days monotonously glum. Edith acted as if she was on a tour of the Greek islands, minus the archeology and the Metaxa (seven-star no doubt). Help her? Moreover, she had been insolent about an old friend of his at lunch, Rochelle. He moved forward.

'We don't bait each other in here,' he said savagely.

She looked taken aback. 'I— She— I'm sorry, I only— I had no idea.'

'She must be incredibly sensitive, damn you. You were rude about Rochelle at noon, too. Rochelle is a close friend of mine, we were together in Group last Spring. You said she had the manners of a prostitute. Who do you think you are? I personally know various duchesses and princesses' (one princess, anyway, that's enough) 'if we're going in for that stuff: they are delighted to entertain me, and I consider Rochelle my social equal. I suppose *you* hobnob with duchesses,' he snapped, and left.

Arita, who had just come on duty, looked up Luriel's room number and Alan went softly down the dark right corridor. He knocked, knocked again, heard a sound, turned the knob and pushed. She was sitting hunched over on the far side of the bed with her back to him, unmoving. He walked around the end and sat down tentatively in a straight chair. Her convulsed face, when she lifted it, was the colour of clay.

'I'm *sorry*,' he said bitterly.

'Everybody makes fun of me.'

'Have *I* made fun of you, Luriel? She told us she was sorry, when I hit her. What was the trouble exactly?'

'I have to eat all the time. I can't help it. I'm an addict.'

'Eat?' Severance was surprised. 'Aren't you an alcoholic?'

'Maybe,' said Luriel earnestly, entering into something with him, 'but the real trouble is my *eating*. I can't stop. Night and day.'

'But you eat practically nothing at meals,' he said puzzled.

'It's not so bad then. It's in between meals I have no control. All night long.' The weird unattractive, even repellent young woman sounded desperate. She was confiding *fear* as well as resentment. 'They have no right to laugh, it's not my fault, it's my body. I'm helpless.'

Severance hurt with her. 'Who laughs, for God's sake? Edith is Bitch One but she certainly did not know about your trouble. Nobody else laughed, I can tell you. They felt bad.'

'They all make fun of me. Even my doctor.'

'Your doctor?' The M.D. was scandalized. 'That's unprofessional! Who is he?'

'Dr Walters.'

'I don't know him. He must be out of his mind. I *have heard everything* about psychiatrists, I've had four or five myself, but this is new to me. What the hell does he laugh at?'

'My problem.'

'What problem?'

'My eating problem.'

'It's no joke. Obesity can be dangerous. Does he deny that?'

'He says I have no eating problem.'

'And you really do? When did it begin?'

'Last week, up on Seven. I began to crave. At first I thought it would go away, but I began to hide food and I saw I was lost.'

My God it's just like bottles, he thought. But he said: 'I never heard of addiction happening so suddenly. What drugs were you on?'

'I forget.'

'Anyway it hasn't got far. At least you have no *weight* problem.'

'That's just what I do have!' she cried furiously.

He was taken aback. 'But you're very *thin*, Luriel.' He did not want to hurt her feelings: she was skin-and-bones plus excited.

She pointed her left forefinger with terrible emphasis to her belly and said ominously, 'Just wait till I weigh four hundred pounds.'

Severance actually seemed to see a frightening *rounding* under the green robe. He knew what could happen with drinking, and he and his wife had a witchy-pretty young hausfrau friend who had mountained under his eyes over the last two years. It was no laughing matter.

'Look. Get another psychiatrist. This is out of my province.'

'I like Dr Walters.'

'But you say he laughs at you.'

'Only about my weight problem.' She sounded both stubborn and strangely happy.

Severance was lost. 'Take it up in Group tomorrow,' he said as a last resort. 'Maybe the counsellors can help, or somebody.'

'But what about tonight?'

"You can't eat yourself to death in one night. Just *don't fight* it and sweat about it. Relax. Eat your goddamned head off if you feel you must. I don't know what to say. It sounds awful.'

'Oh, it's awful,' she stared at him solemnly. At the same time she seemed perfectly content, and as he said goodnight and shook hands he felt entirely out of his depth, not for the first time today.

*   *   *

Stiffly he shed his clothes, drew on soiled pajamas, and knelt down reluctantly against the side of the bed, having switched off the light. His bony knees resented the floor, his scrotum flamed, his head ached, even his toes were not comfortable against the inhuman cold parquet. He was ready, and he was not alone (Alas). The damned room was uneasy with pervading, incomprehensible but all-comprehending all-remembering all-penetrating all-foreseeing *Presence*. Alas!

He did not feel like a fool. He felt pinned: on his mark, get set.

Severance did not know much about prayer, and he knew it (he thought). Anyway he was no good at it. Off and on, fifteen years before, studying a translated selection from the *Philokalia* ordered from Blackwell's in Oxford, he had used the Jesus Prayer, so he had inklings of the heights above him and the depths below him. But now that he was praying every night—five now, six?—he confined himself to the Lord's Prayer, as recommended by Christ ('After this fashion pray ye'), for fear of making mistakes, and frankly it wore him out. Six weeks ago in Mexico City, passing an old sunken church on Madero, his mind brimmed with wishes, and he went in and said or prayed the Lord's Prayer. By the time he had finished, half or three-quarters of an hour later, he found that all the topics were taken care of. Encouraged by this luck or providence, he did sometimes allow extraneous prayer-wishes to flash through the main business, but on the whole he concentrated with his whole power, and Severance when he wanted to had a mind as simple as a hydraulic press.

'In the name,' he said mentally, 'of God the Father' (no doubt about *Him*) 'and of the Son' (amazing, God-inspired, unique, whether a special Son who knew?) 'and of the Holy Ghost' (not clear, far from clear, Pentecost scene misunderstood by Luke unrecoverable) 'Amen' (Let it—this prayer—be established) joining his palms and fingers flat as he had done every bedtime until he was twelve years old.

'Our Father' (fact, and Christ's father, 'my father and your father') 'who art in Heaven' (wherever that may be) 'hallowed be thy name' (no associations except Shaddai, Yahweh, Adonai etc., the clause meant nothing to him, only: Aweful). 'Thy kingdom come.' He came as usual to a full stop, having noticed it once in the AV. *When* was the point. Be it soon. Image of the drummer's flushed face, yellow shoes, in the club-car of his first midwest express streaming through the prairies: they had bought each other drinks and were discussing religion: drummer a member of the Open Bible Church, headquarters in Des Moines and London, hadn't tried to convert him, talk of Second Coming, sense of adventism in the drummer, finally asked without malice just when he thought, heard, 'Well, we think any day now,' say Tuesday next at one twenty-seven. The sense fades out from the later Epistles. We can hope, though. I hope. Let all this horror here and in Asia, and our causing it, cease, let me in particular not suffer any more pride lust greed rage self-loathing despair, Your Honour. 'Kingdom': not the hid treasure or the pearl of great price but the lucky find! the risking *all!* to have *one* thing—Christ to Martha, his gentle and inexorable reproof defending Mary. Wise Mary, the better part. It: sobriety, and a decent end. Maybe years of work first, they didn't bulk for him at the moment. 'come.' 'Thy will be done' *by me* (the only words in Shakespeare's hand, closing the will—except the British Museum Ms.) this afternoon, at last. Contract. 'on earth' (that's here in my cortex, as in Bahrein) 'as it is in heaven' (wherever that may be —in the Local Group or behind some quasar, if quasars had backs). 'Give us this day our daily bread' (I'm ashamed, as You know, of this money, when others are starving, half my engineer friends out of work, help Dale, help Harmon, Andy, help my brother, forgive me, I didn't ask for it, it just came, I was poor until lately, I turned down wealth at twenty-one as You know, I do support Mother besides David, I lend money or rather *give* it, forgive me) 'and forgive us our trespasses' (he was too tired

to go over them, maybe a dozen vanities and attacking
Edith were worst, He was irremediably familiar with them
anyway) 'as we forgive those who trespass against us' (off
the hook! by great rare luck he had no enemies, unless the
old Dean, who had first lost all power over him and then
been forced to resign—long forgiven, though admittedly
long *hated*, Severance had even been sorry for his humiliation). 'And lead us not into temptation' (The Masters, the
Brass Rail, the Bedford, only threats really in the city, and
all airports, insolende, pretty tits and eyes and asses, outrageous demands by mail and telephone, getting better about
these) 'but deliver us from evil' (all these, everything characteristic and inappropriate—Change my life). He paused,
worn, aching. Trouble with final rubric. As a cradle Catholic (a truly *disgusting* expression, like 'let it all hang out'
—image of testicles dangling through zippers) he could
not get used to it. Also, what the *hell* was the point of re-
minding the Lord of the Lord's power (obvious in every
kinked corner of the finite but unbounded Universe) and
glory (whatever that was—with all his Francophile passion he spat on gloire)—still the streaked clouds showed
forth His glory and the great seas His power—okay: 'For
thine is the kingdom' (no sweat there) 'the power and the
glory, for ever and ever' (that is to say, not sempiternally, as
per Augustine, but in an infinite series of uninterrupted mi-
croseconds, Thomistic instants, no doubt about it). 'Amen.'
(Forgive me this lousy prayer, as usual; tired, Lord, for no
reason and with no excuse. If there was anything good in
the day—surely there was!—his spirits pricked up—
thank You).

   With rapid supplications for Ruth and The Baby and
the coming real baby and one of his ex-wives and the
mother of his bastard and their daughter who was nothing
but a name and an infant-shitting-all-over-him nineteen
years ago and the soul of his father, Addressat Unbekannt,

he rose creaking and climbed up on the bed and under the covers.

He relaxed his shoulders, wrists, fingers one by one, breathed two-one two-one, attended to his stomach, paid no attention to his sphincters, worked mentally on his thighs, the backs of his knees, ankles, toes, as his fiancée's father had taught him in London so long ago. Three or four times, some years, he did this. What were his chances? At one point he had decided he was just doomed to slips —he could go a week, ten days, even two weeks, then he drank. One Wednesday evening in August Dr Rome had mentioned for contempt and laughter (will hiss me to my knell) the man who had 'only had nine slips in two years! —I *love* the Programme.' Everybody laughed. Severance did not laugh. With six or seven slips in two *months*, he felt a young-brotherly and horrid admiration. The guy was trying. He wasn't drinking himself to death. 'Until next time.' But with its ten billion nerve cells and incredible pathways, what stability could be *expected* of the cortex, in its endless destruction and replacement, not to speak of alcohol affecting oxygen-glucose processes—'quicksilver' Luther called the heart of man—an ignorant agreement of biology and theology: give him a prohibition and he'll disobey it, *blaming* not only somebody else but God Himself ('the woman *thou* gavest me') . . . his tired thought reeled and his scrotum hurt. The irresistible descent, for the person incomprehensibly (and how many working on it? one of the three worst problems) determined. Relief drinking occasional then constant, increase in alcohol tolerance, first blackouts, surreptitious drinking, growing dependence, urgency of *first* drinks, guilt spreading, unable to bear discussion of the problem, blackout crescendo, failure of ability to stop along with others (the evening really begins after you leave the party, 'my soul ran in the night, and ceased not: my soul refused to be comforted'), support-

excuses, grandiose and aggressive behaviour, remorse without respite, controls fail, resolutions fail, *decline of other interests*, avoidance of wife and friends and colleagues, work
troubles, irrational resentments, inability to eat, erosion of
the ordinary will, tremor and sweating, out-of-bed-in-the-
morning drinks, *de*crease in alcohol tolerance, physical deterioration, long drunks, injuries, moral deterioration, im-
paired and deluded thinking, low bars and witless cronies,
indefinable fears (terror of the telephone, for me—never
mind *who*, menace, out of the house!), formless plans along
with incapacity to initiate action, obsession with drinking,
conformance to it of the entire life-style, *beyond* the alibi-
system, despair, hallucinations—ah! he knew every abyss
of it, as he drifted off. Something white jerked in some
dream, a red figure receded (a woman?), a Vivaldi rallen-
tando was audible off right, just audible. Turn the goddamn
volume up will you. He slept.

It was a good night, he only woke twice. The second
time, he was sitting bleary with Bill S over coffee in the
Snack Room, four o'clock in the morning, when the
frightful craggy face of the retired fire-chief came close to
his face and said: 'Alan, I have more *anger* to control than
most people.' The nurse and deeply graph-absorbed orderly were too far away down the hall, twenty feet. Severance shuddered and did not confront him. 'I know, Bill. I
believe you.'

13

NEXT MORNING he got shot to pieces—in, of all calm *safe*
places, Animal-Vegetable-Mineral. Confrontation was rare

on Saturdays, and leaders who went in for it (like Julitta) were hated as well as feared, but it wasn't the leader who happened to confront Severance. It was everybody.

Saturday morning was not designed as a rest-cure quite, but at least there was no Group, and the patients were comparatively relaxed. First came a talk by a recovering alcoholic ('I have never known,' said Larry T one day, 'a recovered alcoholic'—out of his boundless experience of eleven years' five-state-wide AA sobriety) on some aspect of the treatment Programme; then came exercises, one short, one long, plus a second short if there was time before lunch. Everyone stood in a circle, closed their eyes, walked forward with arms down at their sides, and milled. At a word, they opened their eyes to see where they were, then they resumed their seats and reported, one after another around the rough circle, their feelings. Both last Saturday and now, Severance was bored blind and expected to have nothing to report (though this was regarded as very suspicious and in fact rarely happened). But to his surprise his feelings were strong and different from those last Spring. Then he had detested contact; when he felt people bumping against him, he tried to avoid and generally wound up in the open. This second time in treatment at Northeast, he felt a little lonely on his own and moved eagerly about *seeking* contact—amazing. Odder still, when he found himself, secure in a tossing bundle of bodies (a Group, eh?), being by accident shoved out, he threshed to get back in, and got back in, both times. In short, he enjoyed the exercise. It was pleasant, too, always to find two or three pals hard by when he opened his near-sighted eyes. He decided he was less of a loner than he had always supposed—intensely territorial in his aggressions maybe, but also, somewhat, in his self- and Group-protectiveness.

Eye-stare was the second exercise. All sitting quietly, at a signal each tried to find another pair of eyes and secure their attention, holding it then for what seemed a very long time indeed until at a signal they broke contact. Each then reported (1) what he felt, and (2) what he saw the other person feeling. Severance did not love this exercise either. The first time, however—they did it twice—he had a hair-raising experience. Looking about with increasing eagerness (nobody liked to be left out, as one or two or even three always were), just as he was giving up hope of finding anybody free he found George S looking at him from halfway down the lounge, to his left, with the maniacal velocity of a Japanese train. He thought, 'Fuck him. I am just as serious as he is,' and glared across no space at all like his eight-inch reflector, they locked wills, and supported each other's Programmes with tooth and nail so hard that it seemed only a second when Jerry said, 'Okay,' and he sat back as exhausted however as if he had run a 220. He felt terrific. He had misjudged George—as he was beginning to wonder if he always misjudged everybody, him, with all his experience with men and women and colleagues and students and artists and you name it. He thought George, the short young bullet-headed businessman of his first morning, a smart-aleck, here to dry out, crack a few jokes, and go out to the nearest bar. Couldn't be more wrong—and he delivered an eloquent speech on the subject when his turn came.

Altogether he was way above himself, the doctor, inspired by his triumphs yesterday over the Third and especially the First Step, and he should have seen trouble coming. Maybe he did—yes, he actually in some corner of his self-exposure did—but not vividly enough to avoid it. Indeed he invited it, he set himself up.

His account of his feelings while milling was remarkable. It would have reminded a Jamesian, had any been present (but Jasper was in one of the two other lounges), of what some insolent bitch accused the master of in *The Sacred Fount:* an expenditure of mental force equivalent to what produced for Kant the two *Critiques* on the problem of whether or not there indeed existed between two English upper-class house-guests a relation no more important in their case than it would have been between baboons. But in Eye-stare he went further. He interrupted at will, he corrected, he interpreted, he extrapolated, he reminded, he put words in people's mouths, he read their minds, he *gave advice* (the sin against the Holy Ghost—you were only supposed to say what you felt or what you saw the other person feeling). As the session wore on, he realized gradually that he was out of line; but he could not help it, he felt too good. His motives moreover were of the best: to share his insights. Tension mounted around the room as driving across Long Island into an electrical summer-storm, and broke in Animal-Vegetable-Mineral.

This third exercise consisted in everybody studying everybody else in silence and then, ad lib, uncalled on, saying what animal (or vegetable, or even mineral) someone reminded him of, and why. Severance had three impressions ready at once, and composed out at hilarious or penetrating length in twenty seconds. But he was wary enough to wait until someone else had spoken before he compared Maggie to the Taj Mahal, with data (the illusory white produced though by a spectrum of semi-precious stones, the massiveness with delicacy, its creation by a Venetian *Catholic* jeweller, the reflecting pool vertical in front, the broad Jumna unseen behind—leaving out an excursion into Islamic un-iconographic metaphysics). Nobody cheered. Presently Mike M said: 'I see Alan as a sick old *lion* . . .'

Severance didn't hear the rest, composing his admiring impressions of Mike.

When he heard Mike's voice stop he said, 'I see you as—'

'Wait a minute,' said Jerry, 'how do you feel about what Mike said?'

'Well, nothing particular.' Severance, an inveterate interrupter himself, was annoyed at being cut off. 'It's nice, of course, to be compared to a lion—'

'What about what he *said?*' somebody broke in. 'He spoke of "roaring all the time without meaning it"; it wasn't too pretty a picture.'

'I didn't hear it all. "Sick" and "old" are *true* and besides I'm case-hardened to epithets. I'm a sort of public figure for God's sake. Every time I put a book out some stranger tears me to shreds. I get quoted in the papers, in *Life* magazine—half the time, wrong. Who cares? You get used to it.'

'Bullshit,' said somebody.

'You must be kidding.'

'May I kiss your foot?'

'You *disgust* me.' This was a pretty little blonde nurse new on the Ward. She was glaring at him like a reptile.

'You're not the only person I disgust,' Severance threw at her from a hot broth of rage contempt resignation self-loathing self-pity, meaning him. 'No doubt about it, Miss.'

'You don't even know my name!' she cried exasperated.

'How could I? I never saw you before this morning.'

'We all said our names around in the beginning. You're so superior you make me sick. You think we're all just zeroes.'

'That's it.'

'That's what I see.'

'He's not even one of us.'

'—sky-high—'

'—superior—'

'—'

'*rude* to Mike.'

'—'

Making every allowance for a novice nurse with an MD miraculously under her thumb, and with the mob behind her, he felt crushed by a monotony of injustice and hatred.

He was guilty all right, but, even more, he was innocent. Severance decided he had had enough.

'What are you feeling right now?' Jerry asked.

'Tumultuous.'

He rose quietly from the end of the couch, seething, threaded between chairs and went bow-legged out down the hall to his room. Screw them. Hyperdemocracy. He hacked. His scrotum was worse than ever. He lit a cigarette, to find one already burning in his ashtray. Linda was her name he had heard it after all and forever fuck her. Snip with a uniform, Judge Lynch, hounds baying the bayou, caught redhanded, 'I DID IT!' He was prepared to lay claim to a certain superiority in this and that. Linc far beyond him in the other, Dr Rome elsewhere. Everybody should know their place. He knew his. Nobody better than nobody in *all* respects. Compare not. He felt suffocated, airless, in this room lounge Ward hospital city— gashed. Truth in it, too, though, he was an arrogant man or bastard. He hated his admission to Linda. Linda eh? White-wrapt, lustrous, frigid, crap. Locating himself on the black sand beach at Saint-Tropez in May, mid-afternoon, seventeen years ago, he rêved.

Knock on the door, another, hesitant. Hutch's wife came in. She looked nervous, a heavy-browed solemn short woman he hardly knew, mother of nine and veteran of Hutch. 'Come on back, Alan,' she said awkwardly. 'Everybody's sorry.'

'I bet,' he growled, touched though by this compassion he would as soon have expected from an eggplant. He was getting used to being a bad judge. 'Come back and hear some more "superior." Superior.'

'I don't see why it makes you mad. You are superior.'

'What's so superior about me? Who am I supposed to be superior to?'

'Well, me.'

'It's not so, Wilma. Look. Hutch and I are friends,

we've suffered and stood by each other, we are both so
sick we might die, do you feel I'm superior to Hutch?'

She was very reluctant but it came: 'No.'

'Okay. Now you are Hutch's equal. Right? Come on,
give.'

'I guess so.'

'Then how I can be superior to you?' He was talking
without thinking, reaching down or out to her simplicity,
refusing to give in to this insufferable abasement. People
who treated him with kid gloves made him want to strangle them. *Respect* yes, but self-respect: Severance was hell
on worshippers.

She sounded stubborn: 'You said you felt "tumultuous." '

He felt, slightly, trapped. 'Did I? That sounds a little affected of me, but I'm used to choosing my words, and that
is indeed precisely how I felt. For Christ's sake, you know
what the word means.'

'I'm not sure. Anyway I would never use it. That's the
difference. Also, last Saturday you called Bob an "immobi-
lized badger." I never heard anybody say anything like
that before, except maybe on TV, so I remembered it.'

'I'm *trained*, Wilma, trained. There's a superiority in expression. What of it? I can't help it. Our *feelings* are the
same. It's not my fault.'

'I didn't say it was. Nobody blames you. Linda said she
was sorry for insulting you. They gave her the devil.
Come on back.'

The sun was doing its duty through the dirty Venetian
blinds of the tidy room, though neither of them looking
down saw it. Wilma waited.

Suddenly he could see no reason why not, and he gin-
gerly followed her out, mumbling gratitude. At the end of
the long corridor, friendly glances from various as he
threaded through to the corner of the couch. Even young
Linda gave him a guilty affectionate grin. He could tell
Mike, when they broke up, that he had intended no slight,

and the comparison that had occurred to him and why. He was glad to be back. He felt—chastened.

From Severance's Journal

Sat. aft. Oddly I feel better, after the *hell* this morning.
Why I slip:
1) False pride ('I am unique': *I* am the one alcoholic who can drink and get away with it.

2) Teen-age instability and overconfidence (used to getting away with *anything*, always have done, bec. loved and powerful: *I* can drink and get away with it.

3) despair: so why not? (>suicide) I am wicked: and can't bear it sober.

4) Lifelong rebelliousness vs all programmes (AA) and rules and superiors—neurotic independence (of Dr Sh's saying C might be 'neurotically indomitable')
Refusal to admit failure at *anything* (exc, at last, tennis), e.g. six (hopeless) goes at playwriting. Weirdly inverted, this.

5) Grandstanding—my clockwork slips made me the star turn every week or so, esp in Dr R's Group.

6) Whim. Pure feather whim. All the foregoing is no doubt true, but this is it. I need manacles. I *know* I won't get away with it, I've never had an unconfessed (known to me, i.e. remembered) slip, but off I go. 'Guckenheimer. Make it a double, with water.'

Will I really never pronounce those
frightful words again? Not today,
anyway.
Almost unbearably depressing, though. I need a programme of iron. AA will never do it. Maybe becoming a
Jew?

**   **   **

In the Snack Room an hour ago—we were alone—
Jeree suddenly opened her mouth and said, 'I'm scared.'
Rush of love and pity. For almost two weeks now we have
been sitting there hours a day and I'm not sure she has
said one word since the first morning (been in treatment
before). Later: she's *always* shy, scared—but her psychiatrist helped her yesterday morning. If only she'd talk in
Group; worked on her; you've got to come out.
    Hank Poore tells me (the Theologian of the Slip) that
after nine years is it sobriety he *still* feels now and then
that he can handle it. I have written Step One in the front
of my 24-Hour Book and include it now in the 5 to 20
min. meditation every morning before washing—
    Scrotal fire.

**   **   **

New to me?: 'the Jewish conception speedily became
unique. No other nation of antiquity ever came to the
point of regarding itself as chosen not for its own advantage but *for service.*' A bearing attraction.
    Also find: 'Man may be the crown of creation, but he is
totally a creature. God, not he, made him, his faculties, the
world. What is more, he serves the good, if at all, in no
more than in infinitesimal degree, and then with many an
interval of truancy and unfaithfulness.' Reassuring after

my talk Wednesday (with Dr G and Fr Krueger) about policing my phantasies. I find I get nowhere again and again, almost give up trying. But doesn't *Christ* expect more? I'm nervous sometimes with a faith that never mentions Him or the saints (though the Psalmist uses the word). On the other hand, the over-all sense here of the importance of the Person seems beyond Xtianity really. 'No special privileges' however, and I like that.

**   **   **

David eh? Heavenly older sister he'll have. (Peculiar to see Rachel an *older* any—I'll have to give in and abjure 'Baby.') Always longed for one myself, or, no, younger. Developed them—N, Br, So, M (sooner or later drinking made passes at them. Not invariably. Often enough to be reconciled to not having had one, God help her and me). Young Origen was wise. Odd that just at this point. I wonder when. *Is* heredity a factor? Victimology a real field, with only a German or so and a Canadian doing anything to advance it so far.

I'm not sticking to business. Find out from Dr G how much *delay* is plausible in traumatic response of this sort (*if* he ever heard of a case like this, and is it likely?). Two summers, the brilliant year. Snapshot of me on the sidewalk in white ducks and a blue jacket, arms full of trophies, Graduation day, my plump-spinster English teacher arm around my shoulder, admiring young brother grinning up at me sideways. A menace to him even then. Love. Then all to hell four years.

Stick to business!

Studying these Steps in Chapter Five *appals* me. I can only find one entry to hope: 'Resentment is the "number one" offender. It destroys more alcoholics than anything else. From it stem all forms of spiritual disease, for we have been not only mentally and physically ill, we have been spiritually sick. When the spiritual malady is overcome, we straighten out mentally and physically.' Surely these are the most reassuring sentences I have ever come on, *if* they are right. Now I seem to feel *no resentments* at present, I got rid of all that at Howarden in the 4th Step and last Spring again. Shuddered this summer coming on Scott Fitzgerald's 'When drunk, I make them pay and pay and pay and pay.' That was me. Not just now; hate nobody. Wide experience of alcoholics, and *recovering* alcoholics, behind those four sentences. Hardly likely wrong. Hang onto this. (No merit, by the way, in my freedom from resentment: product solely of all-excluding *gratitude*. I don't deserve the help I've had even so far. Ugly fact radiant, sometimes almost insupportable, that *I* should have a chance.)

**   **   **

Better and better with Ruth. Another long talk about her pupils. She's less afraid of them, and the two little brutes (one broke a girl's arm in class last month, the other hoisted an atlas and slammed it down on the cranium of the little girl in the desk ahead of him—talk about the Generation Gap—in twelve years of mostly public school in the Southwest, Florida, New York, nothing remotely similar happened in any classroom I was in or heard of) have been, one removed, other's parents brought to bear. She too thinks I'm getting on.

Rachel excited, great eyes glowing in her less round, *adorable* face: 'Daddy, do you realize that it's only *nineteen days* till Hallowe'en!' I still hurt from when she suddenly didn't want me to take her out for tricks-or-treats two years ago.

Charley dropped me in my tracks this afternoon: 'Your face is more *serene* the last day or two.' I admit I feel pretty good, though I have no reason to (unless about the resentment-bit).

** ** **

Later. *Terrible excitation, hair-trigger.* Omaha stock-broker: 'Didn't Kafka kill himself?' 'Well, wasn't he insane?' (talked with Rita—he came back and apologized).

Roberta Br, the most elegant pretty woman in Ohio, rushed into the Snack Room and embraced me in my chair. 'I'm a hostile bitch.' She was too; she must be recovering with her marvellous husband. Staggered.

The little hippie Dan: 'Was Washington a revolutionist?' 'Was X the son of God?' 'Who am I/ I'm one of the Revolution!' I said, 'There's a revolution is there. Where? Who are its leaders?' Long long pause—'Abbie Hoffman.' 'Who?' I laughed at him. *'You're* a murderer—National Guard at Kent State, A-bomb and H-bomb, killing Nazis etc.' 'Yes,' I said, 'look at my hands. That's all blood.' No idea that a revolutionary is *learned* (as well as deluded)—Mirabeau, Christophe, Blanqui, Che, Ho—especially the Argentine doctor sans merci, who rejected Cuba's Soviet benefactors on the grounds of revolutionary ethics—namely, they were *rude.* Sweet pathetic exasperating kids, with nothing to put in play but a (temporary—and they don't know that) life-style-in-opposition plus omnipotent *ignorance.* Their chances against the Pentagon-FBI-Ford-Boeing-the unions and the rest of the Establishment tyranny?

** ** **

I did not get either *support or control* from the AA group (they should have thrown me out after the third slip, 'Go and drink yourself to death, Alan. If you want to come back dry three months, fine, welcome.' Maybe this Chapter of Mike's.

I seem to need CONTROL in order not to drink, and a control I *fear*. Ruth kept me safe to, in, and from Mexico. Dr Rome, spectre and fact, kept me sober (or *dry* say) two months; I drank on Tuesday because I was leaving for upstate New York and would not have to face him the next night; I felt free. Imagine! feeling free. Christ.

But where was the resentment? Ah, *ah—of him*. Those men are right right right. *That's* what I've got to lie in wait against. Or rather: come out in the open with. But if I don't feel any?

I feel—good but—perplexed.

14

~~~~~~~~~~~~~~~~
~~~~~~~~~~~~~~~~

TUESDAY MORNING was dull grey out, remote, improbable. Severance, shocked to his root by Jeree's First Step, was working madly on his own, but for some reason, for a change, he listened to Tracy Croy's talk about feelings and defences Monday evening. 'Jeree's terrible Step One (desperate—suicide—one attempt already),' he had written in his Journal, '*brave* and *humbling to me:* ALL-OUT but *no* hope. Gus made one attempt "Do you want to live?" no reply "You *do* want to live."

'Banish *all pride, any* sense of achievement from mine. Separate the history into 1) alcohol 2) unmanageability of *life*. End with *work* on Steps II and III, and XII. The First Step without the Second Step is death, right away or around the corner. There is not one anti-proton of ongoing, esperance, in Step One. What will happen to her? Everybody crushed, except Gus, and Wilbur wasn't listening.'

Tracy, an active amusing self-critical but lounging man in a cardigan with a half-grown beard, used a blackboard, listing down the lefthand side various feelings and across on the right, in no particular order, the defences adopted by the alcoholized personality against not only their expression but their realization by the patient himself.

'mad	minimizing
sad	denial
bad	silence
glad	projection (reading into
hurt	the other person
scared	the feelings you
resentful	deny in yourself)
ashamed, guilty	attacking
embarrassed	explaining
inadequate or confused	humour (ugh)
rejected	chat
accepting (with whatever	intellectualizing (ugh)
pain)	agreeing, complying
warm, cold	(playing Group,
	smug, often hostile)
	shifting'

Sick feelings, he said as lightly as if he were discussing a 'dessert,' produce sick thinking (delusion, masking true feelings) and then sick behaviour (drinking).' The condition aimed at in treatment, over the two-year period, is 'mental sobriety' or 'comfortable sobriety' (= not want a drink). Just being dry was just being in hell. He knew a man who had been dry for eleven years on just the First Step and *fear*, and he was the most ill-tempered and tyrannical son

of a bitch in the community, corroded by self-pity, frustra-
tion, resentment, and vanity. '*Stay real*,' he told them suddenly, and, 'Let go. The more I admit I'm scared, etc., the
less I have to *act* on it,' and, 'Once you're real, you don't
have to be consistent. For instance, stuff like this: I am
kind and loving, therefore I *cannot* be angry. Wow. How
do you like that—which every one of us, every day in
treatment, *does*. Alcoholics are rigid, childish, intolerant,
programmatic. They *have* to live furtive lives. Your only
chance is to come out in the open. Also phony lives, and
they don't know it, once the disease has really taken over
the thinking; so they've got to level. You level with what?
Your phoniness. It doesn't take anybody in. Certain basic
delusions are probably common to all alcoholics, but even
those can be spotted by a patient in a different stage of
recovery—not to speak of your Counsellors. You've got
to help each other, and you *can*, though all of you are
crippled. Say somebody in the Group is controlling anger
(why is he, by the way? because he's afraid of *exploding*
and killing somebody), it's perfectly obvious to the rest.
They confront him with it. He denies it, with the utmost
sincerity, they give him data, he pulls out and deploys his
favourite defences, they are pointed out to him, and in the
end, beaten, if he is lucky he admits it and not only admits
it, he *accepts* it: *he's mad*. Fine. I would be too. Everybody
relaxes, and his long long process of recovery is under
way.' O where the final rout is Victory, thought Severance
illuminated.

   At the beginning of Mini-group he asked Linc if he
could propose a second Contract and heard the long man's
fancy-booted, casual 'Sure. What is it?'

   'My feelings about my father. I used to blame him for
ruining my life; but now I'm not so sure, just lately.'

   'How did he ruin your life?'

   'By killing himself when I was twelve.'

   'But you're not sure.'

'Exactly.'

'If you're not sure, why do you want a Contract?' Linc sounded bored.

'To find out, for God's sake.'

'Contracts are not research projects. They do not deal with the past. They deal with the Present, the real and unreal Present. If you're not sure you have no problem.'

Severance went into double consciousness. Through his mind sprang one of his favorite Zen stories (A Brahmin approaches the Buddha, bearing a gift in each hand. 'Drop it!' commands Siddhartha, and he drops the gift from the right hand. Goes nearer. 'Drop it!' and the lefthand gift falls to the ground. Nearer still: 'Drop it!'—and the Brahmin understands) and *the* Boddhidharma story (the Master arrives in China to introduce Zen, the Emperor builds him a monastery but in some way irritates him, so Boddhidharma encapsulates himself in the monastery with true Zen perversity and refuses to see anyone. Six years pass, before a Confucian sage comes who is really serious, sits at the gate in vain, and finally cuts off his right arm and sends it in by the monk who is portering. Boddhidharma, very reluctantly, agrees to talk with him for one minute. He is admitted. 'What's the matter?' said Boddhidharma crossly. 'Master, I am in pain. Tell me how I can become happy.' 'Where are you in pain? Can you tell me *where* you are in pain?' The Confucian thinks and thinks, at last he confesses: 'No.' 'You are happy') while his voice said, lifted a little, 'But it's killing me. I'm spending most of my time at it, it's interfering with my treatment.'

'This was forty years ago,' said Linc. 'Right?'

'Yes. More.'

'Okay. Why does it bother you?'

'I've got to know the truth. I've got to know why I was a completely uncharacteristic person for the four years after that.'

'I don't see why.'

Severance controlled himself. 'Look. Contracts are about feelings, aren't they? Well, my *present feelings* are hopelessly mixed. I don't know whether he was to blame or not.'

'For what?'

'My wasted years.'

'Everybody wastes years. Nobody is characteristic. But if you want to make a Contract about it, okay. Mildred, have you been thinking about your Contract?'

Mildred, a sweet-faced tidy simple woman of fifty in pink slacks whom it was difficult to imagine sitting in her kitchen stoned, slopping a fresh one out of the lowering vodka bottle, had, and pretty soon she was conversing with the mother she hadn't seen since her parents moved to the Coast ten years before.

Then Letty defended for one hour and ten minutes her attempts to manage her unhappily married daughter's wretched life, disarming even Keg with her wide, caring eyes. Only Harley mocked her; and nothing happened. Wilbur would not agree to go, on discharge, to a State hospital. Finally Keg stood up, with an impatient flip of his right hand, and went over to the board. He drew a long horizontal line, slashed a line cutting its center and marked off five divisions on either side. Above the left end he wrote raggedly, 'playing it safe,' above the right, 'taking risks.' Standing back, he looked harshly around the Group.

'All of you ought to know by now what the goals of in-patient treatment are, the criteria for Discharge, what we look for.' Severance sat up straight, very much surprised, realizing that he for one didn't. Two months altogether he'd been here: why didn't they *tell* you? He had sat in fifty discussions of this all-consuming topic without ever hearing a clue. He did know, better than most of his friends on the Ward seemed to, that Discharge was hardly one damned thing: then the trouble began. He felt none of the anxiety to be released that he had in the Spring or last

Fall at Howarden, none, he was prepared to celebrate Labor Day in W if they wanted him to. Still, he was interested all right. He even half-guessed what was coming, prepared by the transformations—some sudden, most gradual, and fifty percent alas not enduring—observed in others and even in himself as recovery at any rate *began*. 'You come in all clammed up, defences in depth, alibi-systems long established, delusions full-blown. In order to have a chance of staying sober, or rather of staying dry and *becoming* sober, you've got to change. Nobody likes to change. What you really want, when you come into hospital, even for the second or third or ninth time, is to stay just who you are *and* not drink. That's not possible, of course. Jack-Who-Drinks has got to alter into Jack-Who-Does-*Not*-Drink-*And*-Likes-It. The alcoholic is conservative. He hates where he is, certainly, but he can't even imagine being anywhere else. He doesn't *want* to be anywhere else. His chemical is home. That's where he's safe, with a bottle of whiskey or a six-pack or pills. The idea of Elsewhere fills him with panic. How many of you have waited, shaking, for the bars or liquor stores to open?' He looked around. 'Everybody?' Eager or pained nods. 4003 times, Alan estimated. 'But you know they *will* open. Right? What about the morning when you know they *won't* open, for you? For everybody else, but not for you. Freezes your blood, right? It's exactly there that you've got to become comfortable. How can it be done?—for those of you, that is, for whom it can be done. You've got to take risks. You can't stay where you are; if you do, you'll drink. We don't expect miracles here. What we hope for is *enough* openness to establish a continuing chance in out-patient treatment over the two years. One estimate is fifteen percent open. Almost every patient improves *some*, over the self-imposed solitary-confinement he came in. The question is how much, and that's what the whole staff has to determine in each case, and often we're wrong. But we can't keep you here forever. Right now there are seven alcoholics, some drinking, waiting for your beds. Now one of the judges of your progress—this will surprise some of you—is you. You are all deluded, but some of you have begun to recover, and know it, and have begun to feel real fear, and have begun to recover even from that. You think you have come far enough to have a chance. If anybody thinks he has it made, there's no hope for him. But *some* progress, towards self-confidence. You see this scale. I want you to rate yourself on it, Wilbur, and then we'll go around the Group, saying where *we* see you. Take your time, and be absolutely honest. Don't put yourself down, but try not to con yourself either. How open have you been in Group, on the Ward, with your doctor, with your parents on the screwy telephone. Give yourself a mark.'

They all waited. Wilbur's face worked, elongated, lonely.

'Six.'

'Okay.' Keg marked it. 'Hutch, where do you see Wilbur?'

'Two,' Hutch said reluctantly.

'Mary-Jane?'

Her voice was low: 'Zero.'

'Okay. Letty?'

The big eyes stared at the board, Wilbur, Keg. 'Three.'

'Stack.'

'One, I guess.'

'Jeree?'

'. . . Two.'

'Alan?'

Severance was unhappy. 'One.'

Keg looked at Harley. 'One.'

'Luriel?'

'I don't know,' she spat. 'It's none of my business.'

'You have no impression of where Wilbur stands.'

'He's a mean shit, just like the rest of you.'

Christ, thought Severance. Whatever Wilbur was, he was not a mean shit and sister you are even worse than I gave you credit for.

'You won't rate him?'

'—'

'Okay. I give him zero.' He marked it, and studied the board. 'Wilbur, there seems to be a difference of opinion between you and the Group about your progress. Some of us don't believe you've made *any*, and *nobody* believes you've made much—except you. How do you feel about that?'

Wilbur stared sullenly up at the marked line, heavy on the left, so empty on the right, except for his grade. 'I can't help it about the rest of you. I think I've got the Programme. I've levelled as much as anybody.' His voice was stubborn but whining and his gaze dropped to his knees again.

'Bullshit you have,' Harley said with a rare edge on his tone. 'Your old man sits in the kitchen all day drinking and sharpening the ax he keeps down there to sink in your skull one day, as he's promised you sixty times. You sit upstairs in your room drinking, trembling with fear. You come in here and you ring him up morning noon and night out of anxiety for his and your mother's health and fight like hell with him on the telephone. And you want to go home. You've got to go and look after them. You think you've "got the Programme." Get the hell out of here, Wilbur, and drink yourself to death.' Severance had never seen Harley angry before, it was bloodcurdling.

'Well, we have accomplished exactly nothing today,' Keg said, 'and you are all one day nearer to the Promised Land, where booze is flowing just as usual and just as desirable as ever and with just as much blood-sludge and brain damage. Let's say the Lord's Prayer.'

They rose without the usual relief and joined hands in a

close circle and some of them prayed the Lord's Prayer
and at least two of them wished they had never been born
to this unusual fate, common to millions.

*   *   *

'What are you still doing around?' Severance asked.
'Didn't you take your Fifth Step?'

Jasper drew a paper cup from the bottom of the stack
and turned the coffee spigot. It was after ten. Severance
had been alone in the Snack Room for many dreary minutes.

'Sure,' said the poet, 'four days ago. They're whimsical.
I still have kinks to straighten out, it seems. I'm in no
hurry.'

'Nor am I. Christmas is all right with me.'

Jasper sat down across, lighting a cigarette. 'Tell me,
how did you get into this bind?'

'You mean, being a medical man?'

'Yes. Or maybe you didn't know it was a disease?
Wasn't it some time rather recently that the AMA recognized it?'

'That's only the good ole AMA, one generation behind
the planet Jupiter. No, I knew it was a disease all right.
The edition of the Merck Manual I entertained myself
with at P and S, where I trained—this was thirty years
ago—was in no doubt about its being a real disease, "not
merely" (as they put it) "a bad habit." I looked it up this
summer in my attic. There's one charming sentence: "It is
characteristic for an alcoholic to be a veritable museum of
pathology and yet to make but little complaint thereof as
long as he can secure the relief given him by his accustomed narcotic." '

'Droll. But what about it?'

'What about anything? I did not have the faintest idea I
was an alcoholic until my second week at Howarden. It

takes shock, my boy. Tell you a story about one of the lecturers there. He liked flying. Somebody left him some money and he bought a plane and flew about in it. Heavy drinker, long long oldtime heavy drinker. Knew he ought to do something about it (so did I)—say two weeks after the Second Coming of Our Redeemer. What brought him to was this. One morning he woke up and he was in his own bed. *Good*—for he remembered nothing since nothing. Not feeling well, in fact he might die, but he got up and went across to the drapes over the picture-window of his bedroom, drew them apart, and looked out into the bright day. There was his plane in his front yard. "At that point," he said, "I knew I had a problem." For me, it was the imposing and uniform and entirely unacceptable world presented to me by the life stories of eight or ten men during my first twenty-four hours after I was taken out of Intensive Care and assigned to a unit at Howarden. Three-quarters, at least, of every story was my story. Mirrors on every side. It was unavoidable. At least I've had no trouble in *that* direction, as so many patients do.'

'What *is* the disease picture then?' Jasper asked very seriously.

'Well.' Severance gulped coffee. 'Progressive, fatal, incurable. Worse than cancer in items one and three—it attacks the moral sense, and spontaneous remission is unknown. There's a symptomatology. But otherwise they're no better off than they were in 1940—I mean my colleagues: it seems to be *loss of control*. Unpredictability. That's all. A social drinker knows when he can stop. Also, in a general way, his life-style does not arrange itself around the chemical, as ours does. For instance, he does not go on the wagon—except for a joke like Richard Burton, who bet that homewrecker of his he could stay off it three months—the wager was a kiss, I believe—and when I last saw a gossip column he'd gone five months. Sound alcoholic to you?'

'It does not sound alcoholic to me,' and the poet sighed.
They smiled with deep contentment with each other.
Comfortable on the ocean-floor. Plenty of special com-
pany.

*   *   *

After two hours Severance did an unusual thing. He quit
work and got up and lay down on his bed, shoes on,
plumped the pillow once twice and settled back not to try
to nap but merely daydream. An image appeared in his
mind of The Enemy: a transparent colourless mobile and
volatile liquid, having a slight, characteristic odor and a
burning taste, about $5'6''$, $37 + -23 - 36$, with a specific
gravity not above . . . something at $15.56°$ C. Miscible
with water. Decidedly. Inflammable. With amyl alcohol
being approximately 6–8 times as toxic as ethyl alcohol.
No pharmacologist of course but he could read and home
from Howarden in the winter he had looked around a little. Also he read *Time* magazine every week with a ven-
geance and the skepticism with which he faced a lab report.
They checked, though—not only his brother but friends
had worked for them. What killed more young than any
other cause? Cars, cars, with 'measurable alcohol' the criti-
cal factor 60% of the time. What was that: five whiskies in
one hour. Quite a bit of stuff for kids. Only one-tenth of
1% alcoholic content in the blood, technology, and out.
Could happen to the nicest people. Not entirely ignorance,
either (an acid-head *knew* he was in trouble), but substantially. One of his ex-mistresses in New York was on mari-
juana and Librium, and she had the worry—what there was
of it, for a girl whose black lover (elevator boy she'd just
given a car to) wanted her to move in with him and his
wife—upside down: it was the *called* 'drug' she wasn't
entirely comfortable about. The other she got on prescrip-
tion (from one of his orbiting colleagues) so she felt safe,

and the picture he'd given her one afternoon of pill-with-drawal she labelled 'science-fiction'—just as he had done the contingency of convulsions, and had one, five days later.

His colleagues. (And the kids.) Or say, since he hadn't gone on into practice, ex-colleagues. He took a dim view of them privately, on stern grounds. Severance enjoyed statistics, but he *believed* narrative, what you had seen happen. One of the medical fraternities asked him to talk to them about Medical Ethics and he agreed. A little reflection told him he knew nothing whatever, he asked two friends and they not only confessed they didn't either, they denied that there was such a subject. At the medical library he drew a very considerable amount of uplift and blank and only as a last resort before withdrawing his acceptance he went across to the new main University library, scrounged around among the usual crud and pap and peptalk until, sticking to it—bonanza! an actual discussion. Not by a medical doctor of course. The old dean of Harvard Divinity, plagued for decades by friends at Mass General with problems, had finally set down his thoughts. Severance made a rapid digest, rearranged and cut it, threw in cases from his own experience, observation, reading, and gave the young men a goddamned serious talk. They listened respectfully and asked many questions afterward—about fee-splitting. In vain, with growing outrage and scorn, he waited for one question about either any difficulty that he had proposed or indeed *anything* except fee-splitting! which neither he nor the theologian considered material. Their single topic: kickbacks. Not so good. Besides the ignorance, of drugs especially, and in particular pills and alcohol, the legal killers. No, Severance was not happy with his original profession. He knew marvellous men in it, of his own age. The marvellous men not in it but of it were *kids*—the kids whom when he wasn't putting them down he marvelled at. Even the Army—

the most vicious organization in the country, he thought,
not excepting the Air Force and the greediest-of-all so-
long-by-him-admired Navy which he hadn't been able to
get into in 1942 in the wet-heat Washington summer—
knew what the medics were like and had cut their tour in
Nam from the usual year down to seven months, because
after that long of shared suffering they went freaky. Cut
down their water and food to hitch more medical supplies
—stole plasma bottles and walked around on patrol with
six pounds of glass in their rucksacks—wrote home for
medical catalogues to buy their own endotracheal tubes.
Wouldn't leave their units when their tour was up. Kids,
looking after kids. Somewhere down in his left jaw Severance hurt, behind his eyes bitterness accumulated, he didn't
feel good about the world they'd presented to the kids.
The *junkies* proved the most dedicated of all—and got
off the stuff, incidentally.

He sat bolt upright. He and his fellow-Repeaters were
the smashed kids in the paddies; and they were each other's
medics too. His own hope was to forget about himself and
think about the others. And the Enemy was not alcohol
after all, just delusion—the VC dropping the point on
the soldier, shooting not to kill but wound, get him
screaming, so they can get the medic too. He'll come.

Delusion was contagious, nothing more powerful. He
had been taken in by Luriel's. It took last night listening
to the stolid nurse's *not* being taken in by her hallucinating about her overeating to make him look down at her
stomach on his left below the tabletop and for Christ's
sake it was as flat as a board (if not concave) and always
had been and always would be ('400 pounds!') and she did
not have an eating problem, it was a cop-out (sincere
though, real real sincere) from her *drinking* problem and
her psychiatrist and the others had been *right* to laugh at
her, it was not real, she was unreal and he Severance was
unreal with her and things were very bad all over. But not

as bad as he thought last night. *He* had cleared up on that, he had one more ground of self-suspicion, and his motive in trying to help her had been okay, only he hadn't been well enough yet to see through her, as the non-alcoholics (and some of the patients too) did like a flashlight. Okay. Doctors were not so bad, either. The only enemy was Delusion, and her daughters whiskey gin brandy and rum.

15

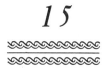

ALAN AND HUTCH made common cause. Each had been accused of being unable to level. 'Okay,' Severance said to the big man on the way down to lunch after Group, 'maybe we can help each other. Let's talk after lecture this afternoon.' They agreed on Hutch's room, and picking up a cup of coffee at two-fifteen he went carefully down the hall and knocked on the half-open door, heard a voice, and walked in.

Hutch was standing on the near side of the bed, with a book in his hand, looking as if he had been about to go somewhere. The bed-table had a book and a magazine on it. The bed was neat and empty. The long windowsill, where patients kept things, was empty. No clothes were visible. The top of the bureau was empty. Severance felt odd before he realized why he felt odd: the room was *all right*. That is to say, all wrong. It looked as if nobody lived there.

'Hutch,' he said involuntarily, 'why is your room so damned neat?'

'What's neat about it?' very defensively.

'Well, look at it.'

Hutch looked around uneasily. 'What's wrong with that? I'm just neat, that's all.'

'You are? You told me the other night your workshop was a shambles.'

'My office is open to inspection at any moment.' He sounded angry.

'I'm not talking about your office. I'm talking about your workshop at home. You said you could never find anything.'

'That's a lie!'

'No kidding, you actually said that,' Alan said sturdily, sorry to be in this, with a pal, but God almighty—

'I may be a little untidy now and then, but what about you? You live in a pigpen, I've looked in through your open door.'

'I'm not too neat. My point is that *no* other patient's room I've seen in any degree resembles this room. You haven't moved in.'

'Damn you, Alan, I come back and *I'm here*. You're making something out of absolutely nothing. Now listen, we'll have to talk later, I haven't read the Big Book yet today, okay?'

Severance was helpless. 'We're supposed to level with each other, you know. In Group and out of Group. You and I have the same trouble, and here it exactly is. You're not levelling with me.'

'I *am* levelling with you, damn it! What about, anyway?'

'Your room! It's too neat. It's not real.'

'I told you, you're out of your mind. Just because I happen to be a neat man, instead of a slob like you, you accuse me of not levelling. Just *how* have I not levelled? Tell me that!' He was as angry as a bull, fists clenched, head lowered.

'Christ, I told you,' Severance said, giving up. 'You're as

slippery as an eel. Listen, I hate to do this, but I may have
to bring this up in Group. I don't know, I'll think about
it.'

'I'm not afraid of you, you bastard!'

'Hutch, that's a lie. Everybody is afraid of being confronted in Group, and *you know it*. Moreover, I'm a
friend of yours, and you know that too.'

'Then why are you making mountains out of nothing?'
Hutch sounded aggrieved now.

'I don't think it's nothing. But I'm as sick as you are, so I
don't know, maybe you do just *happen* to be sloppy at
home and neat here—'

'It's a lie,' Hutch shouted. 'Now will you get out of
here?'

Severance went. Sunk in thought he wandered toward
the Snack Room. What the hell was wrong with Hutch?
if anything was, or maybe it was just himself? Not bloody
likely, he decided irritably. Hutch had not given him *one*
straight answer. Confronted again and again, he had taken
out his Defence Manual, well-thumbed and utterly familiar, and said, 'Ah, page 67 will cover that,' and when page
67 was rejected, 'Ah, page 114,' *and* so on. Screw him,
they were right: he couldn't level. Not wouldn't—Alan
saw that Hutch wasn't to blame—*couldn't:* the truth
was not in him, on the topic of his room's unnatural unin-
habited state. Why not, then? What delusion hid it from
him? The scientist turned into his room and sat down with
a cigarette. He might be as deluded as Hutch, but Gene
had seen through *him*. The truth lay somewhere around
here, available, if he waited. He waited. He heard, *'I'm
here,'* blasted at him, the defence total. Well, it was a lie.
Hutch had not arrived. On the other hand it was true, in
that Hutch was physically present in that deserted room.
Ha! and Severance drew in smoke with light breaking.
He was just exactly *only* physically present—going
through the motions—he had not *entered treatment*—

his position was Defiance, and, 'I'll take off the minute I don't like it.' That must be it—and wasn't it precisely what Gene had seen in his 'being unable to buy' the First Step? that is to say, *resistance:* a self-con: I'm here, I'm taking it, but I'm not having any part of it either. Keg and Harley were on the nose: the two of them were brothers, not identical twins but twins in evasion. Only, with Gene's penetration he had cleared up on this basic topic himself; his treatment was proceeding. He was a little less sick than Hutch. Without enthusiasm he saw that it *was* his job to hit Hutch in Group, just as he had wondered if it might be. Not nice. Hutch would read: Treachery—and unless he cleared up he would never forgive him. Severance uncrossed his legs and felt bad. They had been through Belsen last Spring together. He saw the unjust resentment call it rage coming. Well he would rather see Hutch sober than friendly and that was a fact. He hoped there was nothing noble about this sentiment. Flat minimal duty was the business. Ugh. 'Cut, damn it, *cut*,' he heard Vic's senior telling him as the young surgeon stood paralyzed with the scalpel in his hand before his first incision. Okay. One good friend gone. But Group was utterly different from a dyad: unless it supported his confrontation, his suspicion was merely unjust (*as so often*)—maybe there was some explanation, after all, for what *he* saw as weirdness. Hutch's behaviour would decide. Unhappily he stood up, jammed cigarettes and matches in his shirt pocket and left for the Snack Room, damning all doubt delusion duty and brotherhood. He had no choice.

Charley in high spirits—due for his Fifth tomorrow —was entertaining Mike M, Big Bill and Jeree with his antics at home, midnight, after a grand night out. He stuck his elbows out, miming, broguing. There were two Eskimo Pies left in the freezer and Severance leaned against it munching one and chuckling. He was reminded of a droll tale from Howarden and after Charley had climaxed—

'you see? but then I passed out'—he told it. Jeree's face was brighter than usual.

'A sweet story, friends, and as true as Treatment. Drunk comes home at his regular hour, closing time, and can't find the keyhole. Wife lets him in, embraces him tenderly, says, "Have a good time, dear?" instead of the usual, leads him to his favourite chair, pulls his boots off, asks, "Can I make you a drink?" He can't believe it. She goes to the kitchen and brings back a triple, has one herself, sits at his feet, rubs his knees, cozy cozy, never seen anything like it, pretty soon he gets the message: "Shall we go up to bed, honey?" He thinks it over with his remaining brain-cells. Finally he says: "Well, I might as well. I'm gonna get *hell* for this when I get home anyway." '

The afternoon wore away. Hutch was not at their table at dinner, across from him on the right, but two tables off. After dinner and a tiresome thrice-told lecture on—horrifying to him last Spring—the tiny upper lefthand corner (conscious mind) of the very large blackboard representing the vast Unconscious that says, in terms of *learned* behaviour and with irresistible authority, 'I *want alcohol*'—with only the ittybitty Conscious to make the commitment that may arrest the disease—he groped for The Missing Years and read *Basic Judaism* with four eyes. Around eleven o'clock he came on this: 'I cannot respect my fellow excessively. On the contrary, since he contains something of God, his moral worth is infinite.

'Translated into concrete terms, this means that I may not use him as a mere tool for my purposes but must always treat him as an end in himself. I may not injure him in any fashion, oppress, exploit, humiliate him, or deprive him of anything to which he is entitled. Nor may I deceive him or withhold the truth from him' (Severance was getting used to these 'coincidences' but he was startled) 'since, as the rabbis pointed out long ago, oppression may be through words as well as deeds. Finally, I may not restrain

or inhibit his self-fulfilment according to his talents, incli-
nations, and conscience' depending on his *degree of illness*
and delusion. Severance said his prayer and crawled onto
the bed easier in mind.

He was happy, though, to be taken off the hook when
Keg began Group with *Hutch:* 'What's with you, Hutch?'
and getting an incredible, 'Fine. Fine,' from the closed, resentful face, entered on a fullscale confrontation. Severance
was both relieved and pained to watch his old pal in business at the lemonade stand of yesterday: *angry*—and ad-
mitting it but minimizing, shifting, contradicting himself
—only not attacking of course, not attacking—polite,
smiling, managing, *hurt*, *scared*, so Alan read him. He said
nothing whatever of their dyad and finally, during a pain-
ful silence Severance described it, eyes moving between
Keg and Hutch.

'Your room looked odd to me too, last week,' said Keg.
It was lovely to Alan to be confirmed. 'What about it,
Hutch? Alan's confronted you.'

'Sure! Sure!' Hutch blustered indifference. 'He expects
everybody to live in a stye.'

'But I saw just what he did—oddity.'

'That was a week ago. I wasn't settled in.'

'He's talking about yesterday.'

'To hell with yesterday! We're supposed to live just one
day at a time, aren't we? Well, I'm doing it.'

'You are doing absolutely nothing of any kind whatever
about anything. You're on Cloud Nine, with your feet
planted firmly in midair. I've *never* given anybody such a
hard time before, and you "feel fine," you see yourself as a
"nice guy," you're "*in*dependent." Bullshit.'

Into the stillness that followed, Harley said quietly:
'We're all *dependent* people. Take our chemicals away, we
have to find something else to depend on.'

Nobody else said anything.

Severance took a risk. 'Hutch,' he said in a neutral voice, 'are you a son of a bitch?'

'*No*,' came with the baleful look Alan had once seen in the eyes of a mongoose in the grounds of the famous old British hotel outside Benares just before it attacked and killed a large green snake, while in the same breath

'Me neither!' Stack sang out from across the room. 'I had a wonderful mother!'

Roars of laughter except from Hutch and Keg— Severance couldn't help himself, if Hutch was on Cloud Nine Stack hadn't entered the solar system yet—but though Keg ignored the old boy, keeping onto Hutch, the pressure was lost, and nothing happened. Group was a complete failure. Severance felt like Stonewall Jackson surviving his try. But more ran underground than over on Ward W, and two nights later—Thursday—he saw Hutch seating himself across in the usual place, half-smiling nervous, his face open, and leaning forward to say, 'I can't keep my damned room shipshape after all,' and everything was forgotten between them as their treatment proceeded.

16

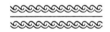

IT WAS AFTER TUESDAY MIDNIGHT, Week III of one of the lesser dynasties of the Middle Kingdom, when Severance, low in the mouth, wandering restlessly about his insufferable room, heard a knock and let Mike M in. He said only, 'I wondered if you'd like to have this,' pushing a sheet of paper out awkwardly, and went away. The scientist sat down with it. Maybe this was Help. He had received two important pieces of advice from Mike already: 'If you pick up one piece a day, you're in business,' and, 'Stop wondering and questioning. If it's working for me, okay.' Instead of reading the paper he thought about these. Neither had done him much good. He was picking up *twenty* 'pieces' a day and here he was in the Seventh Circle, worrying all. Envy, as he often told people ironically, was a base emotion; so he directed it after Mike. Mike had told him about *his* rescue. His own hadn't seemed to stick, though he did feel he had the First Step by its preternatural balls.

The sheet was headed 'God': and ran in loosely printed letters as follows.

> 'I offer Myself to the—
> To Build with Me And Do
> with Me As thou Wilt.
> Relieve me of my Bondage
> of Self that I may Better
> Do Thy Will.
> Take Away My Difficulties
> that Victory over them may
> Bear Witness [word much rewritten] to those I
> would help of thy Love,
> Thy Power And thy way
> of Life.
> May I Do My Will
> Always.'

The University Professor was amused by the tyrannical slip of the executive's pen though the man was moved. Mike was ahead of him all right; you were not responsible for your unconscious. He even tried to construe the clumsy lettering of 'My' into 'Thy' but it wouldn't wash. Severance was expert in various handwritings, particularly Seventeenth Century, and the 'M' was irreconcilable with any of the four 'th's' just above it. The point was the sincerity of the assignation, Mike confirming his give-up. In fact, this was a sort of Fifth Step—'to God, to ourselves, and to another human being.' He was the other human being. Touched.

Mike's rescue had been much like his last Spring. Both had been trying to run their ordinary lives instead of giving their whole attention and force and desire to a treatment Programme. Mike's situation was tricky: he owned his business but he had with supreme unwiseness taken in one employee and one man from outside as partners, and during the month he had been in hospital one was lying down on the job and the other was trying to cut Mike's throat with both their customers and the competition. They were also fighting cat-and-dog with each other. Mike *could* fire the slacker (though he hated the prospect, they were Army buddies) but he needed—at present— the traitor. He walked on eggs, twice or even more often a week when they came in the evening to confer in the downstairs lounge. Now nobody was forbidden to go down there but patients were supposed to stay on the Ward. It was by the Grace of God, then—Severance was with him there—that just as he was about to explode at both of them one evening and throw the firm into chaos, Rita walked in and said harshly, 'What are you doing here?' to Mike. His rage collapsed as a balloon plops. 'What *am* I doing here?' he asked himself. 'Those bastards might cost me my life, the hell with Allied Products'— he seized Rita's rather formidable hand briefly ('Thanks!') and went off upstairs without a word. The partners thought he was crazy, but what could they do worse than they were doing, and from that moment three days before he had dated his beginning of recovery. God bless him.

Bless me too, You. Granted I don't deserve it *or anything*. Severance felt more discouraged than ever, and he did a thing rare for him: he swung into play, on his behalf against the horrors of worthlessness, not his fancy, visible accomplishments and despised honours, but the real stuff, definitive (if anything ever deserved that term—three observers had recently independently concurred on speeds greater than light, so much—perhaps—for *that* cornerstone) but unannounced. Leaving aside this that and the other, what was it? Limit to three. In what order:

I. Alkaline phosphatase higher levels before ovulation. A saliva test had proved easy, and three of those he developed twelve years ago showed correlation with body temperature. Begin with the advanced nations, if the silly sex would do it. Church behind you, for once. Hard to see who wouldn't be.

II. Sacrifice as the key to the relation between Technology and primate Survival. A new American Dream (the old one, Getting On and Doing Good, having turned into The American Nightmare as a friend of his had put it twenty-odd years ago, catchphrase now): Giving Up and being. Leave the ozone in the stratosphere alone, for instance. Spiritual problem as well as biochemical and politico-economic.

III. The Big C was (most likely) a virus. Fantastic simplification, and not even literally true—problems of redefinition—but the *only* avenue in (to date), and he wondered to God why nobody else had stumbled on it during the last eighteen years. Staring them in the face—admittedly, only after 1) consummate invitation, 2) recognizing *the* tool, 3) making one initial connexion, and 4) working their asses off as he had in the winter of '52–3, from a bloody *spectrum* of verification and exclusion.

The three had a common teleology, he suddenly saw: life—or more life anyway. Similar origins too. Severance was a believer in serendipity, like every creative scientist artist and philosopher he knew, but he also believed in the power of frontal attack—not putting up with nescience. The seminal discoveries (recognitions, he preferred to call

them) emerged from that cooperation. Well. Similar des-
tinations? No. The first was frontpage country-wide, but
only III was Nobel likelihood—for which in fact he
sometimes now got mentioned *anyway*, with almost nothing showing. Who cared? Small wonder that for all his
vaunted professionalism his heroes were always the strong
silent men (women too—the unpretentious precision of
old Mrs Mullins) with everything up their sleeve. Give
rare but burn it in. Dr Cushing's father never spoke to his
family for weeks, abstracted, hard-pressed, eminent, came
into the house one day and told his wife he'd given all his
money to and brought home with him a woman who had
lost both arms and both legs, a terrible case, out in the car-
riage right now—bursting with admiration love and
sympathy she ran out into the street and found propped up
in it a bronze replica of the Venus of Milo. Happy days. In
bed at last he drifted off and somewhere later he was shaking hands, though not of course from any position of
equality, with—was it Mary-Jane? yes—'Stronger than
a man's, simpler than a child's, her nature was unique.'

*   *   *

After the rousing lecture next morning on Human Toxi-
cology ('Among the anatomic changes that have been observed are chronic meningitis with thickening, serious effu-
sions into the ventricles, softening of the brain, and
tendencies to hemorrhage and apoplexy. . . . The mental
changes are gradual and progressive, the intellect is ob-
tunded, the judgment overthrown, the moral sense
blunted, and mendacity appears in its most bizarre forms,
delusions may develop . . . combination of peripheral sen-
sory polyneuritis with a peculiar tendency to confabula-
tion. . . . alcoholic pseudo-paresis, which may be distinguished from the syphilitic paresis by the tendency to
recovery if drinking can be controlled'—don't you be-

lieve it) Severance indulged, before Group, in a retrospect.

'3rd Wed. a.m.,' he wrote in the bitter recollection that very very shortly his case would be up for review, and if no progress, *out*. What in God's name would he do? 'First week, increasing selfconfidence, *unjustified:* because no amount of hard and "honest" thinking will keep me sober, even if my brain were not "fogged" (Gus's word) by *withdrawal* (haha, I thought I didn't have any) and *delusion:* it seems to me now that what *may* do that is the simple ability to *recognize* my *emotions* as they occur (I absolutely did not hear Jerry's concern for me until Mike asked me, though) and then the —' what word? he left a space— 'to handle them appropriately—as for years I've handled them *in*appropriately, namely with alcohol.

'Second week, increasing *self-doubt*—maybe a small but definite improvement, because my mental apparatus *is* in poor shape: didn't even recognize Gus (surprised when he spoke of this later, and also minimized both to him and myself my drinking over those terrible days), thought yesterday October 2 instead of 27, etc. etc. "Bewildered" (my own word) by what Linc and Rita said to me. *Emotions* also *stupid* and confused: did not know *how* to respond to Vin's friendly, embracing even, delighted with everything heard about my progress, in the hall—grateful, pleased, but somehow half-blocked and distorted, skeptical, resentful, God damn you. Often catch myself also in *irrelevance*—have to fight it—clear enough in Stack yesterday, but what about me, part of the illness? Evasion?'

He sighed. Severance was a great sigher, they came from way down, and he did not altogether trust people who did not *sigh* a good deal or at least look as if they did. He did not trust himself either, but he started a third paragraph. 'At least I *have* been seeking people a little (Mary-Jane, Luriel, Jeree—not much, and all women!) and welcoming them (Harry, Gene, Charley, Mike—two *greatly*

helped me). Luriel conned me, with a phantom "compul-
sive eating"; at least I recognized this later when she was
trying to con Cathy.'

Prognosis? He was glad to hear the bell for Group. At
least the review, the uneasy review, had spared him his
usual state of mind as ten o'clock approached, which he
put as: cyclonic apprehension. The sooner he got confronted, the better—ghastly ghastly, but better. He
couldn't tell where he stood.

It did not happen.

But in mid-afternoon little Sherry, from Vin's Group
last Spring, walked into his bedroom. She had been drinking for three days. Not much—less than a bottle of
wine—but she hadn't been to work and her Civil Service
job was imperilled for the nth time, though her supervisor
(also an alcoholic) protected her—that is, enabled her.
Little Sherry was tall, slender, very pretty if colourless,
very sweet, entirely passive and fearful except when drinking. In bars she had tried several times to strangle the man
sitting on the stool next her. One night stole a bar-stool
around closing time, simply carried it out, it was foolishly
sitting in the minute kitchenette of her pathetic apartment
when Alan visited her once. She was alone, except for a
mother in Chicago whom she hated and a boyfriend, also
alcoholic, to whom she lent money and laid whenever he
got around to it. One day they had decided to marry but
were both too drunk to negotiate. She hated him, sex, her
job, and herself, though apparently neither Rochelle (another out-patient, a blonde sexpot also from Vin's Group,
now making it) nor Severance. Her life, at thirty (manner:
fourteen), was emptier than any life hitherto presented to
him for inspection. During over a month in treatment he
had explored her lack of interests with the same unbaffled
energy useful to him in lab, and it was rewarded: she was
interested in something. Forty days of denial fell to the
ground when he discovered that not only was she inter-

ested in the history of North Dakota, she had actually gone into two bookshops asking for books on it. He had supported (in vain) this hummock almost lost in the general quagmire of her apathy, and once lent her a hundred dollars without wishing repayment. Now he did a Dutch uncle on her dangerous three days. She accepted everything (haha) but showed spirit when he urged her to pour the remaining inch-and-a-half of wine down her discoloured sink. 'But I'll need it,' she cried, 'the next time I have a slip! That's *money*.' 'Forty cents. Do you want to have to come back into treatment? You're as far out of line as you were six months ago. You're setting yourself up. You're at work on your next slip *already*.' 'I am not,' she said vacantly. But he kissed her forehead with helplessness and squeezed her thin shoulders strongly before she wandered out.

And after Dr Rome's classic lecture on the effects of alcohol on the brain and central nervous system in the evening, talking with another out-patient he heard with horror the recent history of Little Marv. His wife after sixteen years of battling it had finally given in and was *drinking with him*. They had flown madly around two States in his Cesna, landing in Akron with Marv derelict and babbling. Strapped on a stretcher he was rushed off to a straitjacket. 'The brain damage must be something,' Severance said sick. Even last Spring he had noticed Korsakow's syndrome. Little Marv had then already been in treatment all over the Middle West five times, and he was resolute, nobody on the Ward comparable for determination, and his terrible I've-*got*-to earnestness seemed to pay off with immense real strides, reconquest of reality, submissions, relaxation achieved. He went out happy, into a forest of gin and narrow, wide, slowly wheeling airstrips.

17

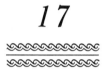

Confrontation

HARLEY SWUNG his hooded eyes lazily around the Group after they sat down following the Serenity Prayer —Keg was staring at his knuckles in his lap, long legs outstretched in a straight line towards the center of the circle—and they came to rest on Severance's, and stayed. The scientist tried to look as if he had absolutely nothing in the world to hide, but his heart rose throat-ward, and the smile he hoped for failed. Once, doing a two-week summer job in Salt Lake, he had been driven with another of the visiting stars to Guardsman's Pass at ten thousand feet in the Wasatch Range by some Utah scientists, they parked, ridge-walked, dropped down a little to a tarn. He and Herb decided to go in, and stripped, while the natives broke out the whiskey, jeering. Herb dived in and came back in a recoil that may have lasted six or seven seconds, splashing on Severance the coldest water he had ever felt. There was Maine, way Down, and there was the north shore of Lake Superior: kid stuff. He had gone in too, stayed a bit. He braced himself.

'Alan, what sort of fellow do you see yourself as being?'

That was all, but that was enough and too much. What

a question. 'Well, I do science. Write books, lecture and so on. Sometimes I give seminars in the Arts College, or away. Serve on boards, train younger men. Various things. I don't do much Government work; some.' His voice sounded to himself defensive, and the list had gone on longer than he intended.

'I didn't ask what you do. We don't give a damn what you do. I asked what you are.'

Alan knew that he *ought* not to get annoyed, still he bristled slightly. It was undeniable that he was not used to being talked to like this, or asked to give an account of himself, except career summaries for reference works (and they went in the wastebasket). He looked around mentally for a wastebasket. No wastebasket.

'I don't know, Harley.' (He wished he could sign his name, as Unamuno did in the hut-book on top of a Spanish mountain, and write under 'Profession': 'A humble man, and a tramp.') 'I'm a useful man, in some ways, rotten with certain successes, hopelessly arrogant. I try to be a decent husband, when not stoned. I'm faithful, except once. No, twice, now. I love my daughter. I work like a maniac. I have a drinking problem.'

'You have a life problem.'

'Excuse me, I have *published* thirteen books.' Despite himself, Dr Severance's voice was very hard.

'And how many unpublished?'

My God, how could he know that. Usually Severance gloried in all his invisible (so far) achievements, like an iceberg—when not tortured by them. But not just now. 'Some,' he said reluctantly.

'Come on, give.' This was Keg, leaning forward from the waist with bright eyes.

'How should I know?'

' "How should I know." You mean you actually don't know how many books you have under way?'

Severance felt rattled. 'Damn it, *I work*. No. I have no

idea. There's one lifelong one, and another twenty years now. Another. Two more far advanced. A new one.' He was sweating as he walked through his monsters.

'That's it? Six?'

'Call it six. No doubt there are others.' (One more jumped to his mind, curse it.)

'You're irritating me. *How many* unpublished books do you have around?'

'God knows,' he gave up. 'I can't think.'

'Do they matter to you?'

'Matter? They're my life work.'

'You are deluded. They are not your life work.'

Severance burst into flame, and stamped it out. There was a silence. 'If it weren't for my drinking they wouldn't *be* unfinished.'

'I wonder. But what about the rest of your life?'

'I have terrible trouble with young women. That's a fact, and it isn't all my fault. I love my wife and daughter. I support my mother.'

'Is that your whole family? You're very hard to track today, Alan.'

'I have a son by a previous marriage.' He felt trouble coming but he was determined to hold nothing back.

'How old?'

'Thirteen. I think.'

'You don't know.'

'He may be fourteen.'

' "He may be." What's your relation with him like?'

'Very poor,' Severance said miserably. 'He lives in the East. I only get there maybe three times a year.'

'And always see him, of course?'

'No. No. I'm always pressed for time. It's awful.' He brooded. 'His letters are very childish, I can't find out anything about him.'

'It doesn't sound as if you try very hard. When did you see him last?'

Severance had to think. He thought, and he hurt. 'He came for a visit once. Two years ago? Three years?'

'Well, which is it?'

'God almighty, I don't know.'

'When did you see him last at his home?'

'I've never been there. She brings him to New York.'

'Well, in New York.'

Severance thought in vain, felt backward for his son's face. 'I don't know. I just don't know. Leave me alone!'

'That's the trouble, Alan. You are alone.'

'It's the drinking. I always drink on trips.'

'Horseshit in all directions all over the place,' said Keg with contempt. 'But it does sound as if you always drink, period.'

He pivoted from pain to rage. 'That's what my god-damned wife said, in a dyad last Spring. It's *crap*.' He glared at Keg's long hard face. 'I've done an incredible amount of work in spite of my drinking. *Sober work*.'

'Exactly: "incredible." '

'It's true,' he shouted.

'Say it is. What kind of a *life* do you have? You go East how often—three times a year—and you can't remember when you saw your son last? You don't know how many *years* it is.'

Severance felt tears coming. He couldn't deny it. What kind of a father was he? He stared at his boots. He wished with all his heart that he could feel sorry for himself, but that was out of the question. It was simple: he was an utter bastard.

There was a long silence. He didn't know whether anyone was looking at him or not. He hoped, without hope, not. He would have liked to shrink into his chair-back taking his shame with him.

'Your life-style,' Harley said gently, 'seems to leave something to be desired. Do all these great accomplish-

ments of yours give you any great pleasure, Alan? You're
proud of them?'

'No,' he heard his voice weary and low. 'No, I'm not.
I'm ashamed of them.'

'Why are you ashamed of them?' Keg asked robustly.
'You ought to be proud of them. Why not?'

'It's not my doing, except the work. I do work some
times. But all my priorities are wrong. I see that.'

'You see it's not just drinking?'

This was hard, very hard. He couldn't think, he just felt.
'I see it. My whole goddamned life is a fucking mess even
apart from the drinking.'

'Me too!' said Stack suddenly. 'The wife confronted me
last night, about all everything I did this last time after I
lost my job. I was a beast in sex. I did awful things! The
wife forgave me!' He raved on—and Severance, who
was also a beast in sex, besides being off the hook now, felt
an obscure gladness to find out that all his trouble was *not
just drinking*. In some way that he could not have stated,
he felt a new hope not just about his son—something
could be done about that!—but also about everything,
including his drinking. If that was not the whole business,
maybe *it* could be put to rights—that is to say, oblit-
erated—after all. The Third Step. He took his mind off
Stack's outburst long enough for two violent, grieving
prayers.

18

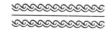

THURSDAY AFTERNOON cannot be declared a glorious time
for Severance. Re-reading the 24-Hour Book for the date,

he flooded on his daughter Rachel, ways he had hurt her almost beyond bearing to him. Then he found that at some unnoticed point he had fouled himself behind, and had to change his clothes and shower. Then, scheduled at last for his First Step Confrontation and believe me ready for it, he found himself when Gus called on him—they were meeting downstairs in an unaccustomed room—unaccountably equipped with a sheaf of papers that were not his First Step. Chagrin, suspense, incomprehension, shame, deafness.

He found the right sheets—just two, with a prefatory note—and put them on his bureau by the door and looked at them every time he went in and out for the next twenty hours. But shaken by a dyad with Mary-Jane at two o'clock when both had wept with fear of 'playing Group' and the self returning and drinking or popping pills, a savage quarter-hour, at the last minute he *wondered* about the First Step set down with such care and okayed, for the last time, each sheet, Wednesday night. Frantically he searched for the merely circumstantial Step that had satisfied Gus One last Spring, just in case. Nowhere. He grabbed his scratchpad and threw onto it rapidly, with no feeling whatever but haste, what he remembered of it. He only hesitated once, over whether to mention that that lecture in Vermont though unpublished had been quoted a year later in a *Life* editorial somebody showed him ('A man can live through his whole life in this country at present without ever finding out whether he's a brave man or not') and rushed on without. All the Repeaters had assembled when he got to the lounge. Julitta was not there, only his friends, and Gus.

'Okay, Alan,' said Gus. 'If you have it.'

'I've got two.' He found himself very cool, after all. 'One satisfies me, but God knows, so I wrote another one.'

'Go ahead.'

'There's a covering note,' Severance said, and he read it. ' "I have lately given up the words 'sincerely' and 'honestly,' as mere con-words designed by my diseased brain to support its lying products. So I won't say this is a sincere attempt—though, friends, *it is*. I haven't knowingly lied, minimized, or omitted."

'Here it is. "I *am* powerless over alcohol. That is not only an historical fact, but an account of the present moment, and an absolutely certain prediction—I can no more ever safely drink than I will ever again play a decent game of tennis.

' "I have *known* this for a long time; but (possibly) I only *felt* it as *fact* last Thursday night, when I wound up, telling Gene Snyder about my six days' drinking two and a half weeks ago, 'So you see, I can't accept the powerlessness because if it hadn't been for the taxi's accidental route and the mere whim of stopping off for a drink or so, I would have been safe.' He said: 'Until next time.' This simple truth came with the force of revelation. It wiped out the final escape clause: I felt *trapped*. Weirdly enough, this came as a great relief, and I have even been feeling rather *free* ever since, in spite of many other troubles. They seem minor. I *have* thought, for the first time, all this two-plus weeks, that Step One was basic and indispensable, only a foundation for sobriety, but that.

' "With the second half of Step One (which weirdly enough I used to think the *harder* half) I have no problem. Walking down after Vin's Group one noon a few days out of treatment, I remember *wondering* whether I would turn off right to the Library and the bus home *or* continue on down to Cleaver and have a drink or so, and thinking that this was an insane way to conduct one's life, to let one's very existence depend on whim or abstract chance; as if one were not even one's own actor but only a spectator. All right, *now* I would turn straight back to Northeast for help, knowing that I was doomed; in fact I drifted on in a sort of trance from which I came to in front of the Library feeling immense relief at what I thought was my narrow

escape. A few days later, of course, I started drinking. My life is completely unmanageable. The fact that I have a highly developed and strong *will* is absolutely irrelevant." '
Ignoring a note to himself (analogy of the uselessness of his checkbook on the locked ward at Ansel) he turned to the third sheet, a postscript set down at noon. ' "My connexion of unmanageability *only* with alcoholism is far too narrow a view as I picked up from Harley *as lately as this morning* (to my mingled dismay and relief). It's the whole story and I know it, as my word 'actor' back there shows. *I* need a manager, I've hopelessly failed as my own. So: *Third Step*—to which in recent days I've given almost as much thought as the First. With *only* the First Step one might not drink but one might *kill* oneself." '

He stopped, a little tired, sharply disappointed. He knew audiences inside out, and with this one he was nowhere. It was without surprise, but with heavy discouragement, that he heard Gus.

'We'd better hear the other one,' sounding restless.

He turned to the other one, and began to read it aloud without interest. 'It's called "Data for Monomania." '

' "A life centered around whiskey (gin, ale, vodka, rum, brandy) may have byproducts but clearly it is *insane*. The first evidence I remember is 1950, when I gave a public lecture drunk; I did not know I was drunk and do not now recall being drunk; I *know* it because somebody wrote down all my replies during the question-period and a friend of his showed them to me years later: they were incredible—irrelevant, violent, long silences, incoherent—' (Severance realized he was gasping, choking, also his vision was blurred with involuntary tears—why, he had no idea, he must be in despair but actually he felt nothing, only the necessity to get on, he forced his voice ahead through the strangling) 'if my chairman had been up there, I would have been fired immediately. A day or so earlier, I staggered up and down a narrow parapet eight floors above the street, until the headwaiter threw us out. Three years later my beloved first wife left me after eleven years because of liquor and bad sex. I then drank fifteen hours a day in New York, once *very* seriously planning suicide if by a certain date money had not turned up—it turned up, or I would not be here—jumping off the George Washington Bridge cannot fail. I gave academic lectures so hungover that I was afraid of falling off the platform; once threw a chair down to the floor of the auditorium to emphasize a point. I had a drunken quarrel with my landlord, he called the police and I spent the night in a cell, press and radio picked up the news and I had to resign. Here, the following winter, my chairman told me one day I had telephoned a girl student at midnight threatening to kill her—no recollection, blacked out. I lost when drunk a manuscript containing scandalous facts about well-known friends' (he was sobbing rapidly, voice coming out in hard jerks) '—couldn't remember where, retraced steps of night before—anxiety so terrible that finally I went to an analyst. Many injuries drunk, three weeks one mental hospital, half a dozen times another. Four or five incomplete homosexual episodes when drunk. Lost all night once abroad, drunk, walking streets, couldn't remember my address. My second wife left me because of liquor and bad sex, taking our son with her of course—nearly killed me. Hallucination once, DT's once (six hours). I had an involuntary bowel movement in my clothes, in a corridor of a public building; got home unnoticed. Drinking a quart of bourbon a day last Fall. Too ill to give an examination myself; had to cancel a lecture. Ruth in despair. Howarden six weeks, discharged December tenth—only two AA meetings—first drink, New Year's Eve party—moderate drinking several months, began a new book, gradually up to a quart a day. Northeast last Spring—on the second Tuesday, amazingly rescued by a personal God—full belief for the first time since childhood—

loved Vin for it—first convulsion in third week—
happy and overconfident in the last of six weeks. See now
that though I conned (without meaning to) Gus Larson, an
astute man, I *never took the First Step*" (my note here in
the margin though says, "Not *sure* about this, maybe I just
lost contact with it"), "made no progress except spiritual.
In four months never missed AA or Encounter-Group, reporting: five or six slips in eight weeks. Sober almost two
months, I suppose out of spite and rage against Dr Rome,
then drank six days here and in New York State—flew
back, blacked out, hiding out forty-eight hours, on the last
day (Sunday) planned suicide for next morning when gun-
shops opened, in afternoon decided I would have to go
home—postponed it with half a dozen drinks downtown, went home, argued with assembled authorities—
campus cops, my Dean, Ruth—gave in and was
brought here, on a stretcher I'm told. Some management of
some life." '

It had taken a long time. He wept on, looking at nothing, the upper part of his body shaking. At last he managed
to get out, 'I don't know what the hell I was crying about.'

Gus Reimer said something in the silence.

'Can't hear,' he gasped.

'Remorse and guilt,' Gus said softly.

He saw it must be so, and felt—nowhere.

Severance's Journal

**Mary-Jane again this evening. Talked over this afternoon's
incomprehensible performance and also why I have, had,
no feeling about the pseudo-affairs with Lo and Re when
anguish years ago over Vera C—she said we're *always*
feeling: I did feel guilt those times but have now masked**

it out. Helplessness. How can you manage what you can't recognize. Step Three?

Surprisingly, Rochelle looked in later. Tight ship, married hell. We agreed marriage can be fine *without:* sex, intellect, children, etc. etc. *but*—in that case what? Gus dropped by, we put it up to him as a dry man. He thinks: areas of dependency (mutual) and individual fear. I felt witless to hear that in his opinion I'm going strong.

So much for my opinion about *anything.*

* * *

There had been no sign or word of the dreaded end-of-third-week 'evaluation' and Severance was comforting himself on Saturday, for all his failures, with a remark of Harley's the day before during a nought-to-ten safe-risk rating of Severance towards the end of Group, shifted suddenly into from a long confrontation of Letty in which the scientist had played second violin to Keg's first and Harley's cello. 'I would have given you seven, I considered seven, instead of five, if you could dump your bad feelings out on the floor in the middle of the Group.' Now nobody in fact had come up to the mark that Severance after a split-second savage struggle had dared to award himself —seven; and this hurt him. On the other hand, there were three sixes and nothing below four. 'Maybe if I can find' (he wrote in his Journal) 'and reveal this cluster of unknown horrors, underlying even them in me I will find God,' and he felt okay. So when Ray, the humourless tall cadaverous man in charge of the AA part of Ward W, stopped by him and Ruth talking in the lounge downstairs (Rachel was not allowed upstairs, as too young), and asked Severance aside and said in a low voice, 'I probably shouldn't tell you this but they may let you go Monday,' Severance was horrified.

Tears of consternation sprang to his eyes: 'It's not possible!'

'Yes, Harley told me so himself after the consultation.'

'What in the name of God will I do?'

'Just go home. What else?' Then Ray's face changed, as he caught on, and Severance caught on.

'You mean I'm *not* being thrown out?'

'No, no, no.' Ray squeezed his shoulder. 'Take it easy. Of course not. Everybody's delighted. Relax.'

Severance swung round to face mentally in the right direction with difficulty. At last he said, 'But I haven't taken my Fifth yet?'

'It's only a rumour, as I said. Anyway, it's good news.'

It was good news.

V

CONTRACT TWO

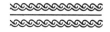

FOUR A.M. SATURDAY/SUNDAY and busy with his past.
They told you to live in the present. But Severance's
thinking was purposive. A pretty woman faithful to her
husband (except for one unconsummated idyl with an
aesthetician from Montana) through eleven years, until she
located Severance, had told him when, surprised by her
lack of interest in History or Science or Art or Religion or
anything else, he had asked her what she did think about,
'Love.' 'You mean you and this man?' 'Among others.' 'All
the time?' he asked incredulously. "All the time.' The scientist shuddered. So much for her four thriving children
and sociological hubby. This was before involvement between them developed. He himself thought about *problems*—putting them through sieves, heating and cooling
them, relating them or detaching them, disverbalizing them,
re-structuring them, hitting them with analogical blind-
alleys and mare's-nests, teasing them, pretending they didn't
exist, pretending they did exist, conjecturing origins, extra-
polating menaces. Why, for instance, for mere instance, was
man righthanded? Fetal position, apparently—and go
into that. And for how long? Seven of the forty-two
baboon skulls certainly, four more probably, had been
crushed from the right by the southern ape in misty an-

cient Africa. Now then, about southpaws . . . Dexter-
ous vs sinister. Two of his wives were lefthanded; gentle
women. He was exacerbated, at this unpleasing hour, by
how little he seemed to remember even of the dozen years
before the four-year prep school blackout.

But as he began to swing his mind through his childhood,
sitting with spread knees under the single lamp in the over-
heated room in the sleeping Ward—it was arrested by a
picture. Herb Poore's long, thin, young face half-con-
vulsed across the table from him one night last summer.
The Encounter-Group was about to break up after two
hours, the first of which had been devoted to Alan's current slip. Herb had asked diffidently if there was time for
'a sort of AA story.' Dr Rome leaned forward smiling,
everyone was relaxed, Herb had been completely dry ever
since treatment a year and a half before, a respected and
soft-spoken veteran hero of the Programme, sessions often
ended with humour. But Herb had no amusing tale to tell.
During the last days of a fortnight's motor-holiday with
his family, he had felt pressure mounting. He thought
about drinking, drinks, bars, bottles, he accelerated past liquor stores, he over-sweated. He did not tell Ann and
waited for it to fade when he got home. It grew worse.
Monday he called in to his office sick. He wasn't sick.
That afternoon, alone—Ann was out with the children
—he churned. He filled with paralyzing fear. He felt he
had to do something but he couldn't think what. He was
too weak to walk up and down. The idea of calling came
to him. He was so agitated he couldn't remember the name
of his sponsor. He couldn't remember anything except liquor. But he got over to the telephone and a blind impulse made him look up the number of Alcoholics Anonymous. There were half a dozen. His hands were shaking so
badly that it took him three tries, dialing, to get the top
one listed. A woman's voice came on. He got out, 'I'm
Herb, I'm an alcoholic—' and fainted. When he came

to, she was still on the line, frightened. She told him the address of the 24-hour clubroom nearest his house and he dressed and went there for the rest of the afternoon and was all right and had been all right since. Severance was amazed with admiration, and as they stood for the Serenity Prayer he wondered if he could ever come to value his sobriety that desperately.

Did he now? Did he right now? Metaphysical question, with whiskey inaccessible. But it was either that, or the death of the craving. A sentence had struck him, lately, in one of the letters of Plato's last years. He had studied all the Dialogues through, in chronological order, under a philosopher at Columbia, as an undergraduate, but not the letters, and he suspected that as a young man he would not have valued the sentence. To a friend, commending his programme of conduct, Plato said: 'Hold fast to the things to which you already hold fast.' So simple. Deep, wise and deep. Maybe, the longer sobriety extended, the dearer it held itself. He gave a long sigh about the disease. As for craving: hard and savagely as he had wanted and 'needed' drinks down the gluttonous decades, he had never suffered the stomachic frenzy he had just heard of with horror from a new patient. Between drinks at lunch and five o'clock, Drew had sometimes to leave his drawing-board for the washroom with projectile vomiting. No such need pleaded for Severance—though he was no stranger to projectile vomiting during drinking.

With an effort he turned to the problem: his skimpy childhood. But at once without effort memories flooded. Himself as pallbearer for his little-older hero, F. J. Callahan, surreptitiously touching the dead hand in the funeral parlor, running screaming night after night to Mother in the livingroom, crossing the street and then re-crossing it to avoid that fearful building, on his way across town to visit Richard Dutcher, with whom did he masturbate in their hayloft?—the pretty Aunt who partly brought him

up in L.A. with bare arms sunlit knitting, her severity
about his collecting all his toys before dinner into his big
quilt-covered chest—Daddy marvellous in his Sam
Browne belt and saber—himself in a uniform, at three or
four, standing on a rock in the yard waving a flag at the
crowded streetcar passing—himself beside tall Daddy in
a rainy dawn of artillery maneuvers at Fort Sill, shellburst
puffs of French 75's on the far hillside through big heavy
fieldglasses—shiny wonders and challenges of his first
chemistry set—every great glossy new Oz book, every
Tarzan from *The Return of* to *The Jewels of Opar*, Tom
Swifts and Don Sturdys galore, the thick red *Three Mus-
keteers* with illustrations by Maurice Leloir (lost in some
warehouse), A. Merritt's horrors and Hugo Gernsback's
Ralph 124C41+ with a high black hair-do, greatest scientist on earth, all for her (met the author in New York),
wasn't Faulkner's chilling "Turn About" (in the *Post?*—
on his delivery route) the first real story he came to?—
Thurston the magician in the Tampa Bay Hotel, things
disappearing—Easter egg hunts in the broad green
grounds there—old *Adventure*'s and *Argosy*'s—dol-
drums of 'Abou Ben Adhem, may his tribe increase,
Awoke one night from a deep dream of a piece'—
despised poetry—trapped up a tree with pants ripped
in the bottom; waiting for the other kids to go home to
lunch—anxiety wobbling snuffing the six high candles at
Sunday mass—revelations (forgotten) by a Bad Boy with
his little sister on a side-street after dark—the mocking-
bird he shot by accident and mourned and with his little
brother buried in a brown cigar-box behind the garage—
bacon and eggs, adult! when it was still dark out, before
being taken duck-shooting—climbing bracing inside the
outside fire-chute at school deserted in summer and
whooshing down—the long long scary glistening slide
down into the blue water at Medicine Park, Wheeeee
. . . . . . No end to thronging images. No, no. The prep

school oblivion following all that was special. Switching off the light and climbing wearily back into bed, with a silent prayer, he saw the problem as narrowed, separated, identified, real.

When Letty knocked on his door in mid-morning, Alan was sitting in a stupor of impotence over some unimaginable point of entry to his problem and he was glad to see her. They shook hands warmly. Refusing the chair and a cigarette, she plumped herself down in a businesslike way, dressed in the standard women's Ward-outfit, a shapeless black sweater and shapeless slacks, on the edge of his bed and said determinedly, 'I can't feel anything.'

'It's a stage of treatment, maybe not a bad one,' Alan encouraged her. 'I think I'm the same way at the moment, as if I weren't going anywhere—though they tell me I am.'

'Hm.' She thought, with her large black eyes on him. 'When I told Dave Harris yesterday, he acted differently from what I expected. He smiled and looked *pleased*.'

'You see? Suppose the picture is something like this. We have terrible feelings to get rid of. They explode out, drain out, whatever—and can't be replaced right away. The stage has to be set for new feelings. It takes time, Letty.'

'There's been one big improvement. I don't resent my mother as much as I used to. I always felt she was trying to sit on me—she's taller than I am, like everybody else. Now I don't think that. I remember all kinds of support she gave me. How do you get on with your mother?'

'Love and hell,' said Severance.

They debated mothers, passing to Letty's attempts to manage her married daughter's life, which she knew was wrong but couldn't seem to do anything about, and Alan's comparatively peaceful, quasi-flirtatious relation in later years with his other mother, the aunt with whom, now widowed, attractive as ever, he sometimes used to stay when he was out on the Coast. 'With my mother,' he switched back, 'in spite of all my admiration for her—

she's had a frightful life, eight or nine operations when she was young, both husbands let her down, she's been dying of cancer for ten years and she's unbelievably brave, Letty—not to speak of my gratitude for all her help after my first wife left me—after a few hours with her I'm ready to climb the wall. Moreover I feel she's somehow afraid of *me*, God knows why, and that paralyzes me.'

'Maybe you bully her without knowing it,' Letty said reluctantly, 'though it's hard to see. You're very kind to everybody. I like you, Alan. I trust you. I think you're the only one.'

'You mean in the Group?'

'I mean in the Group.'

'You don't trust the Group?' He was surprised.

'No. Not a bit. Do you?'

'I feel some doubt,' he admitted, 'except when I'm in Group. Then I feel perfectly confident. We're bound to be able to help each other.'

'Well, we can hardly,' she said rising, 'help Luriel. She's packing to leave.'

'No!'

'Oh yes she is. Bags and clothes all over. She's frantic.'

'I'll talk to her,' he said alarmed, stamping out his cigarette and following Letty to the doorway.

'You do that. Two of us didn't get anywhere. I know she places some confidence in you, she said so when we were arguing at dinner one night. *I* don't know what's wrong with her.'

Severance paused a little in the corridor, to adjust his thought, before knocking. Nothing could be more serious than this. Patients who walked out didn't have a prayer, neither at Howarden nor here had he heard of anyone just raging out—so few did, anyway—and making it. He decided, without wondering why, on straight AA talk, and marched in like St George on the rail-thin grim-faced young dragon bent flurried and desperate over the disordered bed loaded with her possessions. She did not look up.

'Luriel,' he said softly, 'you know this is crazy.'

'That's just it,' her voice was bitter and low, 'I'm crazy and this place is driving me crazy, I've got to get back to a hospital for crazy people and think.' She straightened up and glared at him.

'But you're an alcoholic, Luriel. Where are you with the First Step?'

'Oh I know I can't drink.'

'And how about unmanageability of life? That's what you're showing right now.'

'I know it. All I can think about is how I hate my husband for what he's done to me, and where I'm going to live. I'm a jungle of problems.'

'We all are, or we all were. What about the Second Step?'

' "Restoring us to sanity." ' She said it like a curse. 'I don't believe that. One of the things wrong with me is envy of the rest of you recovering. Also I'm taking up bed-space, people are out there waiting for my bed.'

'You're recovering yourself, Luriel,' Alan said earnestly. 'Listen to me. Sit down.' He shoved back a suitcase half-full and pushed her narrow shoulders down until she was crouching on the edge of a rumpled blanket. He pulled the chair over. 'Can you remember what you were like just two weeks ago? You never spoke, you sat at meals like a dummy and wouldn't speak to me. Look at me. Isn't it true, what I'm saying? And lately we've been talking like friends.'

'I don't know if you're a friend or not. I haven't got any friends. In Group you were just as bad as everybody else about my over-eating.' But she sounded less hostile.

'Your delusion of over-eating. You finally admitted it was a cop-out. Didn't you?'

'Yes I did. They made me.'

'You did it yourself. That's another great improvement
—to begin to concentrate on your treatment for alcoholism. But you've got to get rid of thoughts of Outside, your
husband and the rest. Your job is just in here. Even your
posture has improved recently. Sit up straight now and
look at me.'

And the meagre woman did almost straighten, as one by
one he recollected and proved her achievements to her.
Gradually it seemed to him, urging on her her small, real
gains, without exaggerating, without pleading, that he was
pleading the universal case of hope for abnormal drinkers,
for Hutch, for all despairing and deluded sufferers fighting
for their sanity in a world not much less insane itself and
similarly half-bent on self-destruction—using only the
eloquence of facts he bore her down, till her face softened
and once she interrupted, 'I did, didn't I?' with something
like a child's exultation. Her grey eyes were bright.

'So you've come a long long way from nowhere, Luriel.
Nothing could be plainer than the evidence that you're
building on God's will—that's the Third Step—with
His will, and that He actually wants you to stick with
you, to stay here and submit and trust us to help you.'

'But I don't trust *anybody!*' she cried out.

'You trust what I've been saying to you, or you
wouldn't have changed so in the last ten minutes. How
about Harley, who was so gentle with you in Group?'

'Maybe you two, but not the others.'

Severance was not having that, after Letty. 'We're all
for you,' he said with hard tenderness, liking her as much
as he could, 'you can't stalk out on us like this and destroy
yourself.'

'That's just what I felt like doing.'

'Exactly. That's just what I really was afraid of. Do you
think I don't care about you, Luriel?'

'Well, *I* don't care,' she said roughly, 'but if you do, I

don't mind staying, I guess. I'd have to put all this stuff away'—she looked helplessly round her.

'Get Letty to help you,' he said, standing up with a surge of relief. It had been easy, after all, the work had not been done by him, and he went back to his room and his own work with a better heart.

That night on his bony knees he was visited by a calm joy of prayer, long-lasting: the miracle of me-suicidal three weeks ago to me-now, survivor of renewed access to realities, partly in true touch with myself for the first time in many years, confident (though fear too—of Outside— I won't go home, whatever they say, with my problem hanging), happy, and *useful* to my friends these last days, certain to be so in days to come, goodnight, thank You.

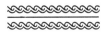

MONDAY WENT SWIFTLY BY, punctuated however with new thoughts of an alarming kind which was not to declare itself until the following morning and of which meanwhile the less said the better, Severance only felt rushed from time to time, and menaced. Nobody spoke of his being discharged, and he was as glad not to face the temptation. Stack was confronted for nearly the whole two hours without result. Accused of self-pity, he chimed in heartily, 'That's right! Self-pity!' but did not see either that he ought to cast it off or that it was grounded in measureless resentment, which, further, he could not name. 'Me? I don't resent anybody or anything! Not me!' boiling with

it, innocent. Keg wrote on the board a favourite aphorism:
'We are as sick as we are secret.' Severance looked at it
with grave doubts. Called out of Group to see Dr Gullixson he took up with him the question, from Saturday's
trouble, of his actual superiority in communication. 'Why
should it matter?' he asked aggrieved.

'How can you ask?' said the older man. 'It's the one
main way in which we know other people and make ourselves known.'

'Is it unavoidably obvious, except in diction?' Alan pursued a lost hope of equality, his mind telling him at the
same time: phrasing, syntax, pace, rhythm, pauses, his sudden great volume (hated by all, including Ruth, an eccen-
tricity no doubt from lecturing).

'—everything that aims at persuading or emphasizing
or dominating,' Gullixson was saying. 'It's your racket,
naturally. Part of how you got where you are.'

'Wherever I am,' Alan said unhappily. 'Then there's
nothing to be done about it. People resent it, or some do.'

'Their affair. Yes, it's a permanent real problem, neither
alcoholic nor neurotic. You don't really think we don't
pay for our advantages, do you? But about this roaring of
yours: you ought to consider whether it isn't a means of
intimidation, and whether whatever satisfaction it gives
you is worth your wife's discomfort, or indeed anybody's,
since you seem to dislike it yourself. I must say you've
never roared at me.'

'It comes out with awful naturalness,' Severance said
grimly. 'But I may as well change my whole way of life
while I'm at it.'

'Hardly that,' Gullixson was smiling. 'Just enough to ac-
quire and equip dryness. Roar away if you like.'

But the scientist roared not all that day, instead he grew
increasingly and mysteriously abashed, until after dinner
he was scarcely able to speak to his wife and daughter visiting, he heard no lecture and half-slept fitfully after a de-

spairing prayer, still without knowing just what was
wrong, until in the darkness of earliest morning he came to
suddenly on a forgotten scene. He was in his aunt's apartment in California twenty years ago. He had come in very
late and very drunk, to spend the night as he sometimes on
trips did, after a loud party for him following his high-
powered evening lecture at UCLA. She had waited up or
got up. They were sitting drinking, a nightcap, nightcaps?
Had he made a gesture, or said something? He felt so, now
stretched in his hospital bed, trembling with horror. Nothing was clear, two lamps shifting, a shadowy alcove, except
that he was drunker than she was. Merciful, that. He
seemed to feel her put a palm on his forehead, smoothing
him back, before he passed out. So nothing had happened,
no kiss even? But the terrible design was clear. His mother's closest sister. It stood before him worse than what he
had remembered last year in the second week of treatment
at Howarden, and begun his Fifth Step with, walking into
the office and saying shamed to Father L, 'The worst
things I have done in my awful life were to make three excellent women utterly miserable with my drinking and bad
sex and to seduce once after we both married my dearest
girl cousin.' Darker still.

Inappropriate and paralyzing sexual images danced before his closed eyes in their dozens, or hundreds or thousands. Vulvas, hands on him, mouths, hot breasts, spread
bottoms, their clenched feet and scissoring, in cemeteries,
parks, cars, sand-dunes, darkness and daylight, floors, beds,
beds. Heavy breathing, gropings back. Once without even
knowing who it was. Friends' wives, virgins. Unspeakable.
And the myriad unacted. He might not be as bad, Severance thought with clenched teeth, as the poor maniac in
Stekel who before speaking to a man had to look fixedly at
him and repeat to himself, 'First I will bite off his nose,
then knock in his teeth, then shove his chest,' while thinking first of his penis, then of his anus; no—but nearly.

With disheartening regularity he phantasised on women in any degree attractive, on busses, sidewalks, in crowds, anywhere. His poor thing shrivelled in his groin as he cursed himself. He envied, not for the first time, the great early Alexandrian theologian who taking, 'If thine eye offend thee,' literally, castrated himself.

Then a thought if possible more drastic entered his tortured head. Should he report all this in Group? Grievous hours raced toward ten o'clock. But it was taken out of his hands.

Confrontation with Letty began, when he felt his head tilting backward, his mouth opening crookedly, his neck-muscles taut, and a soundless sobbing in his throat begin. He prayed not to be noticed or he prayed to be noticed. At length of course he was, and voices stopped. Finally somebody said, 'Do you want to talk about it?' and his body arched forward and down and, gasping, fighting tears, with his face just above his knees, he spilled out in spurts of shame his sordid life. It took a long long time.

He sat sunken, amid dead silence.

'I'm a monster,' he choked out hoarse.

'Maybe it's easier to be a monster,' he heard Harley say, 'than a human being.'

Without attempting to understand this, he burst at last into convulsive tears. When he came back under control, Keg said, 'Don't you want to try to sit up and look at us,' and with deep reluctance and a sudden, growing animosity he slowly did. He looked at the faces without looking at the faces. He hated his grievous confession to these remote bastards, and hardened his heart against them. During the prolonged confrontation that followed, he grew more and more morose, only once snapping bitterly, 'Don't ask me that question any more, Mary-Jane,' and once starting to cry again, leaning his head against Hutch's shoulder on his right—the big man warned in a low voice, 'Self-pity,' and with one rare impulse of gratitude he straightened back up. He heard Harley and her read in his tale 'lonely despair' and felt none, except of the Group. Harley also said he saw the 'rage and hatred of women' that Alan had certainly mentioned with passion at one point in his outburst, as overlying some different emotion. Several people saw fear, and he didn't understand this either, and detested them. When they finally gave up, he heard as from a great distance Keg's harsh summary: 'unable to level with anger, fear, guilt—unable to level.' Nothing mattered to him, surrounded by enemies. Far from any longer trusting the Group or imagining that he could ever expect any help from it, he felt no concern for anyone in it and wondered what he was doing there, listening now, wounded, stony, to the details of Letty's relation with her ambivalent mother.

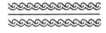

A FAILURE SO ABJECT after the embracement of a risk so great might have been expected to drive a man out of treatment. But Severance had survived something of the sort once before, in the Spring, during his second confrontation, and it did not occur to him to leave hospital. He had developed a little nervous hum, unawares until other patients teased him about it at table one day. Vin noticed it, and—a great natural producer lost to the stage— made him take it out and put it on a chair facing him, and talk to it; and have the hum talk back. Semi-hallucinatory after an hour under high pressure, he conducted a one-man merciless dialogue, with the hum attacking. 'You're doomed!' it roared at him. 'That's right!' he roared back. But later he was unable to describe the hum, and sank into defiant stupor, until at last Vin turned to someone else saying, 'I've seen you take risks in the past, Alan, but today you're playing it safe.' Also Severance was tough, a hard-case if quivering veteran of you name it, with nothing to lose.

Also he had picked up something: that concern is not necessary for help, you can be sharply helped by someone who doesn't give a damn about you or even hates you. Joining perfunctorily, towards the end of the session, in a confrontation of Stack, he had been amazed to find the slit-eyes in the huge face glaring at him and lashing, 'What about you? You say you're hard of hearing! But you always come late to lectures and sit at the back! You can't hear a word!' His first impulse to deny it failed: it was too true, he had been neglecting, without realizing it, an important part of treatment. 'God damn it, you're right, Stack. I've been goofing off, there's no excuse for it. It'll change,' and when they were leaving Group in the hall Stack put an arm around his shoulder, 'Sorry, Alan,' they agreed to look for each other, go down to lectures together and sit together, without exception. Here was a definite gain. He even felt affection for savage old Stack, for Hutch; remnants of, for Mary-Jane who had come in after lunch with, 'You make me mad—the great Alan Severance,' and so on.

Also, he decided, he had as usual set his goal too high. 'Aim high, then,' Thoreau might warn, but character-reformation in a month, at fifty-five? Unrealistic expectations, as usual. This was a hospital, the matter was medico-psychological, the purpose simply to safeguard sobriety as a habit, break apart the delusions that allow (enforce?) drinking. He had swallowed the Group-mystique too far for him—not much of a Group-man after all. Rigorous honest private mental work had brought him wherever he was. He saw no reason to give up. When groups, though, of which he felt part in the past had been beleaguered he had sprung into public action—he was no hermit or lighthouse-keeper or prospector (attractive destinies, however)—and this Group utterly was beleaguered. Look at Wilbur. Maybe after his resentment had faded some, *some* Group-sense might return.

Also there was his problem—not the Jewish aspiration, pursued daily, that didn't have to be solved here on the Ward, but the missing years and his father. *How* had he really felt about him, down the deep backward and abysm? He could not remember ever once being punished by him, though Mother's hairbrush as a paddle was vivid enough and Uncle Jack's declaring, 'I'll never again meet you anywhere,' when as a boy he was late for an appointment on some corner in New York chilled his blood and still did. Could he recall his father ever even angry? Mother said once he had been rather a *cold* man—as Thoreau called himself. Am I wrong about the warm close fishing hunting father-son duo I've always seemed to remember?

He sat up in his chair and reached for the scratch-pad, jotting:

'New problem. Did I myself feel any *guilt* perhaps— long repressed if so, and mere speculation now (defence here)—*about Daddy's death?* (I certainly picked up enough of Mother's self-blame to accuse her once, drunk and raging, of having actually murdered him and staged a suicide.) Lecturer lately on children's blaming themselves for father drunk (=What did I do to make Daddy angry and get drunk?). BLANK, probably odd. He *was* drinking heavily, all four of them were in those last weeks, nightmarish quarrels. Gun-death at dawn, like Hemingway's, imitating his father. Does my fanatical drinking emulate his, and my fanatical smoking (both "manly")? So possibly it wasn't rage/self-pity, but guilt, that were simply driven underground for a year (Why? if so) to emerge after all and cripple my prep school years. Then I "solved" the problem all wrong my first week here!?

'How do I actually now see him: limited, weak, honest (but unfaithful at least twice), prominent only very locally, not a soldier (*fake* soldier, National Guard)—and do I feel guilty about this rather *contemptuous* view, in the face of my real love? Queer that that Faulkner story hit me so hard, hit me *only*, the sole early work of art I remember. Very young hero a British torpedo-boat second officer (my unfailing, planned juniority to somebody), hopeless drunkard between reckless missions, misunderstood by (older) American aviators, thought a sissy (me at St Paul's, because I wore glasses and didn't go out for football my first year—have always seen myself ruined there by this, but is it likely? And the bullying? awful, but adequate to explain an almost-four-year ambition-lacuna?)—anyway, braver than them, cooler in crisis, lost at last. What subtle identifications are worth pursuing? How many models can a grown man survive?'

He dropped his pen, confused. The mystery of what I was reading under the covers after lights-out! Tall handsome Daddy, adored and lost so soon!

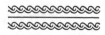

THEN, after several days of increasingly reconstituted hope and better spirits and listening closely to lectures, in the front seats, next to Stack, a cataclysm occurred in Group. Jeree began talking. The soft, plump, still, amber-haired young woman was talking to Harley in the far corner of the room. Her voice was too low for Severance to hear what she was saying, but presently he saw her huddle up and burst into tears! He felt heavy tension and concern around him. 'What is it?' He leaned over to Hutch. 'She had an abortion eight years ago.' My god, he yearned toward her. Even her sobbing was scarcely audible. But when she began speaking again, her voice was stronger. She had talked about nothing else, she said, twice weekly to a psychiatrist for two and a half years. It was why she and her husband couldn't have children. She had finally told him and, a heavy powerful man, coming home every night drunk himself, he beat her every night, calling her 'whore' and 'drunken slob' and hurling her across their kitchen. Hatred against the brute mounted around the room. Jeree felt none.

'You don't hate him,' Harley said.

'Oh no. I love him.'

Then it transpired that he was divorcing her, didn't give her even cigarette-money on the Ward, refused to come and see her, and had told her when she called him yesterday, 'I can't wait to be rid of you so I can have a ball every night.'

Severance ground his teeth. Luriel said, 'Christ.'

Keg got up and placed an empty chair in front of Jeree facing her and stood over it.

'Your husband is sitting here on the chair. What do you want to do to him?'

'I want to beg him to take me back.'

'So he can beat you up again.'

Silence. She stared at the chair.

'Go ahead, beg him.'

'I want him to forgive me.'

'And he will.'

'Oh no he won't.'

'Maybe he will.'

'No no he never has. I used to get on my knees.'

'And you love him?'

Her face worked. 'I don't know if I do or not.'

'Sure you do. You want him to take you back and beat you up again every night for the rest of your drinking life.'

'No!' she cried suddenly. 'I *hate* him!'

A thrill ran through the Group.

'Here he sits.' Keg pushed the chair close towards her knees. 'He called you a whore. Would you like to do something to him?'

'I'd like to hit him!'

'Hit the chair. He's the chair.'

She hesitated, glaring, crouched forward.

'Go ahead, hit it.'

Trembling, the girl lifted her right arm and patted her palm down on the chair seat.

'Harder.'

Pat.

'Harder! Hit him!'

Pat pat.

Keg sprang around to stand beside her, seized her forearm, and brought her palm down sharply down on the seat. Again.

The girl went wild. Snatching her arm away from Keg's hands, she slammed it down and slapped the chair until Severance's palm tingled. Then she rushed forward and grabbed it up, screaming, 'You lousy bastard! You drunken bum yourself! You bully! You beast!' and hurling it to the floor again and again, finally standing with clenched fists and contorted face over it, swelling with triumph, amid clapping and cheers. Luriel embraced her, Harley grasped her hand, Severance was beside himself with pride and love.

Jeree dated her beginning of recovery from this outbreak, and a year later in AA one Wednesday night Alan had a full view of the quality of her sobriety: one of her two alcoholic brothers had gone through treatment and rung her up drunk two days after his discharge—'He just accepted everything,' she told them, 'he never surrendered,' and, 'He did it for his wife. Anyway, now he knows where it is, if he ever wants to do it for himself.' For a selfish disease, only selfish initial treatment.

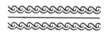

MINI-GROUP was on Fran, whom Alan knew only as a tall handsome ramrod of a girl, late twenties, on pills as well as booze, who was being divorced—'No feelings about it,' she had replied to him in lunch-line one day, 'I couldn't care less about him.' She had a shock of brown hair, energetic regular features, prominent eyes. It was her dying alcoholic father she had feelings about: hatred, grief, fear, They drank together in the family kitchen when she visited home. Cronies—'*You* know I haven't got long, Fran, *you* understand.' She understood that she was being torn to pieces.

'He is really drinking himself to death?' Linc asked lazily, his long fine-booted legs crossed, turning the tape-recorder on. 'There's no doubt about it?'

'I guess not. He puts away two fifths a day, sometimes more. Our doctor gave him a year, this summer.'

'What are you doing about it?'

'I can't do anything about it. I just get drunk too, and shout at him, and then we both cry.' Her voice was savage.

'You don't see him very often. Do you telephone?'

'Three or four times a week.'

'What happens on the telephone?'

'I beg him. It's almost as bad as being there.'

Linc ruminated. 'How would you like to have a talk with him face to face but with both of you stone sober?'

'I can't imagine it.'

'But you must be sober at the beginning, each time.'

'No,' she sounded shamed, 'I have a few before I go, and he's always loaded.'

'Well, you're dry right now. Suppose we put him in the chair here'—he swung an empty chair around to face the girl—'at, it's nine-oh-seven a.m., and he's still sober.'

'No,' she said bitterly, 'he's not even up yet. He's still passed out.'

'Not this morning. Or some time in the past when he *was* sober. You've seen him sober a thousand times, haven't you?'

'That's true,' reluctantly.

'Well, here he is, sober as you are. What would you like to say to him?'

'There isn't one thing on earth I would like to say to him.'

'Look at him, and think. Nothing whatever?'

Linc's lowered, other-worldly voice had its usual effect. The girl looked at her father. Her face softened. ' "Why are you doing it, Daddy?" '

'And he says?'

' "Can't help it, Fran!" '

'His voice sounds cheerful?'

'Yes. He's grinning at me.'

'And you say?'

'What can I say?'

'What *do* you say?'

Her voice tumbled out: ' "Daddy, you remember one morning you took me canoeing up at the lake? It was a blustery day, sun coming and going, but we stayed out hours and you told me about your first wife. I felt so grown-up. Do you remember how close we were?" '

'And he says?'

Silence. Her mouth opened, closed.

'And he says?'

'He doesn't say anything.'

'All right,' Linc's voice brightened, 'he's gone and you're back here with us. Right? Tell us something about your childhood relation with him.' He drew her slowly through a dizzy, sorry tale of savage rejections and unpredictable intimacies alternating in a general cold desert of indifference, and then made her talk to her father again, with the same result, silence from him answering or not answering a plea of hers. Linc shifted to the mother—'She's given up too. She's just waiting'—and then seated the frightful old man in the empty chair again.

'Now. You know he's not going to answer you, right? so you can say anything to him that comes into your head, without any fear of its effect on him. What would you really like to say?'

'Just tell him I'm sorry, and say goodbye.'

'Go ahead.'

'I don't think I can.' Her voice broke on the last word.

'You can.'

She sat up, back into her customary stiff, almost back-leaning uprightness, and stared at the air above the chair facing her. ' "I'm sorry for everything," ' she said suddenly, ' "I'm *sorry!*" '

After a pause, Linc prompted her: 'And?'

' "Goodbye, Daddy," ' came softly out, then strongly, ' "Goodbye." '

'Hey, who's goodbying?'

'I am.'

'Yes. You're the boss. You've decided to live your own life, not his death. This is your place, you're in treatment

here, not him. Would you like to point your finger at him
and tell him to go?'

Silence, immobility, stare. Linc kept at her. At last Fran
lifted a thin arm, sweater bunched above her elbow, and
pointed a long forefinger. ' "Go, Daddy." '

'Does he hear you?'

'Yes, he did. He's gone.'

'How did he look when he heard you?'

'He had . . . a little devilish smile . . .'

'What do you make of that?'

'Maybe . . . to con me back in again,' she said doubtfully.

'Exactly. Are you going back in again?'

'No!'

'Good. Now I want you to put *yourself* in the chair,
your old self, and tell her goodbye. Can you do that?'

'It seems I can do anything,' she said without humour.
'All right. I'm there.'

'No. *She's* there.'

'Yes.'

'Tell her goodbye.'

She looked fixedly and resentfully at the spectre, and
said firmly: ' "Goodbye, Fran." '

'Is she gone?'

'She just disappeared. I can't see her.'

'But she'll always be *with* you, too. Only not in control
any more, unless you let her back. She's more dangerous to
you than your father is. Was.' Linc re-crossed his long legs
as always before exposition.

Alan had been mysteriously moved by the final scene.
He felt that there must be something in it for him, if he
could find out what. But *he* was not threatened by a dying
father. Farewells with fathers affected him anyway. It was
one of his crosses that he had not been able to say goodbye
to Daddy. One of his most acute memories was of his son's
baby face contorted through the back car-window as his

mother drove the boy away from the mental hospital where Severance had been confined for two weeks, on the visit when she told him she was divorcing him and wanted him to move his stuff out as soon as he was discharged. A stunning afternoon. He had ground-privileges by then, and had walked out to the curving driveway to see them off, feeling at the end of the possible. David, two, had been all right when he kissed him through the open side-window, but then his little face had broken up, waving through the glass. Severance heard nothing but the car accelerating.

Linc was talking about the Victim ('I feel worthless') getting strokes from Rescuers (wife, doctor, Fran) and then defying them. 'When he dies, he achieves final victory—equals "*I am worth*" your sacrifice—"Sorry I had to make you all uncomfortable, but—" '

Severance could see an insane game, played for keeps, but where in his case were the Victim and the Rescuer? Daddy in hell (if there was Hell), himself fighting for life not death. He walked away gloomy and baffled from Fran's lonely triumph.

VI

SELF-CONFRONTED

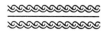

Become a methodical man, seeking non-chemical salvation, Severance had taken to reading with all his strength a Psalm or two every morning along with the 24-Hour Book and his modern Jewish studies later in the day. He had once familiarized himself with Gunkel's revolutionary typology, but paid no attention to it or pre-Exilic or post-Exilic now; he was listening for the word of God and the inspired cries of genuine sufferers. He marked 'O that my ways were directed to keep thy statutes!' But a little they were, at last. Wishing no credit for it, he had confronted Hutch, kept Luriel in treatment, worked almost a month daily on Jeree to speak out in Group, and she had. He marked, 'I will keep thy statutes: O forsake me not utterly.'

He found himself back in what he thought of as his pre-Casey or post-Casey days, full of trust. He read as if the whole truth might lie open before him in the next verse. Casey was a legendary teacher at the College in Alan's time, in the Thirties: a tall, spare man, remote, most of a large white handkerchief dangling out of his breast-pocket, who not only paid no attention to the students who jammed his lectures but was said never to have looked directly even at his assistants. His course appeared in the bul-

letin as Sociology 3-4, Severance recalled, but was widely
known as Caseyology. The readings were conventional
—Vaihinger's *Philosophy of As If*, Lippmann's *Public
Opinion*, Wittgenstein's *Tractatus*—and the examination
was based on them. He never referred to them in lecture,
or to any intellectual source, indeed, except a detective
magazine called *The Shadow* and the letters, from corre-
spondents all over the country, of which he kept a selection in his inside coat-pocket. His lectures were devoted,
one by one, unpredictably, to problems. The most devas-
tating was on Keats's 'Ode on a Grecian Urn.' Sparkling
aggressively with terms like 'cortex' and 'negative feeling-
tone' and 'referent,' it climaxed against 'faery lands forlorn,'
and its listeners gave their English instructors a hard time
for months afterward. He would stalk in, with the bell,
at ten o'clock, stare out over the silent assemblage crowding
even the windowseats, and announce with an edge in his
high voice: 'Today, we'll be investigating The League of
Nations Problem.' Ah! the students rubbed their hands with
glee, leaning forward with destructive joy, in the certainty
that by the end of fifty minutes there would *be* no League
of Nations Problem—no further enquiry necessary, that
is, into why the United States had never joined the
League. At a certain high point, after salvos of irony towards both partners of this historic non-cooperation, he
reached conclusively inside his jacket and drew out a letter. Ah. 'I have here,' he said solemnly, 'a letter from a
farmer in Wisconsin.' Now this might not be impressive in
Ohio, but in upper Manhattan?—grass-roots! And he
read part of the letter aloud, a denunciation of the Prince
of Wales for being unable to stay on a horse. 'The worthy
farmer,' Casey intoned, 'is unaware that the Prince is in
fact an excellent horseman, but' and so on—'Hence we
never joined the League of Nations!' with crushing final-
ity. Alan had partaken of the course, he considered later, at
exactly the right time, in the first half of his sophomore

year, and recovered by the following summer. The spell-binding amalgam of analytic method and theatrical sampling remained, strongly subordinated, one corner of his approach, and it was useless here, against his addiction, against his Christian doubts, against the mystery of his occluded teens. No sampling there: the question, the genetic question, was how the two towering failures of his life, the negative one and the positive alcoholic one, were connected—if they were—and they had got to be. They seemed to hover before him, as he sat musing, smoking, in his hospital chair, like the Platonic essences Professor Edman used to intuit in midair at Wednesday night seminars. High in the air, left, dull and black, formless: the four-year hiatus, while his contemporaries in various countries were thriving their way ahead towards careers. Why had Alan Severance, after joining the League of Nations at eight or nine, resigned at fourteen? Why, for that matter, had he ever rejoined? Above him on the right, nearer and lower, opposite, glowing rich brown, three-quarters full, the globular decanter his mother had given him, crystal, flat-stoppled, shimmering with silky drifting snakes of light, inviting and repellent: the alcoholism that seized him fifteen years later, spawning all his failures since, Father of Lies. He shuddered. In the dark of the left and the bright horror of the right, how had he ever contrived to accomplish *anything*, much less what he undeniably had done? Did it matter? Straining to hold both images, wall-eyed, losing them, he felt as they slid away and the breakfast bell came faintly through his closed door an unaccountable thrust of actual joy that sat him upright. He was going, this time, to make some connexion, or break, break some fantastic connexion, and get out of the whiskey business altogether, clear quite off, empty of urge and fear, his own man again, a decent servant. He could see it, guidance would come, he looked ahead at dry dry dry.

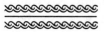

AFTER MENTIONING some official's estimate that it would
take, with present facilities, five hundred years to treat all
the alcoholics in Iowa alone—this was the fourth time Alan
had heard this talk but he was listening, listening—Father
Krueger leaned forward a little over the lectern. Tall, gentle, black-robed, he did not lecture to the patients, but
merely spoke quietly towards and in them, with the kindness of a recovered priest dry now twelve or fifteen years,
God knew how long. He was the most beloved of the lecturing staff of Ward W; Alan wondered, often, whether
his fate would have been different if he had been able to
take his Fifth Step with Father Krueger—whose schedule
had made it impossible—instead of with the perfunctory
priest he had taken it with, Father Grame, who hardly listened to him, asked no questions, told him to pray, and ex-
tolled AA—one hour or less, and out. He thought with
satisfaction of the high news that Charley Boyle had *confronted* Grame during his Fifth Step, a new world record.
'It's not how much,' Father was saying, 'or over how long,
we drink, but *why* we drink—in our case, we drink because of what it will do for us,' and he told the story of his
sacramental wine. Over-estimating the spiritual readiness
of the congregation, he had found himself left once with a
whole half-chalice-ful. 'I was appalled, but it was necessary
to drink it down, and I did. It was not until four hours later,
when next I thought of the circumstance, that I realized
that it had had *no effect* on me.'

Alan suspected that he had in fact prayed and had his prayer answered, suppressing this out of humility. He thought of his shame over his own pride the day before, alleviated only, and not much, by a chat in the Snack Room with Charley at 3 a.m. 'Why, the whole world's as proud as Satan, Alan. I'm a very proud man meself.' The cheery cocky furrowed blue-eyed eyebrows-lifted old face grinning up at him across their white paper coffee-cups comforted Severance in the silent night. Still he remembered what his counsellor had said to him angrily at Howarden— 'Alcoholics can't afford pride'—and he identified heavily with Stack's shame when it emerged in Group later that morning. Stack had been raging at his step-daughter for her bedroom walls festooned with film stars. Very high-minded and explosive he was, until under Keg's and then Harley's pressure he switched sharply round. 'I'm a hypocrite!' he cried. 'I have bad thoughts myself! The daughter's okay! I don't know what's wrong with me, Harley!' I'm a hypocrite myself, thought Severance, I only pretend to take pride in anything, actually I'm ashamed of it. And besides it's all self, self.

'The Third Step,' Harley said sideways in his lecture after lunch, his right hand as ever in his back pants-pocket, sounding like an older brother, 'is to go from where we know what the answer is to where we don't know—now, or ever will know. That is, it involves taking the biggest risk of our lives. We do it: out of utter misery with our *self*-government, and out of trust in God.' Harley was one of the few speakers, clergymen apart, ever to name Him, and Alan felt comfortable. 'The Fourth Step is *where I am*. The Fifth equals "Here's the material *You* have to work with, Lord."'

ARABELLA was a bright-faced, plain, tidy woman of forty, short, dressed in a grey sweater and black slacks, who had sat quietly in Mini-group for two weeks looking, except that she smoked as compulsively as Alan, as if she hadn't a care in the world. She had a care in the world, it appeared when Linc asked her on Tuesday morning if she had been thinking about her Contract. She had.

'Tell us about it.'

'It's this thing inside me.'

'When is it inside you? Right now?'

'All the time.'

'How does it make you feel?'

'I want to scream.' Her voice was flat but some of the colour had left her face. Severance was dumbfounded.

'Is it there when you're asleep?' Linc asked casually.

'I guess so. Anyway it's here whenever I wake up.'

'And you want to scream?'

'All the time.'

'For how long now?'

'God knows. Years.'

'You don't remember a time when you didn't have it?'

'Drinking sends it away.'

'But you can't drink, can you? You know that?'

'Yes.'

Linc reflected. 'It's in your body. Can you say exactly where?'

'In the lower part of my chest and stomach.'

'How big is it?'

'Bigger than I am.'

'It's bigger than your whole body?'

'Oh no. Just bigger than inside.'

'I see,' he said as confidently as if he had been a banker arranging a small loan with a valued depositor. 'Can you *see* this thing?'

Hesitation, then: 'Sort of.'

'Suppose you take it out and station it in midair, facing you, your arm's length out in front. Can you do that?'

'It's very heavy.'

'Sure, but we're just imagining making it float out there. Can you do that?'

'I guess so.'

'Do it.'

She closed her eyes, and a little tremor moved her narrow shoulders. Her eyes opened slowly, fixed.

'Is it out there?'

'Yes.' The word came out half relief, half fear, with a sigh.

'What shape is it?'

'It's square. It's a cube, sort of.'

'Has it any colour?'

'Oh yes, it's black. It's very ugly.'

'Shiny black or dull?'

'Dull black.'

'Rough or smooth?'

'In between.'

'What does that mean?'

'Well, it has smooth ridges all over it.'

'And how big is it now?'

She put her hands out, about eighteen inches between the palms.

'The same distance high and wide and deep?'

'Yes.'

'How does it make you feel, hanging out there?'

'Well, it's nice to be rid of it for a minute.'

'You don't sound as if it was nice.' Severance, too, had picked up an undertone. 'How does it really make you feel?'

'Scared.'

'Scared of what?'

'When it comes back in.'

'But you know it has to come back in.'

'Does it have to?'

'Of course.'

'Okay. Now listen to me.' Linc re-crossed his long legs and leaned forward. 'Before you put it back in, I want you to make an agreement with me. You spend a great deal of time worrying about this thing, don't you? You wish it wasn't there inside you, right? You pretend it isn't, but in fact it is, and nothing you can do will make it go away, right?'

'That's true.'

'Okay. I want you to quit. I want you to put it back in, and instead of trying not to think about it, I want you to think about it as much as possible, without worrying about it. Just carry it around with you, for the next twenty-four hours, till we meet tomorrow morning, giving it your whole attention. Don't try to forget about it and don't pretend anything. Keep saying to yourself, "Here it is, and there's absolutely nothing I can do about it." Do you think you can do that?'

'I can try.'

'I don't want you to try. I want you to do it. Will you?'

'Just till tomorrow, you say?'

'Twenty-four hours. After that, you can go back to worrying your head off. Is it a bargain?'

'Where's the bargain? What do I get out of it?'

'I don't know. That's up to you.'

'All right. I'll do it.'

'Good. Now put it back in.'

Arabella closed her eyes, and the thing seemed to Alan to be sucked off into nothingness, as he felt himself in the grip of an inspiration like Pope John's when wondering what use to make of his brief power he said suddenly one day to an attendant '*Consilium!*' He Severance would call an anti-Council all by himself. For weeks he had been worrying sweating torturing his problem with no result that he could see but extensions of mystery. He would give it a twenty-four-hour rest. What was one day lost? He determined, with joy, to *do nothing about it.*

The rest of Mini-group and Group and lunch and the lecture passed with such a rare sense of freedom, energy set loose, that by mid-afternoon he decided to extend the moratorium by an extra day, to forty-eight hours, and as he climbed into bed that night he felt so unusually comfortable that he resolved to abandon the problem forever. He slept like a baby, poor Severance. When he announced to Linc that he was giving up Contract Two, the long man nodded with satisfaction, 'Okay,' and Alan found himself with no new contract to propose and he felt that he had never done anything so wise before in all his harried dishevelled wicked life as here finally to confess failure. Long afterwards, dry through many difficult months and wondering one evening how *that* had been so easy, he was tempted to ascribe the major praise, not to himself of course but to the luck of this renunciation, and he thought for the first time in many years of a story told by St Augustine—apparently a joke making its way round the churches of North Africa in the last decades of the Fourth Century. Question: Why did God create Hell? (It was, Alan swore to himself, a damned good question.) Answer: He needed a place to put the impious who enquire into his mysteries. The great sweet Bishop does not find this funny, but Severance considered it a riot—best explanation available, though of course nearly all significant human behaviour, like his sobriety, was over-determined too, Freud was right about that. Einstein might once have been whimsical enough, in a letter to Bohr lately published, to venture doubts about causality altogether, but the universe sparkled and geared with it, with Command, the order of intimate forces. As a crypto-medievalist Severance had always been impressed by the scholastic warning against multiplying causes beyond necessity, indeed he found this useful in his work, but in the bewildering worlds of bio-psycho-socio-spiritual disease and recovery one went as far as possible, with Freud, and then surrendered to a self-respecting nescience. The disappearance of the drive was as weird as the drive itself.

VII

DRY-DRUNK

Z ING, AND EVEN VOOM, distinguished Severance from this moment in his (no doubt about it) ultimate treatment for chronic alcoholism. Afire with goodwill, he welcomed new patients limping in, entertained his friends with outrageous stories, confronted in Group and out, took—privately—everybody's temperature, assessing their degree of progress like the veteran he was, who had been told ten days ago he was about to be discharged. He felt ready, now. But with his tender feelings towards most of his fellow-Repeaters restored, he was in no hurry. He wanted *everybody* to get well, or well-er. He was not alarmed by a minor setback on Wednesday morning.

Joining in a confrontation of Letty, his expression 'my little students' was picked up by Keg as significant. Alan defended it as merely habitual and affectionate. But when the matter recurred to him late that grey afternoon he wondered. By an arrangement between the two deans concerned, Severance sometimes gave eccentric courses in one or another of three departments or programs of the Arts College and the Graduate School, and one afternoon the previous winter, teaching *Hamlet*, he had lost his temper with half his seminar when, first, they couldn't see a fully justifiable fatherly concern for Ophelia's chastity in Polonius' forbidding her to receive the Prince's visits (they thought it was none of the old man's business) and, second, when one lofty young man characterized Polonius' famous parting advices to his son Laertes as 'a series of clichés.' He tried, patiently enough, to make clear to these midwestern democratic children the threat posed by royal amorousness to the nubile daughter of an inferior, but at the sneer 'clichés,' smoldering, he scrawled, 'Give thy thoughts no tongue,' on the blackboard and glossed it for ten minutes with everything from the Greek sage sitting against the wall with his left hand on his genitals and his right over his mouth, as the worse danger to Christ's, 'Let your communication be Yea, yea, and Nay, nay, for whatsoever is beyond these cometh of evil.' No visible effect, and he blew up. He read them the riot-act for smugness, immaturity, inability to apply their knowledge of life (most were in their early, some in their middle, twenties) to literature, disrespect for traditional wisdom, gross willingness to take for granted what was in fact profound, and other abnormalities. He calmed himself in short order, and went on to expound the gap between Hamlet's political hostility to the usurping King's tool and Shakespeare's half-contemptuous half-sympathetic serial presentation of the anxious father and decaying-statesman-turned-sneak (necessary, the first, for a family-group to spotlight the Prince's isolation, and the second, for the plot), but Ruth when he described the affair that evening was less sympathetic than he expected, and two students dropped the course. (Question: Had he had one or two drinks before the seminar, as sometimes in recent years he did, and if so, had he got partly out of control because of drinking?) On the other hand, several students troubled to tell him in conference that his charges had been true and that they personally intended to approach things differently from now on. The lofty boy apologized for 'clichés' and wound up with a splendid paper on the source, for some of Polonius' aphorisms, in

Sidney's *Arcadia;* four other student-papers were so much abler still that Severance planned to publish them as a symposium in a new Texas quarterly that had sought his counsel. Still, a sorry business. Was he really far less sympathetic with his students than he liked to suppose? Examples down the years of impatience contempt intolerance thronged nervously to him until he sat huddled in his chair an image to himself of Mr Generation Gap. Was the strain of suppressing the aggressive (lower) half of his feelings for them responsible for the fact that he *always* drank after teaching? This idea came with a certain force of relief, as of a menace that could be handled, out in the open. But then he reflected that it wasn't so: when drinking he drank every afternoon anyway. He taught hard, as he experimented, as he researched, as he wrote, hard; the strains were the same.

Besides, the picture was wrong. He had been made uneasy again and again, uneasy to the point of disdain, by younger colleagues around the country fulminating against their students; just as, at a faculty luncheon for him after a guest lecture at CCNY, long ago, he had been disagreeably impressed by the professors' complex attitudes to their students, who had just asked him such brilliant questions, the professors sitting in around the lecture-room. Themselves tweedy types, socially anti-Semitic to a man, they were yet partly boastful about their able young Jews, and above all fearful of their superiority—correctly, if the level of the two discussions, before and at lunch, indicated fairly the intellectual thrust of the taught and the teachers at City. Severance was amused but disgusted. And now contrary instances of his care and call it love for his students came happily to him—the suicidal boy recovering at Berkeley whom he walked up the hill every afternoon to visit in hospital—warring young husbands and wives reconciled (one failure though)—a boy in the Arts College supported in his resolve to join the police, against the united

rage of his girl-friend, his parents, and his best friends one
of whom offered him a $10,000-a-year partnership in a li-
quor supply business—two suicidal girls, one of whom
barely made it back from forty Vallium. His office hours
over the years a sort of clinic. Vulnerable young faces, al-
ternative-haunted, anguished, glum. Canada or jail? Practice or research? Science or religion? Service or money?
Here or abroad? Sometimes he could pass them on, but
mostly he was a last resort and mentally he had Mr Tru-
man's desk-sign on his desk: 'The Buck Stops Here.' Ab-
solving himself, for a change—he had generally done his
best, and forgotten about it. Letters came from ex-students
thanking him for this or that long-past 'generosity' or 'salvation' without awakening memory. A note passed to him
in flight from somebody invisible further down the plane
had begun, 'I just wanted to say that fourteen years ago
. . .' This rare recollection calmed him now, and dismiss-
ing the subject he turned to Judaic study with fresh humility.

He smoked and read, quietly, until he came to a sharp
sentence about 'obligation.' Feeling brought up short, he realized it was high time he did something about the 'amends'
Steps—got on, altogether, with his Programme. He
looked them up in the back of his 24-Hour Book. Step
Eight was, 'Made a list of all persons we had harmed, and
became willing to make amends to them all.' Well, he had
done that at Howarden a year ago, a gratifyingly short list,
too. He was almost never violent, drinking. It wasn't until
last Spring at Northeast that he noticed the Step said nothing about 'while drinking' or 'by drinking' and the shock
of this so lengthened his list that when he went on to Step
Nine he quailed. He read it again: 'Made direct amends to
such people wherever possible, except when to do so
would injure them or others.' He had *not* done so, except,
some, to Ruth and their daughter. A large smooth face
drifted before him, cold, detestable. Alan could not re-

member anyone he had ever hated but Graham Weeks. At one time, when he first moved to C——, they had drunk together at parties, once the Weekses had taken him home with them and he and Graham had drunk and laughed till breakfast. What had happened to chill the relation he couldn't say, never knew, but later when Weeks had shifted into administration a far from unusual change had come over the scholar, power transformed him into a tyrant. A complication of appointment brought Severance partially under his authority for several years: he was in a position to do the scientist harm, and he did it. At a large garden party, Severance very drunk, they had quarrelled —what about?—he recalled chaotically saying to the taller man's face, 'We'll never speak to each other again,' before his wife dragged him away. Then his final promotion put him out of Weeks's power, his rage died, and he was actually sorry when general discontent forced the man out as associate dean and he returned to harmless teaching, though his abuses and injustices particularly to some of the younger men Severance was glad to see at an end. What harm had he done Weeks? He had hated him—that was wicked—never mind the long-standing provocation, his drunken outburst (nothing was right done drinking) could by inflaming have assisted the other's moral deterioration. He felt guilty. Begin here. It was true that they were often warned, the patients, against beginning amends until their sobriety was well established, for fear of the effect of the occasional inevitable rebuff, but here on the Ward he ran no risk there. Moreover, his eyes dropped to Step Ten. 'Continued to take personal inventory and when we were wrong promptly admitted it.' Promptly. An image, frequent and adorable to him, of Charles Darwin's alacrity in this, came before him: the great man, old, knocking on a house-guest's door in the middle of the night to apologize for some mistaken view. He leafed his scratch-pad to a fresh sheet and wrote painfully.

One of Severance's bad habits was reading his letters over and over before enveloping them. He was made uneasy now by the end of one sentence: 'though many others, to my knowledge, besides myself, felt that you strained justice in the exercise of the authority of your office'—without, however, being aware that it was this surviving hostility, expressed under the guise of doing his duty to the truth, which caused counsellors to warn against precipitate amends. He also felt vaguely ashamed of giving the hospital as his address, lest he seem to make a claim on Weeks's sympathy, but he wanted to hear back immediately.

He needn't have worried. The reply was icy, hypocritical, complacent. 'I do not remember the occasion you refer to with such shame. I am entirely familiar with the University regulations for its administrative officers, and am not aware that I ever in any degree deviated from them in the performance of my duties.' Severance, though disappointed and hurt and outraged, recognized at once that he had been an ass to hope for a different response. But it was weeks before he tried any more Step Nine, months later still before he concluded that he had been partly grandstanding, even seeking revenge. He got what he asked for.

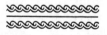

'You've never even levelled with *me*.' This charge of Keg's had perplexed Alan for days, after astonishing him. He thought his feelings, admittedly not simple, were clear enough, and that he had made them plain enough: admiration, grateful affection, healthy fear, trust. But he had never yet, except once in Mini-group in a detail, found Keg wrong about anything, whereas bitter experience had accustomed him to being wrong about everything himself. He went inside.

Finding Keg just ahead of him, among three patients moving slowly down the hall toward the Group-room on Wednesday morning, he took hold of the young man's thin arm. 'I think I've finally seen,' he said hurriedly, 'what you meant by saying I'd never levelled with you—'

'Save it for Group,' Keg grinned back at him, and began, sure enough, when they were all assembled and looking nervously about at each other or at nothing, with 'Well, Alan?'

Severance swallowed. Confronting a counsellor was not unknown, just as Kanchenjunga had been climbed once or twice. Everybody waited, with no idea that an assault on the summit was in prospect. 'You said last week,' his voice stronger than he expected, 'I'd never really told you how I felt about you. That's not entirely true. There are all sorts of strong good feelings towards you that you know very well.' He named half a dozen. 'There's also, of course, envy, I mean of your sobriety and your insights about delusion. But I wonder if you don't get a charge out of torturing people. You've got a killer instinct, which just happens to be employed on the side of health. I admit I feel some aversion. You use Vin's method but I don't think you have his warm heart.' Well, it was out—and Alan, who felt sorry already, would have felt worse if he had known, as he did not know until he was thinking Group over that evening, that he was 'attacking' not levelling.

Nobody said anything—Keg looking at his shoes—until Harley's soft, 'How does that make you feel, Keg?'

'Hurt.' The tone was dejected, inward.

'I'm *sorry*,' Alan said stricken. 'I may be wrong. I generally am, lately.'

Then everybody was all over him, with 'squeamish' and

'a bully yourself—you're projecting,' and he made a
sorry spectacle for twenty minutes, defending, shifting,
sarcastic, belligerent ('I'm an expert in the English language'), attacking even the nurse Leta, who was sitting in,
for her description of his impatience the day before as 'alcoholic behaviour.' But Leta was very calm, besides having
the invaluable credential of an alcoholic ex-husband, and
nobody supported Severance's objection to the phrase as
'non-professional' from a nurse to a patient. He felt more
and more isolated, finally saying, from a silence, 'I'm wasting the Group's time.'

'It's your words,' said Harley.

It was little enough, but it touched Alan. 'You mean not
yours. That's a lifeline, anyway.'

'You threw me one,' Luriel said suddenly, warmly.

The atmosphere changed, with this. Confrontation
switched to Jeree, and then to Hutch, and by the time
Hutch—Hutch!—had crouched over with his face in
his big hands sobbing, Severance felt back at home with
everybody but Wilbur, absolutely silent throughout.
Hutch was in agony over his children. 'I never show my
love for any of them,' he groaned at one point, and, 'I take
food-money for booze. With seven kids! How could I love
my children and do that to them?'

'Maybe you don't love them,' Harley suggested.

'No, he loves them,' Severance said strongly. 'Hutch,
right now you know where you are: *you love your children*. Otherwise you wouldn't feel the way you do.'

'Not like my brother loves his!' Hutch half-cried.

What followed was more like Mini-group than confrontation.

'How do you feel about your brother?' This was Keg.

'He's a wonderful man. He's better in every way than I
am.'

'Better how?'

'Well, he's bigger.'

'You're a big man yourself.'

'You ought to see him. Six-four, two-thirty.'

'Ever have a fight with him?'

'God no. I was always scared of him. Once he almost killed me.'

'How was that?'

'I'd done something. I forget what. He picked me up and threw me on the floor.'

'And you felt?'

'I was scared shitless. I couldn't get my breath back.'

'What happened them?'

'Nothing, He just stood looking down at me. He said, "Next time I'll kill you," and walked out of the room.'

'No other trouble between you?'

'No. I believed him.'

'How do you feel about that time now?'

'Well, it was so long ago. We were kids.'

'It seems pretty fresh in your mind.'

'I haven't thought about it for years.'

'I don't believe it.'

Hutch glared, and twisted in his chair. Silence. He looked down at his hands twisted together. 'Maybe I do.'

'When drinking.'

'Sometimes.'

'And how do you feel about it?' Keg persisted.

'Maybe a little resentful.'

'But you've forgiven him, of course.'

'No I haven't!' Hutch flared out.

'What would you think about somebody who picks up his younger weaker brother and nearly kills him?'

'He'd be a damn bully!'

'Who is the main person in your life, Hutch?'

'My brother.'

'So you've got a damn bully for the central person in your life. How do you feel about that?'

'It sounds crazy.'

'It is crazy,' Harley came in. 'Who ought to be the main person in your life?'

Hutch looked lost. 'I don't know. My wife?'

'No. You. You are the main person in your life.'

'I've always felt like Number Two.'

'After who?'

'After everybody.'

'So you can feel sorry for yourself and drink.'

'I guess so.'

VIII

THE JEWISH KICK AND THE FIFTH STEP

[UNWRITTEN]

Selah

[UNWRITTEN]

Author's Notes

He was an inveterate note-taker,
note-maker, self-analyser.
For once the vice would serve a purpose.
JOHN BERRYMAN,
ON A FOLDER MARKED "NOVEL NOTES"

[The text of *Recovery* printed in the preceding pages is basically that of the typescript John Berryman left, on his death in January 1972, with handwritten additions and corrections. There is no doubt that he would have revised many portions of the novel substantially, in manuscript and—following his habit—during the various proof stages. But except for several fragments he explicitly labeled *"end of book,"* no manuscript for the concluding sections, "The Jewish Kick" and "Selah," has been found. Although he was not given to unwarranted claims about his work, Berryman wrote in one of his letters (July 28, 1971): "I worked hard to become a Jew myself last Fall in hospital—the write-up in my novel will kill you laughing." No trace of this material has been located. For this and other reasons, we have decided to print here some of the notes he left behind. Since he also refers in these notes to his short story of 1945, "The Imaginary Jew," we are reprinting it in full. Such fragmentary material can hardly replace the portions of the novel that are unwritten, but it affords some insights into the techniques and concerns of John Berryman.

—THE PUBLISHERS]

16 Sept 71

RECOVERY

| | Vol. II *THE PRESENT* |
| Vol. I   *WARD D* | *SICK WHITE WORLD* |

Selah

I. First Day	Relapse of the Second Step
II. The First Step (I-IV)	(BVM!)
III. Contract One	Slip
IV. Confrontation	The SST and Renunciation
V. The Last Two First	Fidelity
Steps	Hareford & VT (Assumption)
VI. Contract Two	Pike's Peak
VII. Self-Confronted	Berkeley 2 Cor. 5^8
	Traumata at Home
Dry-Drunk	'As It Comes'
	God's mercy and the Eleventh
The Jewish Kick and the	& Ninth Steps
Fifth Step	Higgaion (12th)
300 pages? in 9 sections	
(6 weeks)	9 sections (9 months)—30 pp.
	av. = 270 pp.

HAPPINESS (euphoria)

his 2 seminars
cancer-work

*   *   *

Higgaion

There is no such thing as Freedom (though it is the most important condition of human life, after Humility,—which does not exist either). There is only Slavery (walls around one) and absence-of-Slavery (ability to walk in any direction, or to remain still).

Slavery is man's condition (the Adam-fall story is right, which required man to walk out of happiness, equipped with his evidently ruining self-will). But it is undesirable. (Why? because it makes me unhappy—unlike the rest of natural existence, stones, stars, flowers, animals, lightning, waterfalls, etc.) How then to escape? (Is escape possible? Yes, because some men have.)

First, is escape difficult (i.e. beyond my powers—too difficult)? Evidently, for (1) the walls are strong and I am weak, and (2) *I love my walls*. That Outside may be Hell worse than the hell in here, and I am too afraid of it even to begin action toward it. Existential immoral crisis: *angst*. Effort not only would not avail but is not available. Situation seems desperate. Yet some *have escaped*.

How?   (1) historical;

(2) refusing to accept Walls as God's will (the Redemption story—Moses, Buddha, Christ—is true too). With an effort we lift our gaze from the walls upward and ask God *to take the walls away*. We look back down and they have disappeared. We are "free." But now we are really terrified, because we are programmed-for-walls.

But *are* we now? No, we find to our surprise that we are programmed-for-happiness. So we *happily* find ourselves without walls.

We turn back upward at once with love to the Person who has made us so happy, and *desire to serve Him*. Our state of mind is that of a bridegroom, that of a bride. We are married, who have been so lonely heretofore.

Life lies open before us, with commitment, its interesting and difficult (but He will guide us) choices, its sweet rewards, its delightful (for we will have become so weary) end: immortal rest.

6th Friday, 20 November, 6–7 a.m. [1971]

Father's suicide [for Severance's journal?]

He had not exactly lost his faith. He had gone into violent rebellion. God was a son of a bitch who had allowed Daddy to
go mad with grief and fear. This sentiment subsided very
gradually into a sort of not quite indifference, but two senses
remained vivid and even strengthened in adult life. He had no
doubt at all about God the Creator and Maintainer of the Universe: the original giant hydrogen atom or whatever and its
descendants down to the cortex. And it was perfectly clear to
him that God intervened occasionally in the affairs of crea-
tures, for good: heroes, saints, artists, scientists, ordinary people. No sweat. He also believed in the Devil. He believed in
miracles and felt indeed not only impatience but contempt
when their possibility was denied. The Resurrection—
appearances, say, those at any rate to Peter and the other
disciples—no Church otherwise, eh?—and to Paul. What
he did not buy was any regular attention to human affairs on
the part of His Majesty. Screw that. Because look at them.
Still, he was keen on New Testament criticism. It constituted
his only hobby, excluding the arts and star-gazing, and he read
the bloody commentators with a sharp eye and desperate envy.

What is the meaning of life?
It must lie in *our* performance
of *God's* will, *our* free-will being
one indispensable tool.

1) mate & > children.
2) work = *solve problems* (vs. boredom)
    sleep, eat, excrete; keep warm
    enough or cool enough, dry
    enough or wet enough; wash?
3) play (for some, the lucky, = 2)
4) worship; resist temptations.
5) *help* (others) *& accept help:*
    Group, Family, Tribe, Nation.
6) confront & survive ordeals.
7) *become, thro' dependence*, FREE.

He desires us to penetrate < the universe
                                ourselves

    but he has made both
    mysterious, & banned access
    to certain all-important
    key problems (for instance,
    the Resurrection).
8) Forgive: all, including ourselves.

Severance's re-socialization

SST and Renunciation. Congressional rejection of the SST was the most important thing that has happened in this country for many years, and amazing, for the SST was (1) possible, (2) useless, (3) evil. On all three counts it seemed immensely desirable to many Americans besides those very few who stood to benefit from its further funding. Let me explain.

I agree with those who think our country has been performing not merely wicked actions for many years now but *sick* actions, and I agree with Henry Steele Commager (testifying recently before a Senate committee) that the name of our illness is Power. So, perhaps, do hundreds of thousands, perhaps millions, who respond with rage to the invasion of Cambodia but with apathy merely to the invasion of Laos. Some observers have remarked a certain national despair, the response of a patient who learns at last that what he has is progressive and fatal. But the hospital patient does not feel *responsible* for his condition, whereas, though we don't either and so resent it, also we *do*. Our feelings are right. We are not responsible. 'Men are not evil-doers: they are sleep-walkers' (F. Kafka). Knowledge is good for its own sake, power is good for its own sake.

But we are responsible. (Cf. R. Guardini in 1955 to students in Munich.) Only this was wrong. The body politic itself is a victim of disease, producing *sincere delusions*—that is, lies which the liar believes. However, to be deluded is far worse than simply to be wicked. What is finally scary about our murderers just now, like Charlie Manson's girls and Lt Calley and his collaborators, is their motives—they killed at random 'with love' and 'for duty'—and their judgment: the massacre of Asiatic human beings herded into a ditch, Calley testifies, 'wasn't any big deal.' This is the self-appraisal of a maniac. Millions of worthy Americans share it.

[*Letter mailed to the editor of The New York Times but not printed*]

10 April 1971

Dear Sir:

With regard to the agony or outraged or complacent denial or apathy of millions of us over our share if any in the guilt of Lt Calley for what happened at My Lai 4, and over our share of responsibility for other things (a word about that presently), we might seek what consolation is to be found in the wise analysis of the Roman Catholic theologian (now Bishop) R. Guardini. I extract from a complex argument (reported in *The Bridge*, vol. I, ed. John M. Oesterreicher, 1955) a few sentences. Addressing university students in Munich twenty years ago on the responsibility of the German people for the Nazis' crimes, he rejected the view lately (*very* lately) adopted with dismay by many Americans: that which assigns 'collective guilt'. 'There is,' he told his audience, 'no such thing. Never can a man be guilty of another man's crime, unless, of course, he co-operates in it or fails to do what he can and should to prevent it. There is no "collective guilt", but there is collective honor, the solidarity of the individual with his people and of all individuals with one another. If a member of my family commits some wrong, I may say, I am not guilty; but I may not say, It is no concern of mine. For I am part and parcel of my family, and its honor is, within certain limits, my honor. Similarly, each one of us must accept a share of responsibility for the wrong done by our people, since this wrong touches each one's honor and demands of him that things be put right. This is our duty, because injustice must not be left standing: it must be dealt with till nothing of it remains, and this for two reasons. First, it violates the sovereignty of the good, and it is man's nobility to know of this and bear its burden. Second, injustice is real: if not conquered, it continues to work in the ideas begotten by it and in the people formed by them.'

So no American is off any hook, fellow-actors. The hook is thick and dug deep. Notice '*in the people formed by them.*' We are obliged to hold ourselves responsible not only for a de-

cade of Asiatic corpses and uninhabitable countryside and gen-
ocidal 'resettlement' of whole populations of Asiatic villagers,
but for what we are doing to the survivors with (for instance,
a grant of $21 million last fiscal year; this year: $30 million) to
the police of the South Vietnamese regime for whom our men
have been dying,—police whose 'timely and positive action'
(so a high American official officially boasts to our ambassador
in that desperate country) 'effectively contained civil distur-
bances including war veterans, students and religious groups'
(so the director of a finely named Agency for International
Development, Mr John Mossler, quoted in *The Minneapolis
Tribune*, 9 April 1971). This aid of ours, by the way, to the
enemies of the progressive elements in their country, is six
times as great as our aid to education in South Vietnam. Surely
we *did not know* these things. Surely we cannot responsibly
continue to support an administration which is thus, by a natural, if loathsome, sympathetic conformation, repressing exactly those possibly democratic elements that all or some of us
wish to encourage. Not that any of all this ought to be any of
our pretentious Government's *business!*—not even the education bit, when our own schools are at most levels radically
unsatisfactory and thirty million Americans are right this
bright Spring morning slowly starving.

Yours, etc.,

in-patient

Severance was not very good at Natha(?) and yoga. He had mastered lobhastana and [*indecipherable*], but the instructions of his guru, a banker in Calcutta, went largely neglected.

3 or 4 months 'out of' treatment

Severance was not happy about his money. He was paid a very high salary by the University for teaching three hours a week, his publisher sent him handsome cheques, often sums drifted in from foundations and Government, the place was crawling with dough. He sweated with guilt. He had been poor most of his life, many of his friends, including his brother, were actually unemployed at the moment—some for many months now—and though he supported half a dozen people and 'lent' money to still others, he couldn't reconcile himself to his good luck. He didn't feel worthless, much less Franciscan, but

5th month out of treatment, Severance in his Want Ad cheaply buys himself in Des Moines a black star-sapphire ring from a young Thai sculptor, giving himself seven plus-strokes for only half of what the guy paid for it—sixty dollars, in Bangkok.

6 months out. Author interrupted at breakfast by phone. Liz is back in treatment!

He felt some hurt. Liz was a foxy intelligent sumptuous woman, rich, with four splendid girls, a bad but unassuming portrait-painter, a great friend of his. Towards their discharge, a year ago, he had proposed that the three of them—R. Wall was the witty snobbish advertising director for the second largest department store in the city—start their own AA group. Incredible? Yet at the time he hadn't understood at all when Jerry Croy, to whom he mentioned the gorgeous project in two sentences on the wing, had just said, 'Sounds selective to me' and vanished down the corridor towards some meeting.

Delusions (major 'activity')

   I. Drive to solve his failure with the 1st Step (he hadn't)

  II. Drive to solve mystery of OK 5 years (real, and very odd because so long delayed and so long lasting—well, the joke reported by Augustine, *Confessions*)

 III. Drive to become a Jew (expiate imaginary transgressions—cf. Guardini—join son and dead friend (Delmore Schwartz)

 IV. . . . . Effort of > 3rd Step

   I. Sacrifice.   of vainglory (*not* 'amphitheatre')
                    of self-knowledge (*not* 'Fa>SKS-X)

  II. Selflessness, in Group-Labour (find a term for this) entails:
                    sacrifice of *pride*; secrets! as 'incest' and attempted ——— (drunk—barely escaped)

So, it wasn't only Mini-Group that did the work, but *both*—especially Keg bringing me out to 'level' with him (= attack, & so remorse) and Harley trapping me in D-D at the last minute!

Only realized, 7 June 71, on noticing the "Sacrifice" of Hastings *encycl.* in a 2nd hand cat.

"The Jewish Kick"

The priest genuflected and kissed and mumbled. In chapel Severance suddenly felt a resistless hostility, akin to mother's in Rome, against the gabbled masses. (Succumbed to thru awful laicism in old age, though.)

9:25 a.m. Fri. 13th

I become a Jew—the wonder of my life—it's possible! Rabbi M. is coming at 2:30.

My uneasiness with Xt'y (Christianity) came to a head in Mass with George this morning. Worship God but where? how? *want company* (George—Mike with his wife).

Passion over Rose's John saying to her at last "I love you" —Severance: 'You never could say it to her before, could you?'—I thought of P. *wanting* to say it to *me*, maybe, but held off by disappointment with me (rage, perhaps?)—baffled, hurt—how will he take my letter?!?

Left and came to my room and incredibly thought of *becoming a Jew*. Always held it impossible because of inadequate concept of God. Ok since Vin's rescue—but hostile to Trinity, dubious of X (Christianity?), hostile to the Blessed Virgin, anti-Pope, deep sympathy with Church, but *not for me*.

alone with God, yet *not* alone, one of many worshippers, like them except in blood (who cares?)

Somebody in Snack Room even said to me recently, 'You ought to become a Jew!!' —Bud? (Irish-Jewish wives—my *son*, perhaps the nexus just now.)

I feel apprehensive—joyful—can I? Will He receive me? I know I must prepare, be ready for all.

[NOTE ON SIDE OF PAPER] The Cantor's letter helpt me, unknowing by me. (Maybe as far back as "Imaginary Jew" *— and no wonder I was the N.Y. Jew in Hong Kong story) and overjoyed by *The Bridge* of Will Herberg!!

All has pointed HERE.

I. In my old story *, a confrontation as Jew is resisted, fought, failed—at last is given into *symbolically*. I identified at least with the persecution. So the 'desire' (was it?) is at least 25 years old.

II. PLUS after that, *The Black Book* **—abandoned— obsessed—perhaps now take it up again? *My position is certain.*

III. Horror of anti-semitism.

Excitement over Babel! Buber! the Hasidim! Bloch's music! Pascal's *Hebraism* in 'conversion'! WCW's Jewish blood!

love for S., first doctor I ever felt *anything* for.

resentment of Cal's tiny Jewish blood, Daiches' *full* heritage.

flourishing of Freud and Einstein.

Jewish girls.

Yiddish stories and slang.

my Hebrew effort. Peret and Bargebecher(?).

regular Old Testament study at last, this year.

my anthology of Yiddish poetry! (till lately—why kept?)

unique devotion to *Job*—texts, study, translation begun.

resented/liked name 'Berryman' *being thought Jewish.*

---

* See page 243.

** Three poems from *The Black Book*, a verse sequence about the Jews under Hitler, are preserved in Mr. Berryman's *Short Poems*, pages 106–9.

End of Book

LAST SIX PAGES? Book ends (put the Assumption stuff the *week* before) on the bus descending Pike's Peak. Put the 'pros. distance', [*indecipherable*] and the 'great sacrifice' bits the day *before*. Plus tooth long loose—to lose. P: in here better or worse. S: there isn't enough of it to form an opinion. With understanding of his special awareness earlier, growing up. Prem. of Death—controlled by: Medicine. Value. Still . . . Well, okay with him. He could see a good deal of pain coming up. No sweat. Sorry to leave dygs. so much work unfin'd. Oh sorry sorry—hard to leave [*indecipherable*]. Headache and lassitude gone. P's question and his answer. —P. slumpt in seat, M. sleeping. 'He felt fine'

[Note on back of a yellow card in Berryman's hand] 'END OF NOVEL: TURN THIS CARD OVER.'

∴ by Christmas

The goals of psychotherapy *were char'd by remembering*. The goal of alcoholic treatment, he only had really grasped after six months out, was oblivion. 'The passion of a free and truthful life.' [*Indecipherable*] Five minutes on waking, twenty seconds gratitude at bedtime,—'the rest is silence.' He might, certainly, at any time drink again. But it didn't seem likely.

He felt—calm.

[On a separate page, in Berryman's hand] 'LAST PAGE OF BOOK (EXCEPT SELAH).'

On Pike's Peak, coming down.

He was perfectly ready. No regrets. He was happier than he had ever been in his life before. Lucky, and he didn't deserve it. He was very, very lucky. Bless everybody. He felt—fine.

The Imaginary Jew

The second summer of the European War I spent in New York. I lived in a room just below street-level on Lexington above 34th, wrote a good deal, tried not to think about Europe, and listened to music on a small gramophone, the only thing of my own, except books, in the room. Haydn's London Symphony, his last, I heard probably fifty times in two months. One night when excited I dropped the pickup, creating a series of knocks at the beginning of the last movement where the oboe joins the strings which still, when I hear them, bring up for me my low dark long damp room and I feel the dew of heat and smell the rented upholstery. I was trying as they say to come back a little, uncertain and low after an exhausting year. Why I decided to do this in New York—the enemy in summer equally of soul and body, as I had known for years—I can't remember; perhaps I didn't, but was held on merely from week to week by the motive which presently appeared in the form of a young woman met the Christmas before and now the occupation of every evening not passed in solitary and restless gloom. My friends were away; I saw few other people. Now and then I went to the zoo in lower Central Park and watched with interest the extraordinary behavior

[Mr. Berryman's short story originally appeared in *The Kenyon Review*, vol. VII, no. 4 (Autumn 1945), pages 529–39. It was awarded first prize in the magazine's story contest.]

of a female badger. For a certain time she quickly paced the round of her cage. Then she would approach the sidewall from an angle in a determined, hardly perceptible, unhurried trot; suddenly, when an inch away, point her nose up it, follow her nose up over her back, turning a deft and easy somersault, from which she emerged on her feet moving swiftly and unconcernedly away, as if the action had been no affair of hers, indeed she had scarcely been present. There was another badger in the cage who never did this, and nothing else about her was remarkable; but this competent disinterested somersault she enacted once every five or ten minutes as long as I watched her,—quitting the wall, by the way, always at an angle in fixed relation to the angle at which she arrived at it. It is no longer possible to experience the pleasure I knew each time she lifted her nose and I understood again that she would not fail me, or feel the mystery of her absolute disclaimer,— she has been taken away or died.

The story I have to tell is no further a part of that special summer than a nightmare takes its character, for memory, from the phase of the moon one noticed on going to bed. It could have happened in another year and in another place. No doubt it did, has done, will do. Still, so weak is the talent of the mind for pure relation—immaculate apprehension of K alone—that everything helps us, as when we come to an unknown city: architecture, history, trade-practices, folklore. Even more anxious our approach to a city—like my small story—which we have known and forgotten. Yet how little we can learn! Some of the history is the lonely summer. Part of the folklore, I suppose, is what I now unwillingly rehearse, the character which experience has given to my sense of the Jewish people.

Born in a part of the South where no Jews had come, or none had stayed, and educated thereafter in States where they are numerous, I somehow arrived at a metropolitan university without any clear idea of what in modern life a Jew was,— without even a clear consciousness of having seen one. I am unable now to explain this simplicity or blindness. I had not escaped, of course, a sense that humans somewhat different from ourselves, called "Jews," existed as in the middle distance and were best kept there, but this sense was of the vaguest. From what it was derived I do not know; I do not recall feeling the least curiosity about it, or about Jews; I had, simply, from the atmosphere of an advanced heterogeneous democratic society, ingathered a gently negative attitude towards Jews. This I took with me, untested, to college, where it received neither confirmation nor stimulus for two months. I rowed and danced and cut classes and was political; by mid-November I knew most of the five hundred men in my year. Then the man who rowed Number Three, in the eight of which I was bow, took me aside in the shower one afternoon and warned me not to be so chatty with Rosenblum.

I wondered why not. Rosenblum was stroke, a large handsome amiable fellow, for whose ability in the shell I felt great respect and no doubt envy. Because the fellows in the House wouldn't like it, my friend said. "What have they against him?" "It's only because he's Jewish," explained my friend, a second-generation Middle European.

I hooted at him, making the current noises of disbelief, and went back under the shower. It did not occur to me that he could be right. But next day when I was talking with Herz —the coxswain, whom I found intelligent and pleasant—I remembered the libel with some annoyance, and told Herz about it as a curiosity. Herz looked at me oddly, lowering his head, and said after a pause, "Why, Al *is* Jewish, didn't you know that?" I was amazed. I said it was absurd, he couldn't be! "Why not?" said Herz, who must have been as astonished as I was. "Don't you know I'm Jewish?"

I did not know, of course, and ignorance has seldom cost me such humiliation. Herz did not guy me; he went off. But greater than my shame at not knowing something known, apparently, without effort to everyone else, were my emotions for what I then quickly discovered. Asking careful questions during the next week, I learnt that about a third of the men I spent time with in college were Jewish; that they knew it, and the others knew it; that some of the others disliked them for it, and they knew this also; that certain Houses existed *only* for Jews, who were excluded from the rest; and that what in short I took to be an idiotic state was deeply established, familiar, and acceptable to everyone. This discovery was the beginning of my instruction in social life proper—construing social life as that from which political life issues like a somatic dream.

My attitude toward my friends did not alter on this revelation. I merely discarded the notion that Jews were a proper object for any special attitude; my old sense vanished. This was in 1933. Later, as word of the German persecution filtered into this country, some sentimentality undoubtedly corrupted my no-attitude. I denied the presence of obvious defects in particular Jews, feeling that to admit them would be to side with the sadists and murderers. Accident allotting me close friends who were Jewish, their disadvantages enraged me. Gradually, and against my sense of impartial justice, I became the anomaly which only a partial society can produce, and for which it has no name known to the lexicons. In one area, but not exclusively, "nigger-lover" is cast in a parallel way: but for a special sympathy and liking for Jews—which became my fate, so that I trembled when I heard one abused in talk—we have no term. In this condition I still was during the summer of which I speak. One further circumstance may be mentioned, as a product, I believe, of this curious training. I am spectacularly unable to identify Jews as Jews,—by name, cast of feature, accent, or environment,—and this has been true, not only of course before the college incident, but during my whole life since. Even names to anyone else patently Hebraic rarely suggest to me anything. And when once I learn that So-and-so is Jewish, I am likely to forget it. Now Jewishness may be a fact as striking and informative as someone's past heroism or his Christianity or his understanding of the subtlest human relations, and I feel sure that something operates to prevent my utilizing the plain signs by which such characters—in a Jewish man or woman—may be identified, and prevent my retaining the identification once it is made.

So to the city my summer and a night in August. I used to stop on Fourteenth Street for iced coffee, walking from the Village home (or to my room rather) after leaving my friend, and one night when I came out I wandered across to the island of trees and grass and concrete walks raised in the center of

Union Square. Here men—a few women, old—sit in the evenings of summer, looking at papers or staring off or talking, and knots of them stay on, arguing, very late; these the unemployed or unemployable, the sleepless, the malcontent. There are no formal orators, as at Columbus Circle in the Nineteen-thirties and at Hyde Park Corner. Each group is dominated by several articulate and strong-lunged persons who battle each other with prejudices and desires, swaying with intensity, and take on from time to time the interrupters: a forum at the bottom of the pot,—Jefferson's fear, Whitman's hope, the dream of the younger Lenin. It was now about one o'clock, almost hot, and many men were still out. I stared for a little at the equestrian statue, obscure in the night on top of its pedestal, thinking that the misty Rider would sweep again away all these men at his feet, whenever he liked,—what symbol for power yet in a mechanical age rivals the mounted man?—and moved to the nearest group; or I plunged to it.

The dictator to the group was old, with dark cracked skin, fixed eyes in an excited face, leaning forward madly on his bench towards the half-dozen men in semicircle before him. "It's bread! it's bread!" he was saying. "It's bitter-sweet. All the bitter and all the sweetness. Of an overture. What else do you want? When you ask for steak and potatoes, do you want pastry with it? It's bread! It's bread! Help yourself! Help yourself!"

The listeners stood expressionless, except one who was smiling with contempt and interrupted now.

"Never a happy minute, never a happy minute!" the old man cried. "It's good to be dead! Some men should kill themselves."

"Don't you want to live?" said the smiling man.

"Of course I want to live. Everyone wants to live! If death comes suddenly it's better. It's better!"

With pain I turned away. The next group were talking diffusely and angrily about the Mayor, and I passed to a third, where a frantic olive-skinned young man with a fringe of silky beard was exclaiming:

"No restaurant in New York had the Last Supper! No. When people sit down to eat they should think of that!"

"Listen," said a white-shirted student on the rail, glancing around for approbation, "listen, if I open a restaurant and put *The Last Supper* up over the door, how much money do you think I'd lose? Ten thousand dollars?"

The fourth cluster was larger and appeared more coherent. A savage argument was in progress between a man of fifty with an oily red face, hatted, very determined in manner, and a muscular fellow half his age with heavy eyebrows, coatless, plainly Irish. Fifteen or twenty men were packed around them, and others on a bench near the rail against which the Irishman was lounging were attending also. I listened for a few minutes. The question was whether the President was trying to get us into the War,—or rather, whether this was legitimate, since the Irishman claimed that Roosevelt was a god-damned warmonger whom all the real people in the country hated, and the older man claimed that we should have gone into the f..ing war when France fell a year before, as everybody in the country knew except a few immigrant rats. Red-face talked ten times as much as the Irishman, but he was not able to establish any advantage that I could see. He ranted, and then Irish either repeated shortly and fiercely what he had said last, or shifted his ground. The audience were silent—favouring whom I don't know, but evidently much interested. One or two men pushed out of the group, others arrived behind me, and I was eddied forward towards the disputants. The young Irishman broke suddenly into a tirade by the man with the hat:

"You're full of s. Roosevelt even tried to get us in with the communists in the Spanish war. If he could have done it we'd have been burning churches down like the rest of the Reds."

"No, that's not right," I heard my own voice, and pushed forward, feeling blood in my face, beginning to tremble. "No, Roosevelt as a matter of fact helped Franco by non-intervention, at the same time that Italians and German planes were fighting against the Government and arms couldn't get in from France."

"What's that? What are you, a Jew?" He turned to me contemptuously, and was back at the older man before I could speak, "The only reason we weren't over there four years ago is because you can only screw us so much. Then we quit. No New Deal bastard could make us go help the goddamned communists."

"That ain't the question, it's if we want to fight *now* or *later*. Them Nazis ain't gonna sit!" shouted the redfaced man. "They got Egypt practically, and then it's India if it ain't England first. It ain't a question of the communists, the communists are on Hitler's side. I tellya we can wait and wait and chew and spit and the first thing you know they'll be in England, and then who's gonna help us when they start after us? Maybe Brazil? Get wise to the world! Spain don't matter now one way or the other, they ain't gonna help and they can't hurt. It's Germany and Italy and Japan, and if it ain't too late now it's gonna be. Get wise to yourself. We shoulda gone in—"

"What with?" said the Irishman with disdain. "Pop pop. Wooden machine-guns?"

"We were as ready a year ago as we are now. Defence don't mean nothing, you gotta have to fight!"

"No, we're much better off now," I said, "than we were a year ago. When England went in, to keep its word to Poland, what good was it to Poland? The German Army—"

"Shut up, you Jew," said the Irishman.

"I'm not a Jew," I said to him. "What makes—"

"Listen, Pop," he said to the man in the hat, "it's O.K. to shoot your mouth off but what the hell have you got to do with it? You aren't gonna do any fighting."

"Listen," I said.

"You sit on your big ass and talk about who's gonna fight who. Nobody's gonna fight anybody. If we feel hot, we ought to clean up some of the sons of bitches here before we go sticking our nuts anywhere to help England. We ought to clean up the sons of bitches in Wall Street and Washington before we take any ocean trips. You want to know something? You know why Germany's winning everything in this war? Because there ain't no Jews back home. There ain't no more Jews, first shouting war like this one here"—nodding at me

—"and then skinning off to the synagogue with the profits. Wake up, Pop! You must have been around in the last war, you ought to know better."

I was too nervous to be angry or resentful. But I began to have a sense of oppression in breathing. I took the Irishman by the arm.

"Listen, I told you I'm not a Jew."

"I don't give a damn what you are," he turned his half-dark eyes to me, wrenching his arm loose. "You talk like a Jew."

"What does that mean?" Some part of me wanted to laugh. "How does a Jew talk?"

"They talk like you, buddy."

"That's a fine argument! But if I'm not a Jew, my talk only—"

"You probably are a Jew. You look like a Jew."

"I *look* like a Jew? Listen," I swung around with despair to a man standing next to me, "do I look like a Jew? It doesn't matter whether I do or not—a Jew is as good as anybody and better than this son of a bitch—" I was not exactly excited, I was trying to adapt my language as my need for the crowd, and my sudden respect for its judgment, possessed me —"but in fact I'm not Jewish and I don't look Jewish. Do I?"

The man looked at me quickly and said, half to me and half to the Irishman, "Hell, I don't know. Sure he does."

A wave of disappointment and outrage swept me almost to tears, I felt like a man betrayed by his brother. The lamps seemed brighter and vaguer, the night large. Looking around I saw sitting on a bench near me a tall, heavy, serious-looking man of thirty, well dressed, whom I had noticed earlier, and appealed to him, "Tell me, do I look Jewish?"

But he only stared up and waved his head vaguely. I saw with horror that something was wrong with him.

"You look like a Jew. You talk like a Jew. You *are* a Jew," I heard the Irishman say.

I heard murmuring among the men, but I could see nothing very clearly. It seemed very hot. I faced the Irishman again helplessly, holding my voice from rising.

"I'm *not* a Jew," I told him. "I might be, but I'm not. You

have no bloody reason to think so, and you can't make me a
Jew by simply repeating like an idiot that I am."

"Don't deny it, son," said the redfaced man, "stand up to
him."

"God damn it," suddenly I was furious, whirling like a fool
(was I afraid of the Irishman? had he conquered me?) on the
redfaced man, "I'm *not* denying it! Or rather I am, but only
because I'm not a Jew! I despise renegades, I hate Jews who
turn on their people, if I were a Jew I would say so, I would
be proud to be: what is the vicious opinion of a man like this
to me if I were a Jew? But I'm not. Why the hell should I
admit I am if I'm not?"

"Jesus, the Jew is excited," said the Irishman.

"I have a right to be excited, you son of a bitch. Suppose I
call you a Jew. Yes, you're a Jew. Does that mean anything?"

"Not a damn thing." He spat over the rail past a man's head.

"Prove that you're not. I say you are."

"Now listen, you Jew. I'm a Catholic."

"So am I, or I was born one, I'm not one now. I was born a
Catholic." I was a little calmer but goaded, obsessed with the
need to straighten this out. I felt that everything for everyone
there depended on my proving him wrong. If *once* this evil
for which we have not even a name could be exposed to the
rest of the men as empty—if I could *prove* I was not a Jew
—it would fall to the ground, neither would anyone else be a
Jew to be accused. Then it could be trampled on. Fascist
America was at stake. I listened, intensely anxious for our fate.

"Yeah?" said the Irishman. "Say the Apostles' Creed."

Memory went swirling back, I could hear the little bell die
as I hushed it and set it on the felt, Father Boniface looked at
me tall from the top of the steps and smiled greeting me in the
darkness before dawn as I came to serve, the men pressed
around me under the lamps, and I could remember nothing
but *visibilum omnium . . . et invisibilium?*

"I don't remember it."

The Irishman laughed with his certainty.

The papers in my pocket, I thought them over hurriedly. In
my wallet. What would they prove? Details of ritual, Church

history: anyone could learn them. My piece of Irish blood. Shame, shame: shame for my ruthless people. I will not be his blood. I wish I were a Jew, I would change my blood, to be able to say *Yes* and defy him.

"I'm not a Jew," I felt a fool. "You only say so. You haven't any evidence in the world."

He leaned forward from the rail, close to me. "Are you cut?"

Shock, fear ran through me before I could make any meaning out of his words. Then they ran faster, and I felt confused.

From that point, nothing is clear for me. I stayed a long time—it seemed impossible to leave, showing him victor to them—thinking of possible allies and new plans of proof, but without hope. I was tired to the marrow. The arguments rushed on, and I spoke often now but seldom was heeded except by an old fat woman, very short and dirty, who listened intently to everyone. Heavier and heavier appeared to me to press upon us in the fading night our general guilt.

In the days following, as my resentment died, I saw that I had not been a victim altogether unjustly. My persecutors were right: I was a Jew. The imaginary Jew I was was as real as the imaginary Jew hunted down, on other nights and days, in a real Jew. Every murderer strikes the mirror, the lash of the torturer falls on the mirror and cuts the real image, and the real and the imaginary blood flow down together.

The Twelve Steps

Step One
    "We admitted that we were powerless over alcohol—that our lives had become unmanageable."

Step Two
    "Came to believe that a Power greater than ourselves could restore us to sanity."

Step Three
    "Made a decision to turn our will and our lives over to the care of God as we understood Him."

Step Four
    "Made a searching and fearless inventory of ourselves."

Step Five
    "Admitted to God, to ourselves, and to another human being, the exact nature of our wrongs."

Step Six
    "Were entirely ready to have God remove all these defects of character."

Step Seven
    "Humbly asked Him to remove our shortcomings."

Step Eight

"Made a list of all persons we had harmed, and became willing to make amends to them all."

Step Nine

"Made direct amends to such people wherever possible, except when to do so would injure them or others."

Step Ten

"Continued to take personal inventory and when we were wrong promptly admitted it."

Step Eleven

"Sought through prayer and meditation to improve our conscious contact with God as we understood Him, praying only for knowledge of His will for us and the power to carry that out."

Step Twelve

"Having had a spiritual awakening as the result of these steps, we tried to carry this message to alcoholics, and to practice these principles in all our affairs."